THE JUDGE SERIES

Book 1: THE HILL
Book 2: THE ISLAND
Book 3: SILICON BEACH
Book 4: THE BAY
Book 5: CABO
Book 6: THE STRAND
Book 7: THE LAKE
Book 8: THE CRUISE
Book 9: THE DARK WEB – VEGAS
Book 10: CITY BY THE BAY
Book 11: THE FINAL HORSEMAN
Book 12: MONTECITO

To purchase the complete series, search **Davis MacDonald** under 'books' on Amazon.com. Or go to our website. Google 'Davis MacDonald – Author' to learn more about each book, and to download a free electronic copy of BOOK 1: THE HILL.

All are available in paperback and on Kindle. Books 1 through 6 are also available as audiobooks. ENJOY.

Davis MacDonald

MONTECITO

A Novel of Mystery and Suspense

by

DAVIS MacDONALD

"…if you gaze long enough into an abyss, the
abyss will gaze back into you."
*Beyond Good and Evil: Prelude to a Philosophy of the
Future (1886), Chapter IV. Apothegms and Interludes, §146.*
Friedrich Wilhelm Nietzsche.

"Laura… is the face in the fire's glow.
The girl… you never quite meet.
The laugh… in the wind's soft flow,
That caresses your dreams in your sleep.

And there's Laura… across a crowded street,
Disappearing in the busy throng.
The girl you never quite reach, But memories of
her smile… linger on.

You glimpse Laura… on the floor above,
Those eyes… how familiar they seem.
She could have been your very first love.
But that's Laura… she's only a dream."

"It doesn't actually make any difference whether the President is Republican or Democrat. The genius of the American ruling class is that it has been able to make the people think that they have had something to do with the electing of presidents for 200 years when they've had absolutely nothing to say about the candidates or the policies or the way the country is run."
—Gore Vidal

"Sometimes in a burst of Greed and Hubris we swim out beyond our normal depth, not recognizing the monsters in deeper waters who wait,… watch… calculate… and… strike!" –
-Davis MacDonald

Davis MacDonald

CHAPTER 1

The man's silhouette slowly snaked its way up the steep hill, nimbly avoiding the holes of the gopher communities which riddled the bank, though his bent-over climb suggested he was old and tired.

It was late in the day and the sun was just setting behind the distant hills that ringed the Montecito Valley, shifting the vista toward tints of dark shadows and dusty greys and greens. He wore a floppy camouflage hat with a large brim, a faded green face mask, and camouflage khakis in greens and browns. He had a leaf blower slung over one shoulder.

He seemed just another Montecito gardener, arriving a little late to complete the last leaf blow of the day. The beat-up rusting green Ford pickup parked on the street at the bottom of the hill confirmed his status, its back bristling with rakes, shovels, a weed cutter, an old dirty chainsaw, and several black plastic bags filled with leaves.

He shifted the load of the leaf blower on his shoulder with one hand, suggesting that it was considerably lighter than a standard leaf blower. *It should be*, he mused. He'd taken the heavy electric motor and battery out, leaving only the shell of the thing that he now wore on his shoulder, a counterfeit badge of identity. He helped himself up the bank with a long narrow pole sheathed in khaki canvas. It was a tad too thick to be a walking stick. He was careful to keep the open end of the canvas away from the trees and brush.

Near the top of the grade, just below the narrow sundeck that connected to the sliding glass door of the residence there, he sat down for a rest, apparently exhausted by his climb. But his fingers were agile, sliding with loving care the canvas sheath off the pole; it was no pole at all but rather an oiled and maintained .22 caliber rifle. He pulled the rifle free and ran his hand affectionately along the barrel's smooth, polished black steel. Then he unsnapped the leaf blower's plastic engine housing, exposing the small compartment that contained no motor, but rather a high-tech gunsight. He pulled the sight out, mounted it carefully on the rifle, and brought the gun to his shoulder.

His target was there, just above, close. He could feel him, feel his energy, his warmth, his hubris. God, he hated the man.

He'd learned to shoot from his dad as a boy. His dad had been a hunter by avocation, and a perfectionist. Many a time as a boy he'd been slapped, knocked on the head, pushed to the ground, if he didn't do everything just right. Each little detail. Creating the ammunition with a super load of powder, cleaning the .22, loading the rifle, tracking the animal, putting the animal in his sights, squeezing the trigger just right and at the right time, analyzing the result, retrieving the cartridge, smoothing the ground where he'd lain so there was no record of his passage. And if he missed something, or God forbid missed the animal, there was Hell to pay. His dad had been a rough man, an alcoholic, driven by his own demons, demanding, belittling, sarcastic, never warm, never kind. But he turned out a kid who could shoot.

He'd joined the army, trained as a sniper, and gone off to Desert Storm. He found he liked extinguishing the enemy; it was as close as you could get to playing God; deciding who lived and who died. He'd extinguish several of the enemy, then disappear, leaving no trace. He'd just evaporate into the mist, to strike again from a different angle. There was satisfaction in it, even a thrill, almost a sexual thing. He flat out enjoyed it. Just like he was going to enjoy this, now.

His target he knew well, hated him for twenty-five years with a flame of anger that never diminished. He was going to do something he should have done years ago. It felt all so satisfying, so right; that special serendipity when your work and your passion merge together to create a perfect complement to action. Life was good.

He felt the bloodlust in him now, a haunting need to destroy that made his trigger hand shake a little. He steadied himself; he was a consummate professional. He'd do this task and be on his way, it was just the sweet taste of it that would linger on his tongue for a while; an old vendetta settled.

There was a younger man with his target, a man he hadn't seen before. A stranger. Anyway, the guy had to move. There was no clear shot to his target with the bozo standing in the way. He waited, very still, patient, like a coiled snake, ready.

CHAPTER 2

Blaine Forbes stood on the back deck of the modest ranch-style house on its one-acre lot, looking out across the Montecito Valley with its lush estates, and beyond to its hills and ring of mountains. The sun was starting to settle, and the tan hills were picking up shadows, showing the steep folds and crevices that had been hidden in the direct sunlight. A light ocean breeze drifted from the west, snuggling around the single hill that hid the sea from the house, slightly stirring the leaves on the tall eucalyptus trees to either side of the deck, scenting the air with a slight musty fragrance.

Blaine was an even six foot, tall and slender, with startling blue eyes and black hair that hinted of Irish roots, and an engaging smile. Twenty-eight years old, he was a private eye, partnered with the Judge, an old curmudgeon widely known for solving important and difficult cases. And Blaine was having the time of his life assisting the Judge, although it was often difficult to keep up with the old man, who tended to jump from issue to issue and topic to topic in conversation like a machine gun rattling away at facts.

It was so peaceful here in Montecito, the home to vast estates and large mansions. Some part of Blaine just wanted to find a lazy hammock and settle in for a nap.

But he was here on business. Not the time for lollygagging. Tom Flanders was the new Undersecretary for the U.S. Department of Energy's Office of Nuclear

Energy, and he'd been threatened. Someone apparently didn't like his views on atomic energy. The Judge was a fraternity brother from Flanders' U.S.C. days, and had asked Blaine to drive up the coast from L.A. to hear Flanders out. See if there was any substance to the threat and thereby a case their detective agency should take on. Or whether it was just some crackpot one-off threat from some tree-hugger that could be ignored.

The disappearing sun was leaving a chill in the air that seeped into the soul. Flanders suggested that they go inside. Blaine swizzled his drink in his glass, followed Tom back into his living room, and closed the sliding-glass door behind him.

Flanders, mid-fifties and medium height, was a scientist by training, but had been a bureaucrat all his career. He had a soft, pudgy face with a body to match, squinty blue eyes with laugh crinkles around the edges, and strands of grey hair combed up and over a balding pate and matted down in place. He wore distressed blue jeans that emphasized an expansive tummy, held together by an antique silver buckle of which he was obviously proud. A red-checked shirt collar peeked out above his white cashmere sweater, the sweater now a bit short, barely reaching his belt.

His house was festooned with pictures of him shooting big game in Africa, apparently his passion. Blaine didn't really see the point in hunting unless it was for food. Even the few times he'd been fishing, he came to realize that he preferred catch and release.

Flanders was living alone. According to the Judge, he was in the middle of a rocky divorce, pounded on by the Ex, two sets of lawyers, and a daughter in her early twenties who sided with her mother.

He was congenial, easy to talk to, and had poured Blaine a stiff Tanqueray and tonic that Blaine would have been fearful to set down near an open flame.

Their time on the deck had been spent exchanging banal chit-chat about Montecito, the weather, the Judge, and Washington politics, sprinkled with an occasional oblique reference to Flanders' recent change in marital status. Now Flanders was ready to get down to business; to discuss the threat he'd received.

"It's about the program I'm pushing as the Undersecretary for the U.S. Department of Energy's Office of Nuclear Energy, to move to small box atomic power," said Flanders. "It's known as a molten salt reactor, a small modular reactor invented by a bunch of ex-navy nuclear sub guys. Our fleet of atomic subs prove small reactors really work. Atomic submarines and atomic aircraft carriers have been operating with small modular reactors for years. You combine their small box technology with a molten salt design, and a lot of experts think we get the most attractive next-gen technology to solve our power problems. And it's basically walkaway safe."

"What about green energy?"

"Wind, solar, tides…. Green energy will never be sufficient to meet our spiraling power needs."

"Oil and gas?"

"They're the mainstays now, but most of the cheap carbon resources have already been found and mostly developed. It's going to get more and more expensive as we go deeper and farther to find hydrocarbons. No. It's going to have to be atomic energy. You'll see."

"Isn't the technology you're talking about pretty far off still?"

"That's the thing. We have small modular reactors that vary radically in size. And then you get into microreactors. And consider this. If you build another massive light-water reactor, like we used to do, and they're still operating in parts of the country, then how do you get the power to market? You do the transmission line thing, which is the grid. The grid is just so overloaded now, and it's vulnerable. You may have read recently that the Chinese tried to hack in and basically shut down parts of the grid. And there are concerns that a nuclear device detonated at the proper altitude could take out the entire grid. Or it could be a massive solar flare that does it. It's happened in the past."

"Okay. The grid's vulnerable, but I don't see…"

"One of the advantages of small modular atomic reactors… especially the microreactors, is that you can do distributed power. So, you actually have the reactor close to where the need is, initially military bases, hospitals, but then for entire communities, to assure stable power for each separate community. And because molten salt technology is so safe, it can be placed anywhere on a small footprint. Of course, some so-called experts, scientists paid to be experts in this area by certain industries, criticize the molten salt technology as being too corrosive, but my folks are adamant that they've been able to refine the technology. You can now have a long-lasting microreactor that works and is safe. And manufactured at a reasonable price point in bulk."

"What exactly is a molten salt reactor?"

"They use molten fluoride or chloride salts as a coolant. The coolant can flow over solid fuel like other reactors, or fissile materials can be dissolved into the primary coolant so that the fission directly heats the salt. Molten salt reactors are designed to use less fuel and produce shorter-lived radioactive waste than other reactor types. They have the potential to significantly change the safety posture and economics of nuclear energy production by processing fuel online, removing waste products, and adding fresh fuel without lengthy refueling outages. The systems are used for electricity or hydrogen production. They also can be tailored for the efficient burn-up of plutonium and minor actinides, which could allow them to consume waste from other reactors."

"How does that relate to your death threat?"

"I'll show you the letter, so you can read between the lines. There are certain industries that have been fighting tooth and nail to stop the development of small box atomic reactors, and particularly the molten salt design. They're enraged that I am trying to lead the Department of Energy around to my modern thinking, fearful of what it means for their industries. And probably rightly so. They want to stop me at any cost."

"Is there anyone in particular you suspect as making this threat?"

"I don't know. There's Dr. Emma Broadwell, a mean bitch who very much wanted my appointment; she hates me. It was a year and half fight between us, each pulling strings behind the scenes. She was in shock when I beat her, snatched the Undersecretary appointment out from under her nose. She's very much in the pocket of Big Oil. Gets grants, does speaking engagements, writes books, and gets paid very well by Oil and Gas interests to quash any proposals for use of atomic energy that might undermine the business of oil and gas."

"You think she might be behind this threatening letter?"

"Her, or the interests she represents. Come look at this letter."

As Flanders bustled through a stock of papers on his coffee table to find the letter, Blaine turned to take another look through the glass at the enchanting valley now laid out in twilight. He took one last sip of his gin and tonic, feeling more and more mellow by the second, only half listening as Flanders rattled on about a new defense contract he'd pushed through for small box atomic reactors. Flanders stood over the coffee table, a single-page letter in hand.

CHAPTER 3

There was a low-key crack as the Marksman pressured the trigger, and a mild recoil he absorbed into his shoulder. He watched through his sight as his victim was spun sideways by the impact of the super-charged .22 round, and toppled backward on to the floor. The Marksman dismounted the gun sight, secured it in the leaf blower case, shoved the rifle into its canvas, then scrambled downslope, displaying the vigor of an athlete.

This was a special kill indeed. It had been different, personal, deserved. It felt so… so good. He wondered why he'd not offed Flanders before. He supposed he hadn't realized how much anger he'd suppressed all this time.

He lapsed into his slow, old man gait as he slid toward the bottom eucalyptus trees and approached the road, becoming again the toddling old gardener as he put the leaf blower and shaft of canvas in the back of the stolen pickup, hoisted himself into the truck, and slowly pulled away, driving as an old man would.

He quietly abandoned the truck in a vacant lot, well wooded, near where he'd taken it. No worse for wear. Hoped the gardener quickly found his truck and had enjoyed his hour of free time before the truck was returned. He'd been tempted to put some gas in, but better judgement prevailed. He'd not risk being seen at the gas station just to square his karma with the unknown gardener. As for Flanders, the Marksman felt no remorse, no guilt. A dumb overfed animal had roamed Montecito for a time.... Now it roamed no more.

CHAPTER 4

Blaine watched through the glass as dark descended like a curtain across the valley to hide its fall colors. There was a sharp plopping noise, like a champagne bottle uncorked. He looked down at the glass in front of him, surprised to see a small hole about chest level, cracks running away from the hole like an unfolding web. Blaine looked closer, puzzled.

There was an enormous crash behind him. He turned to see Flanders, all two-hundred-thirty pounds of him, flopping around on his back on the floor where he'd fallen like some distressed marlin out of water. Bright red was pumping across Flanders' chest above his heart, staining his white cashmere sweater.

Blaine instinctively dropped to the floor and crabbed his way over to Flanders, who had stopped thrashing and was now lying flat. Blaine put two fingers to Flanders' neck, feeling for a pulse like they did in the movies. He felt nothing there. But then he had no idea what he was feeling for.

Blaine lifted his arm to turn the only table lamp off, then with unsteady hands fumbled his cell phone out of his inside coat pocket, still staying low. He had difficulty keeping his fingers steady as he dialed 9-1-1. Was the shot meant for him? Or for Flanders? He didn't know. He decided to crawl into the kitchen, out of sight of the big sliding glass door, just in case.

He tried to be calm as he rattled off his information and situation to the emergency operator.

She told him help was seven minutes away. It sounded like an inordinate amount of time.

Blaine decided he'd better crouch his way back into the living room to see if he could do anything for Flanders, hoping he wasn't exposing himself to the shooter.

Flanders didn't look good. His face was gray, his eyes glassy, staring unblinkingly toward the ceiling. His chest didn't seem to be moving at all. It didn't look like a situation to apply CPR, given all the blood. Blaine wasn't quite sure how to do CPR anyway. He decided he'd wait for help.

The minutes seemed to stretch on endlessly. Blaine picked up the fallen letter Flanders had been about to show him. He got one sentence into the letter before it occurred to him that he'd better go open the door and flag the paramedics in. He fiddled the letter into a fold and stuck it in this back pocket, then scuttled back through the kitchen into the entry hall, and cracked open the front door to peek out, not wanting to expose himself in any way. It was dark, hard to see anything.

Then the Fire Department's rescue truck rolled up onto the driveway, siren silent, all lights flashing. Two paramedics jumped out in their colorful suits. Blaine's mind drifted back to the colorful clowns he'd seen as a boy at the circus. Anything to avoid thinking about Flanders.

Send in the clowns, he thought. *And get me the fuck out of here!*

Soon the driveway was filled with three police cars and an ambulance; uniforms scurrying around in all directions like disturbed ants.

CHAPTER 5

Ted Olson came tearing up his steep driveway, which was divided from Flanders' drive by a one-foot space of earth filled with spindly young plants that would never quite be a hedge. He skidded to a stop at the top, leaped out of the red Mercedes rag-top, and pushed through the scraggly bushes to Flanders' property, demanding to know what was going on.

An elder sergeant with flat feet gingerly walked over to him, his large belly a tribute to his donut regiment. "Sergeant Holt," he muttered in a practiced rough voice. "And you are?"

"Ted Olson. I live next door. What's happened?"

"Been some kind of incident here. Not at liberty to say more. But for your safety I suggest you go inside your house, lock all your doors, and wait for the all-clear. Someone will be over to talk to you."

"Is Tom Flanders okay?"

"Can't say. There's been a shooting."

"He do it?" Olson said, pointing to the tall young man in an expensively cut grey suit, sporting a purple tie, standing between two officers. The man's face was white and there was blood smeared across the front of his coat, his white shirt, and the ugly tie.

"Not at liberty to say."

"Look, I'm the neighbor. I live right there. I'm entitled to know what's going on."

The sergeant just looked at him. Then, as though a light bulb suddenly went off, the sergeant's brown eyes snapped to Olson's. "You see any strangers in the area tonight?"

"I just got home from the market. All I've seen is this sea of red lights."

"What about before? Before you left for the market. See anybody?"

"No… ahh… yes. The gardener."

"Nobody else?"

"No."

"Okay. You should return to your house. Lock your windows and doors. Wait for our guys to clear the area. On second thought, let me get one of the patrolmen to accompany you to your house and check the inside. Be sure you've got no unwanted guests."

Olson looked startled, then fearful. He gulped. "Yes, sir. Yes, let's do that." Then he stood nervously, alternating his weight on one foot and then the other, waiting while a patrolman was selected to accompany him back through his hedge, across his driveway, and into his house.

CHAPTER 6

Blaine watched numbly as the ambulance team came rushing out of the house, pushing a wheeled stretcher which had a huge lump under a sheet, a bubble sized oxygen mask protruding from one end, and a normal saline bag mounted midships, its I.V. line running under the sheet. In seconds they were in the ambulance and gone.

"Come with me, sir, I want to take a statement," said the hefty sergeant to Blaine, gesturing with his hand to follow, then turning on feet that could no longer comfortably support his bulk toward a police cruiser with its doors open.

The sergeant deposited Blaine into the backseat of the cruiser, then walked around to bend and slide with difficulty into the other rear seat. He leaned over close, trying to be casual in what was an obvious effort to smell Blaine's breath, then tried to look nonchalant as he backed away from the scent of pure Tanqueray.

"Can I see your license?"

Blaine fumbled out his wallet, then dragged out his license with trembling fingers. Then it occurred to him to fish for his Private Investigator License.

"Private Dick, huh? Look a little young. You the one called it in?"

"Yeah."

"You okay, Mr. Forbes? You seem to have blood all over you."

"Yeah. I leaned over Flanders' body to try and take his pulse."

"Did he have one?"

"I… I… I couldn't tell."

The sergeant pulled out a small flip notebook and a mechanical pencil. "Okay. Let's hear your story, Mr. Forbes. From the top. Don't leave anything out."

Blaine was made to repeat what happened three times, slowly, while the sergeant took notes each time. Then the sergeant requested Blaine's cell phone number and his home address.

"Why don't you stick around here tonight in Santa Barbara, Mr. Forbes? Get a room; come into our police station in Montecito tomorrow when you're fresh. The detectives will want to talk to you some more."

Police cars were pulled aside, and Blaine shakily got into his car, maneuvered a turnaround in the narrow parking area, and slid down the steep driveway, leaving officers with flashlights still searching the surrounding grounds and bushes.

CHAPTER 7

After check-in, Blaine dropped onto the stool at the "O" Bar in the lobby of the Ritz-Carlton Bacara, Santa Barbara, and shakily reached for the drink menu. He glanced up at the sculpture that hung over him, a massive mess that looked like old, twisted metal fencing someone had sprayed silver and hung from the ceiling. He wondered if he was safe to sit under it. He looked out at the sea, hoping it would calm him. But it didn't. He no longer felt safe… anywhere.

He treated himself to a Dragon Bomb, a cocktail made with rum, vodka, several sweet liqueurs of unknown proof, and a drop of CBD oil. Given its price, he was a little disappointed it didn't come with a pink umbrella, but he gobbled it down anyway. It seemed to help, so he ordered another. The bullet had been damn close to his chest. Too damned close. Three inches over and he'd have been dead. This detective work was dangerous. Just out of nowhere, standing looking out across the valley from someone's living room, you could be mowed down. The second cocktail disappeared as fast as the first; he could feel his shattered nerves calming as a healthy warm glow developed in his belly.

A brunette slid onto the stool next to him, shifting her fanny in her bright red silk dress with the low decolletage around the stool for maximum comfort and display. She was young, slender, with a small chest that didn't need a bra, early twenties. She glanced at him speculatively out of the corner of her sparkly eyes while posturing disinterest. He thought of his old college roommate, who'd often opined, *"Ask a hundred women, and at least one will say yes."*

He looked at her straight on and decided she was worth an 'Ask'.

"How are you? Want a drink?"

She turned to look at him full on, soft brown eyes scanning his, taking in his expensively cut blue suit, starched white shirt, and cherished purple tie. He was glad he'd changed clothes in his room. Then she smiled, perfect teeth surrounded by ruby red lips.

"I'm Dani," she said in a low voice, offering out a small hand, perfect clear polish, no rings.

He took the hand carefully; afraid any normal shake might sprain it. Her hand was soft and warm; the faint scent of strawberries wafted over him as she leaned over to extend it, displaying the tops of small ivory breasts cupped into the top of her dress. Blaine could feel interest rising in his lower extremities.

"Hi, Dani. You live here, in Montecito?"

"In Santa Barbara. I go to college at U.C.S.B."

"Go Gauchos," said Blaine, at a loss for a moment as to what else to say.

"I'm twenty-two," Dani said, her chin coming up. "And I've just been dumped by my boyfriend."

"Oh. I'm sorry. That must be tough." Blaine tried to look warm and sympathetic, not a rooster sizing up the entrance to a hen house. He suspected he failed.

"He was my first boyfriend," explained Dani. "I thought we'd last forever."

"What happened?"

"The usual. Dumped me for a cheerleader with big tits."

"That hardly seems fair. Must be a very shallow guy. You're stunningly beautiful."

Dani sat a little straighter in her chair, sucking in her tummy, perking up. "You seem like a real nice guy. Yes. You can buy me a drink. I think I'd like that."

"The Dragon Bomb is good."

She smiled. "Is it sweet? I like sweet."

"Oh, my God, is it ever. I'm ordering my third. Not overly strong either," he lied smoothly. "Safe. Very calming on the nerves. I was shot at this afternoon."

Brown eyes fluttered wide with shock and concern. "You aren't hurt, are you?"

"Just a little shaken. You can try to intellectualize it. But you never understand the shock of it until you've been actually shot… or almost shot…. Shot at. Like what happened to me today!" Blaine shook his head and stared mournfully into his Dragon Bomb.

"Oh, my God. It must be awful." Her small hand reached over and patted him reassuringly on the knee. "Are you a cop or something?"

"A private eye."

"Woah. You must have had some really interesting cases."

"I've had my share." Blaine cast his eye out into the space of the bar, working to paste a nonchalant smile on his face.

After that, somewhere in the middle of his fourth Dragon Bomb, Blaine lost all sense of time and space.

He was awakened the next morning by the rattle of his hotel room door as Dani tugged on it to get out. "Running very late for class, Hon. Sorry. I'll call you."

Her hips churning, Dani bolted out the door like a sleek gazelle. Blaine suspected it would have been a beautiful image to remember if he could have focused, but his head was too painful. Damn Dragon Bombs. He remembered settling his head on her small breasts, warm and smelling of strawberry… then nothing. He couldn't even remember if anything happened. He might have just collapsed into bed. God, his head hurt!

CHAPTER 8

Overlooking Houston's skyline, The Oil and Gas Club was a crusty institution with its own dining room, spacious bar, a famous wine cellar, and very private rooms for special meetings. Dating from the mid-Forties, its club facilities were nestled on the penthouse level of a downtown high rise. Some attributed its survival in an age of disappearing clubs to its founding motto, even more relevant in a climate of pervasive government regulation. *"A tradition of business deals sealed with a handshake."*

The famous 'Doctor', Dr. Armand Hammer, had sat here and made deals on a handshake, as had Fred Hartly, UNOCAL's outspoken Chairman, famous for allegedly being mis-quoted as saying about the Santa Barbara oil spill, *"Who gives a damn about a few ducks?"* At the club's secluded conference room the next morning, Fred had been presented a small trophy, inscribed *"To Fred Hartley, the only man who opened his mouth this week just to change feet."*

This morning it was an unusual group of people who quietly ghosted their way into the conference room and settled into the brown leather seats surrounding the long oblong blonde wooden table, pockmarked and knot-strewn, an antique from Houston's pioneer days. They were all expensively dressed, they all had the sheen of money and power about them that came with their positions in D.C., and, for the most part, they were congressional lobbyists. They offered no objection when one of the lawyers met them at the door and insisted their cell phones be deposited outside in the hall in a basket. In fact, they expected it, would have been concerned if such precautions hadn't been taken.

What was unusual, in fact extraordinary, was the breadth of the businesses they quietly represented. There were people representing the major oil companies, the major pipeline companies, the major public utilities, and the largest of the solar and alternative power companies. There were also representatives of the major manufacturers of generators and electrical components.

The ad hoc Chairman of this discreet group, the man who had summoned its membership, was Buck Jennings, a former senator from the state of Texas and a longtime friend of oil interests. He stood up, took off his Stetson hat, laid it on the table next to the small podium, and clinked a water glass with his fork. He waited patiently for his breakfast group to settle. He was of medium height, with skin bronzed from the Texas sun. Intelligent, dark eyes stared out intensely at the room, testimony to a mixed marriage some four generations back. He wore a wraparound beard, clipped short, and a small mustache. His tailored blue suit, matching tie, and pocket square spoke money…lots of it. But his old scuffed leather boots, well-worn and loved, suggested a trail ride, not a breakfast at the Oil Club.

He still had a full head of hair, long, thick, and black with lines of silver creeping through. But his most notable feature was his smile. He had a wide mouth which quickly became a warm smile all the way across his face, drawing people to him, attracted to his humor and his warmth. He'd been plying his warm smile, and the way it dropped defenses, for many years in the lobbyist trade, and before that as a senator.

Buck produced his special smile now as he tinged his water glass with his fork, bringing instant quiet and attention. "We all know why we're here and I don't need to spell it out."

There were nods of assent up and down the table.

"But I'm pleased to report that thanks to the generous contributions you arranged from your respective clients, we have sufficient funds to continue forward with our agenda.

Also, by good fortune or destiny, a significant irritant we've had to tolerate, the man we installed as Undersecretary for the U.S. Department of Energy's Office of Nuclear Energy, Tom Flanders, is no longer able to perform his duties. The ingrate double-crossed us, but I believe we'll no longer have to put up with his crack-pot ideas and idiot proposals." Buck produced a broad smile for the group.

"And we've made progress through our friends in the Executive Branch with our campaign to encourage many of the major media companies to put the right slant on his extreme proposals. I don't think we'll be hearing much more about wild-eyed ideas to build atomic plants the size of boxcars and place them in major cities. We've hand-picked a replacement for the Undersecretary's job, who will be far more realistic about the limits of atomic power and the holocaust that could occur were the country to use such dangerous and untried technologies. She's been a loyal team player for years; we'll be able to count on her. I'll want to meet separately at the end of our meetings today to huddle with the leaders of our PACs to work out the network of campaign funding needed to assure our gal becomes the replacement Undersecretary.

Now, we're having more difficulty with the Department of Defense. They seem to be more concerned about the military's convenience than about the economic health of our country. So far, the D.O.D. has been unwilling to cancel their contract given to a company in Virginia to build portable atomic plants that can be transported on planes and boxcars to any active military theater. That's a childish response since we've proven in the past the viability of our air freight of fuel and generators to anywhere in the world, to any theater. Our current energy support methods are effective and efficient and provide jobs for our country. But you know how these generals like to spend money on the next shiny thing.

I need you to each go back to your chief executive officers and develop plans and funding commitments. Come back with some strong ideas about where we can lay our money down politically to turn this stupid D.O.D. plan around."

This brought a rumble of agreement around the table as members shook their heads and looked at each other with disgust for the D.O.D.

"Gentlemen, we'll now break into smaller groups by industry for some off-the-record discussion." He flashed his smile again and left the podium,

Buck stepped over to put his arm around Jose, their long-time maître de, and leaned down so Jose could whisper in his ear. "Your special guest has arrived. I put him in the wedding suite."

Buck nodded and quietly headed for the elevator. The wedding suite indeed. It was quite fitting since this was a wedding of interests so to speak.

Buck knocked on the door to the suite, and it was immediately opened by Franklin Ross, the distinguished

Senator from Missouri. They shook hands cordially, Buck splashed some aged bourbon from the bar cart into a couple of glasses, and they settled into the deep sofas across from one another, overlooking downtown Houston.

"How do we stand?" asked Ross. "I've heard conflicting rumors."

"I think he's dead, or as good as. There's no way to sugarcoat it."

"Good God. Who did it? Do we know?"

"No. And I don't want to. We stay as far away from this unpleasantness as possible."

"Right."

"Here's your monthly stipend, Franklin. Don't spend it all in one place." Buck reached into the inner pocket of his coat and produced a very thick envelope, the assurance of Ross's loyalty to the oil industry. It went into the hands of Senator Ross and smoothly disappeared.

"Now," Buck said, "I've got two people here for you to meet. One's an Oil guy and the other's in windmill farms. They each control very large PACs with lots of campaign money looking for a home. I figured it was best you meet them here and not in D.C. That town has eyes everywhere. You stay here and I'll send them each up separately. I've prepped them and they know what to expect; they understand that the time and interest of a U.S. Senator doesn't come cheap."

Buck flashed his famous smile and was gone.

CHAPTER 9

The Judge leaned against the outside wall of the Terminal Building for the Santa Barbara Airport, tapping one foot in agitation. He was a tall man, broad-shouldered and big-boned, with just the beginnings of a paunch around the middle, hinting at an appetite for fine wines and good food. He cut an imposing figure in his dark blue corduroy sport coat, outfitted with casual patch pockets. Under it he wore a light blue dress shirt, its oversized collar open at the neck, and disreputable-looking jeans of unknown vintage, faded and threadbare here and there. He had the ruddy and chiseled features of Welsh ancestors, a rather too-big nose, large ears, and bushy eyebrows on the way to premature gray.

He had a given name of course, but when he'd ascended to the bench some years before, people had begun calling him just "Judge". Even old friends he'd known for years affectionately adopted the nickname. He hadn't been a Judge for a long time now. But his nickname still stuck.

Right now the Judge was agitated. Where the devil was his young detective partner? Blaine Forbes, his ride from the airport, was characteristically late, now fifteen minutes late. The Judge was thinking about saying to Hell with it and tagging one of the yellow cabs lined up in front of him, when Blaine came tooling around the corner at breakneck speed, the tires on his old Mini Cooper squealing in protest. When the Judge saw the car he instantly regretted not jumping into a cab. He'd forgotten about this derelict of an auto Blaine insisted on driving, too cheap to invest in a real car.

Blaine rumbled to a stop and leaned over to throw the passenger door open. He looked hung over, his eyes a bit bloodshot, dark circles there, his hands on the wheel a little shaky.

The Judge surveyed his ride with disdain, then leaned in to grab the two empty French fry containers and the empty Starbucks cup off the passenger seat and toss them into the back. They landed with a crunch, scattering the empty Big Mac wrappers, potato chip packages and assorted debris already piled there.

Blaine was oblivious to the Judge's displeasure, busy in the rear-view mirror, desperately trying to adjust the knot in his fuchsia tie and then mash his hair down with a little spit so it didn't look like he had horse-tails. The young man was a clotheshorse for sure, and dressed well, although this morning he looked a little rumpled. He spent his funds on fancy pants and cared less about riding around in a tiny beat-up car that served as a trash dumpster.

The Judge bent over and pretzeled himself in, bumping his head against the ceiling before shifting the seat farther backward and tilting its backrest even further aft, throwing new pressure on the Judge's iffy lower spine. At barely six feet, Blaine just fit; the Judge's six-foot-four bulk didn't.

Blaine muscled the gears, which ground in protest, and the little car shot out into the airport traffic to a calliope of horns and rude finger gestures from competitive drivers, all trying to leave the airport in a hurry. The Judge grit his teeth. Blaine was oblivious to the turmoil around his forced entry into the traffic stream.

28

"Let's go to Tom Flanders' house first, Blaine. I want to see the lay of the land."

Blaine pulled onto the 101 and headed south, toward Montecito.

"So, you don't think the bullet was meant for you, Blaine?" asked the Judge.

"What?... No…. Of course not. That's crazy, Judge. Flanders got the note."

"I don't know, Blaine. Have you been messing around with a young married woman again?"

Blaine snorted. "She'd been a mistress, not a wife. Why do you always bring that up?"

"Just rattling your cage a little, partner."

Blaine muttered something unintelligible.

A man stood at the side of the road just past the off ramp and glared at the Judge as Blaine slowed the Mini to a stop at a stop sign. Somehow, the man sensed the pomp and ceremony, the power and privilege, which the Judge represented. Of course, the Judge was retired, but he still carried himself in a regal way, there was still crispness in his thoughts and actions, a certain way he held his head, the way he paused to speak, the authoritative gestures with his hands, and if he was truly stirred up, 'the voice' emerged, the gravelly voice, down deep and dark, that he'd barked in his courtroom to keep order and dignity while administering justice.

The man didn't know about "the voice". Didn't care it was an unwashed Mini that had pulled up at his stop sign. The man knew enough. In the man's mind the Judge was the enemy, the authority, the state, the lawgiver, the primary reason there was so much misery in the world.

The man dashed toward the car on the Judge's side, pressed a heavily gummed poster against the passenger window near the Judge's face so it stuck, then slowly moved backwards and away from the car, never taking his eyes off the Judge's face.

"Useless lazy bastard," muttered Blaine, angry at the attack on his Mini, the only thing of substance he owned.

The Judge watched the man back away, dirty tweed overcoat over a white T-shirt, threadbare jeans well past 'designer distressed', a tired red ball cap on his head with the Rams emblem partly missing. He looked the part of a homeless, and that's certainly what he was. Then the Judge looked at the paper now pasted to a portion of his side window:

NO MORE ATOMICS
NO MORE DAMAGE TO OUR PLANET
AND OUR CELLS.

It was a sophisticated message. One the Judge was sure the homeless man didn't write. But it gave the man comfort to believe in it, a cause to justify his existence, a stone to lob at those who seemed to have everything. The Judge wondered what it would be like to live homeless in 21st Century America. There would be freedom from all the worries responsibility brought. An end to striving, an end to collecting things, at least things too big to fit in your shopping cart, and he supposed a whole social set of those equally impoverished to hang with and discuss blame for your condition. It all made the Judge quite sad.

Twenty minutes later the Mini chugged up the steep driveway to Flanders' ranch-style house with difficulty, slipping and sliding on the moist asphalt, threatening to careen backward at any moment.

They parked on the pad at the front of the house and walked over to the front door. It was locked. A notice posted there proclaimed the house the subject of a police investigation and not to be entered.

"I think I can get us in around back, Judge."

They tramped around the side of the house through tall moist grass to the back with its long narrow sundeck overlooking the Montecito Valley and mountains beyond, mostly muted this morning by fine mist. The hole in the sliding glass door glass was clearly visible. The Judge went over to poke a finger through it, turned, muttered, "Small caliber, maybe a twenty-two."

"Would you normally use such a small caliber gun to kill someone?"

"Not usually. But maybe he wanted to keep the noise down. The neighbor's house is pretty close." They turned to gaze at the neighbor's home, built on an adjacent pad at the same level on the hill, a much larger house styled in the Spanish tradition, all white stucco with a red tile roof.

"You said you could get us in?" the Judge said.

Blaine brought out his wallet, selected his lone credit card, and slid it between the sliding glass door and its latch. After 30 seconds of twisting and fiddling, there was a click, and Blaine slid the door open. They stepped in. Blaine shuddered a little, recalling his last time in the living room.

There was no outline of where Flanders had fallen, like in the movies, but the carpet was black and stiff where blood had pumped out and dried black. Near the dried blood the Judge hunched down to put his eyes about the height of Flanders' chest when Flanders had been standing, and sighted with one finger to the hole in the glass and the yard behind.

"Probably rested his rifle on that large stone sitting beyond the deck at the edge of the bank, took his time, waited for the right moment, then squeezed off one deadly round." As they peered out the window at the rock, a head suddenly appeared next to it, making Blaine jump. They opened the slider and stepped out on the deck to confront a wizened old man, Japanese, his dark eyes staring at them from beneath a coolie's broad-brimmed straw hat, a leaf blower in hand, its apparatus strapped to his shoulder.

"Who are you?" he asked, jabbing a finger at them, steeling himself for fight or flight.

"I'm a fraternity brother of Tom's. I'm looking into who shot him."

"Police?"

"No. Private."

"Oh. Okay, I guess. I'll just finish the garden."

"You the gardener?" asked Blaine.

The man just looked at Blaine, seeing no need to answer a stupid question.

"They call me the Judge." The Judge stepped off the deck and reached out a hand, offering to shake, and the gardener accepted it, both of them ignoring the grime of oil on his hand.

"I'm Minato."

Suddenly there was a growl to their left, and a Siberian Husky came out of the bushes, trotted to Minato's side, then turned to face the strangers. Its startlingly blue eyes focused on the Judge as the primary threat, narrowed, and another warning growl came, low and dangerous.

"Hush, Handsome. Be quiet." The dog shut up immediately, turning to look at Minato, expectantly. "He doesn't like strangers."

"Did you like working for Tom Flanders?" asked the Judge.

"No. Not particularly. He was an arrogant prick."

"How so?"

"Always bitching about my work. Always squeezing my price down for trimming and cleanup projects."

"You know he is the Undersecretary in charge of Nuclear Energy?" asked Blaine.

"Yeah…so…if we'd won the war, all your politicians would have been hung for their war crimes!"

"What? What did you say?" asked Blaine, leaning closer, trying to understand the significance of Minato's outburst.

"My older brother died at Hiroshima. Your Truman was a terrorist of the first order. As bad as the Nazis, as bad as Stalin. Should have been hung. A hundred and sixty thousand people died with my brother at Hiroshima. Another hundred thousand at Nagasaki. Civilians! Not combatants." Minato looked grim.

"Tom Flanders wasn't part of that," said the Judge.

"No…but he's a politician pushing for more use of atomic energy, deliberately ignoring the lessons of Hiroshima and Chernobyl and Three Mile Island."

"Did you dislike Flanders enough to kill him?" asked Blaine.

Minato gave Blaine the same look he'd given upon Blaine's first stupid question. Then he turned, waving his hand over his shoulder, and strolled down the bank through the eucalyptus trees toward the old truck parked on the road.

The Judge turned and walked back into the house, Blaine following. They wandered through the kitchen, around the dining room, across the living room, and down a long hall, two bedrooms and a bathroom to the left, and a master bedroom and master bathroom to the right. The master had a hastily made-up king-size bed. A stack of papers was piled beside the bed on a small chest of drawers. The Judge picked up the pile and leafed through, mostly white papers and articles about atomic energy and D.O.E. programs, stuff Flanders hadn't gotten around to reading. Underneath the stack was a small thin book with a colorful cover: *Zen and Atomic Energy*. The Judge picked it up. As he meandered through its pages a small bit of white paper fluttered out and landed on the carpet. Blaine snatched it up and read out loud, "'To Tom, my special pal' signed, 'Iris' in a woman's hand."

The second bedroom was clearly a guest bedroom, everything in place and neat. It looked like it hadn't been used in a long time. The third bedroom was set up as Flanders' office. A massive desk at one end had two computer screens and two telephones, a white one and a red one.

Blaine stepped past the Judge to pick up the red telephone, rolling his eyes at the Judge as he said, "Certainly, Mr. President, I'll get right on it. Did you want it black, or with cream?" his blue eyes twinkling, showing the tall boy he really was. The Judge smiled back. Blaine was impossible to resist.

They each took a side of the office and shuffled through papers, notebooks, yellow pads filled with notes, and old mail, some opened, some not. The Judge took a deep dive into Flanders' filing cabinet, found Flanders' medical history and doctor's bills, his utilities, his credit card and banking documentation, his tax receipts, notecards from a lifetime of speaking engagements, a very well-organized collection of vintage gentleman's magazines, a manilla envelope with photos of a naked young woman who was definitely not Flanders' wife, and a flimsy unlabeled folder with a handful of email print-outs and handwritten notes. The Judge browsed it as he watched Blaine bloodhound Flanders' desk drawers. The recurring theme was something called Complex Atomic Solutions, a guy named Lance Kelly, and a dispute between Kelly and Flanders over the sale of corporate shares. The dispute appeared to grow hotter and hotter based on the progression of details in the emails.

Blaine, having finished his search of Flanders' desk drawers, ran his hand across the bottom of the center drawer, looking for anything taped there, like in the movies. The Judge watched him with amusement, knowing Flanders would never hide something in so obvious a place. And was amazed when Blaine's face changed to a victorious expression as his hand came up with a small piece of tape with a camera SD card stuck to it from the underside of the drawer.

"I'll be damned, Blaine. You actually found something."

Blaine smiled, tucking the card in his shirt pocket.

"That reminds me, Blaine, did the police give you a copy of the threatening letter?"

Blaine blinked. "Shit. I think the original's still in my back pocket. I forgot to tell them about it in all the commotion; the shock of being shot at and all; seeing Tom lying in a pool of blood."

Blaine reached into the right back pocket of his designer jeans, looking startled when his hand came up with only a soiled handkerchief. "Christ, I'm sure that's where I stuck it." He fished around in his other back pocket, then his front pockets, moving more and more desperately, then ransacked all the pockets in his tweed sport coat. His cell phone came out, Kleenex, some change, his keys, and his wallet, looking woefully thin. That was all.

"Maybe in the car, on the seat or something," Blaine said as he turned to dash down the hall to exit the house and check.

The Judge walked leisurely after him, shaking his head in disbelief. He found Blaine leaning on the side fender of his car, face red, hyperventilating a little, upset.

"Jesus, Judge. I don't have it. I had it. I'm sure. I shoved it into my back pocket while I was huddled over Tom to see if he was alive. I… I… I forgot it when I talked to the police, but it was still in my back pocket. This back pocket." He pointed around his butt.

"You sure those are the same suit pants, Blaine?"

"They're the only ones I brought."

"What did you do after you talked to the police?"

"Well, I was a stressed-out wreck. I checked into the Ritz-Carlton Bacara, Santa Barbara, because the police said I had to stick around town, and had a couple of drinks in the bar."

"Could it have slipped out there?"

"I don't see how. I mean…. No, absolutely not."

"Perhaps you took it out for safekeeping when you got back to your hotel room?"

"No. I'd put the whole miserable afternoon out of my mind by then. I was focused on…on…well…other stuff."

"Were you with someone?"

"Why do you ask that?"

"Because I know you, partner. Did someone pick you up in that bar?"

"No. Well…I might have made a new friend."

"So, you picked someone up?"

"Well…yes."

"And you took her back to your room?"

Blaine nodded, turning even redder.

"Did she spend the night?"

"Yes." Blaine's voice was a whisper.

"And now the letter is gone."

"Yes."

"Who was she?"

"Dani. Dani something."

"You don't remember her last name?"

"I…I…I don't think she ever told me."

"Phone number?"

"No. Oh my God, my cash."

Blaine pulled his wallet out again and opened its back pocket, exposing empty space. "Shit…shit…shit!"

"Jesus, partner. I think we better put you on the wagon and keep you out of bars. Come on. We've got to visit the police station right now. Flanders sent me a copy of the letter. It's on my laptop."

CHAPTER 10

As Blaine slid into the Mini Cooper, and the Judge put his body into various contortions, trying to determine how best to squeeze his bulk in, a voice called out from the other side of the hedge dividing Flanders' driveway from his neighbors. "Hey there! Who are you? Do you belong on Flanders' property? There's been funny stuff going around here the last couple of days. We have a Neighborhood Watch around here and I'm Committee Chairperson!"

The shrubs in the middle of the hedge parted and a middle-aged man stepped out. The man was not quite six feet, mid-fifties, stocky, brown hair and eyes, with a beard rapping around a square jaw and continuing into sideburns that framed his face. He wore loose-fitting robin-blue running pants, a matching T-shirt, clearly designer, but was still in his slippers. He walked toward them across the driveway lightly, measured, confident; a guy who could take care of himself.

Blaine and the Judge looked at each other. Blaine slid out of the Mini, and the Judge straightened.

"We're private investigators," said Blaine, "helping the police investigate who shot Dr. Flanders," instinctively raising his empty palms outward.

"Is he okay? Did Tom make it?"

"We don't have any updates on his condition."

"Oh. Poor Tom. I didn't think the police worked with private investigators. Got any identification?"

They both pulled out their private investigator licenses and flipped them open.

"I'm Ted Olson, live next door. "You've got to admit, guys, you're a strange-looking pair. Are you gay?"

The Judge started to bristle, but Blaine stepped forward with a warm smile on his face. "We're not. Are you?"

"Hell no. Watch your mouth, man." Color rose in Olson's face.

"Did you see anyone or hear anything the afternoon Flanders was shot, Ted?" asked the Judge.

"No. I told the police. I wasn't here. Off at the market doing my shopping."

"You live alone?"

"Yeah. Had a wife for a while, but she left for sunnier pastures a few years back."

"What about before you left for the market, Ted? See anyone around?"

"Just the gardener. Pulled up in a beat-up truck as I left. An old guy, moved slow. Or maybe he was just on the clock, charging hourly. I don't know."

"Was he Flanders' regular gardener? The one working in the back now? Guy named Minato?"

"I don't know…now I think about it, maybe not."

"Did he have a dog?"

"I didn't see any dog."

"See his face?"

"Naw. I wasn't really looking. I think he had a hat pulled low."

The Judge and Blaine looked at each other.

"So, you don't think you'd recognize him if you saw him again?"

"I doubt it. Gardeners are a dime a dozen in Montecito."

"Thanks for the help," said the Judge. "And nice to meet you."

They returned to the Mini and crawled in, neighbor Olson continuing to watch with suspicious eyes as they drove from the pad down Flanders' long driveway to the street.

CHAPTER 11

As Blaine drove the Mini, the Judge showing white knuckles and gritting his teeth, the Judge's cell began playing the opening strands of 'Danny Boy', announcing a call.

"Hello. This is the Judge." The Judge put the call on speaker.

"This is Jill Flanders, Tom's mother," said a crotchety old voice.

"Mrs. Flanders, we were so sorry to hear about Tom. I'm in Montecito and we're all pulling for Tom to make it."

"Yes. It's absolutely awful, Judge. Tom told me he was going to consult with you about his threatening letter. And now this. I'm just so upset, I'm beside myself. And they won't let me see Tom. I couldn't come anyway, of course. I live in assisted living now and don't get around much. Don't even have a car. Do they know who did this to my boy?"

"The police are working on it. There's not a person of interest yet, as far as I know, Mrs. Flanders."

"Yeah. That sounds typical for our police department these days. Mostly useless unless a speeding ticket needs written to bump up City coffers. They're always Johnny on the spot for that."

"Yes, Ma'am."

"So, here's the deal Judge. I've got plenty of money. More than I need. More than I could ever spend in two lifetimes. I'd like to hire you to find the person who shot Tom from ambush and see he goes to jail. I'll pay your standard retainer to start, and monthly billing for your time and expenses will be paid within ten days of bill receipt. Does that sound okay?"

"I'm sure you have better things to do with your money, ma'am, than spend it on us. We are poking around a little on our own, helping the police out with their analysis. We don't mind doing that on our own."

"No, no, no Judge. That's not acceptable. I want you to accept my retainer, and I want you full tilt into an investigation. Find out who did it and why. I'm his mom. I'm entitled to know. I've already put a five thousand retainer check in the post to your L.A. office. So, you get right on it and call me with a report once you've got the guy. Thank you so much." The line went dead.

CHAPTER 12

The Judge marched into the Montecito Sheriff's Substation with Blaine shuffling behind, his head down, like a small boy forced to return shoplifted goods. They were shuttled into the small office of the captain who was supervising the investigation of the Tom Flanders shooting, the most significant case the Department had had since the murder of Violet Evelyn Alberts.

Captain Johnny Marks was a tall man, broad-shouldered and just big. He had a broad face, a chiseled nose, and a square jaw, punctuated by bright blue intelligent eyes. He had the look of a German tank commander from World War II, except he'd never have fit through the hatch into the tank. He stood up from his desk and stalked around it to the center of the tiny office to meet the Judge and shake his hand, looking a bit like a caged lion in the tight space.

"I've heard a lot about you Judge, all good. Understand you're something of renowned sleuth."

"Oh, well, you know…" muttered the Judge, but still puffing up a little like the proud bird he was. He loved to be stroked. "And this is my partner, Blaine Forbes. Blaine is the one who was with Tom Flanders when he was shot. Any news on Tom's condition? Is he going to make it?"

"We don't know for sure, but it looks grim. He's in a coma and on life support. The doctors say we just have to wait and see how he does. Nice to meet you, Mr.

Forbes. I read your statement. Sorry your visit to our town became such a harrowing experience."

"Yes, well…thank you, sir." Blaine ruefully shook hands, his small ivory hand disappearing momentarily into the clutch of Marks' sunburned claw.

The Judge, never known to waste a minute, dove immediately into the heart of the matter. "Blaine needs to further elaborate on his statement from last night, Captain Marks."

"Just call me Johnny, Judge. Everybody does. Sit down, gentlemen. Tell me what's changed, Blaine."

"Well, uh…you see…here let me show you." Blaine reached into his pocket and pulled out a copy of the threatening letter sent to Tom Flanders, a copy printed at the hotel from the Judge's computer.

Johnny picked up the letter and took his time reading it, studying each word. His eyebrows narrowed as he read:

Mr. Flanders. You're a fool and a snake. Trying to sell the public on small-scale atomic plants you know will pollute the ground, the air, the groundwater, the sky, and cause millions to sicken and die. You have seriously offended the powerful people who put you where you are. Now you must step down and resign as Undersecretary for Nuclear Energy. There will be serious consequences for you if you do not resign. Consequences with finality.

"Wow. This is for real?'

"Yes," said the Judge. "Tom Flanders was concerned enough that he called our office and hired us to investigate the threat privately for him. Blaine was conducting the initial interview about the threat letter when Tom was shot."

"Very interesting. Where's the original letter? We didn't find anything like this when we searched his house."

"Well, that's something of a problem," Blaine said softly.

"Oh…?"

"Well, Mr. Flanders was about to show me the original when he was shot. I…I…After he'd been shot, I crawled over on all fours and saw he was gravely injured. And then, well…I…I…well just automatically I guess, I just took the letter and shoved it in my back pocket. Then with all the police and the ambulance, and the getting dark, all the lights, and my realization of how close that bullet had been to my chest and telling my story over and over in the back seat of a police cruiser, and maybe because I was in shock…"

"Yes. Yes. Where's the original letter?"

"I forgot to tell the officer about it."

"Yes. I see that. Give me the original letter now, Blaine."

"Well…err…that's the problem."

"What do you mean?"

"I don't have it. I lost it."

"How in the Hell do you lose a letter that's tucked into your back pocket? Probably jammed beneath your cell phone?"

"Well…that's kind of the embarrassing part."

Johnny was sitting up straight in his chair now, not looking at all pleased.

"Go on, Blaine. And this better be good."

"Well…I was shaken last night you know, the bullet coming so close to me and all. And so I went to the bar in my hotel for a drink."

"Okay."

"And I met this young girl in the bar, see, a student at U.C.S.B. And we started talking, and we hit it off, and we decided to go up to my hotel room for a nightcap. And, well, one thing led to another, and...and we spent the night together." Blaine's words came in a rush now, trying to get the whole story out in five seconds.

"The letter, Blaine. The letter!"

"In the morning the girl left. Later, I remembered the letter and checked my pockets, but it was gone."

"What? You've got to be kidding."

"I wish I was."

"Damn, that's great. Just hunky dory. What was the girl's name?"

"Dani."

"Dani what?"

"I didn't get her last name," whispered Blaine.

"You didn't get her last name?" Johnny's voice was incredulous.

"Well, the heat of passion and all. I...no. I didn't get her last name."

Johnny slumped back in his chair, all the excitement evaporating from his face. Blaine looked sick. The Judge sat back in his chair, nonchalantly enjoying the drama.

"You searched your room, your pockets, your car, the parking lot, asked at the bar?"

"Yes." Blaine's voice was very small.

"Nothing?"

"No."

Johnny gave a big sigh. "Okay, come on Blaine. Let's get your statement updated."

"Young Blaine here also needs to report a theft," the Judge put in.

"A theft?"

"Yes, Blaine, tell the nice captain what else is missing. Besides the letter, and your pride."

"She…Dani…I think she took the cash from my wallet."

Johnny stiffy walked Blaine out of the tiny office, out into the office pool, and asked one of the detectives to take Blaine's statement down again.

Stepping back into his office, Johnny whispered under his breath, "What sort of partners are you hiring these days, Judge?"

CHAPTER 13

The Judge settled back in the chair in the captain's office as Johnny slumped behind his desk again. "What can you tell me about Tom Flanders, Judge? You were his friend?"

"We were friends at the fraternity house at U.S.C. years ago, in the loose way all your frat brothers are friends. We shared meals, sometimes went drinking together in rotating cliques of threes and fours that formed and unformed as young boys evolved into men. And we kept in touch through graduate school and after, Christmas cards, occasional emails, and rare class reunions where we both attended. So yes, we were casual friends. But we were never really close. I didn't go to his wedding or anything. He called me out of the blue a week ago, wanted help."

"With the letter?"

The Judge nodded. "He said the more he thought about it, the more concerned he became. He'd received threats now and then over the years, and just ignored them. But for some reason this letter had him rattled. He wanted me to look into it. See if I could find who sent it."

"And you sent Blaine."

"Yes. I was in the middle of a trial. I couldn't come."

"Did Flanders say why? Why this letter caused him to call you?"

"No. But I had the feeling there was something more he wasn't telling me. Perhaps a more complicated situation he found himself in and needed advice. There seemed a touch of desperation in his voice when we spoke on the phone. Just a feeling I got."

"Not a dead horse head in his bed?" Johnny gave the Judge a tight smile.

"No. Nothing like that. I'm sure he'd have told me; and your department would have been called in at once. How is Tom's family taking it?"

"I talked to them briefly. They're in shock. But I guess there have been long-time hard feelings between Flanders, his soon to be ex-wife and his daughter. Spoke to his girlfriend as well."

"Tom had a girlfriend?"

"Oh yes. A pretty Irish girl a quarter century his junior, Iris McGinnes. Once the divorce was filed, he flaunted her around town like an Irish poodle. It was hard to miss."

"I have a stake in this case now, Johnny. It happened kind of on my watch. And we've been retained by Flanders' mother to investigate who shot him. Hope you don't mind. Blaine and I want to nose around a bit to see what we can learn."

"I can't stop you, Judge, and of course, I'll welcome anything you turn up. Just as long as you keep me informed on what you find. Let's make this a team effort."

"Sounds right to me."

"Here are the addresses of Tom's family and Iris, his special 'friend'."

Johnny's door opened without a knock, and a small man in an expensive grey suit stepped in. The Judge and Johnny stood up. The man was heavily balding on top, which was especially unfortunate since he was so short everyone could see the top of his head. He had a mildly disagreeable look on his face, as though having recently sucked a lemon, and sharp narrow eyes that darted around the room and seemed to miss nothing.

"Sorry to disturb you gents," he said. "I'm Craig Barker, FBI." This information was thrown out as though he expected a bow, or at least a curtsey. His hand went to his shirt pocket; a small plastic case with an I.D. in it, likely his credentials, was flashed too quickly to be read.

Johnny and the Judge looked at him blankly.

"So, they sent me over to help 'cause you guys have a shooting of our Undersecretary in charge of Nuclear Energy. Did I get that right?"

Johnny nodded. "The victim is alive, in a coma. Uncertain how he's going to do. It's wait and see right now."

"As long as he's not dead there's always hope. Maybe he can point us in the right direction if he comes around," said Barker, smiling. The smile didn't quite reach his eyes. "I know you by your picture, Captain Marks. You're supervising the Flanders case. But who are you?" Barker stabbed his finger at the Judge.

"Just an old friend of the victim. My partner was with Tom Flanders when he was shot. He'd asked us to investigate a death threat he'd received."

"A private dick?" Barker's mouth curled in distaste.

"Sometimes." The Judge gave Barker his full name. "Most people use my nickname, 'The Judge'."

"Heard of you, Judge. Something of a pain in the ass as I understand."

It was the Judge's turn to provide a smile not quite reaching his eyes. "Oh well, you can please all of the establishment some of the time, and some of the establishment all the time, but you cannot please all the establishment all the time."

"Didn't someone smarter than you already say that?" asked Barker. "Anyway, just stay out of the way of my investigation."

Barker pulled another small wooden chair across the room to be in front of Johnny's desk, squeezing the Judge over a bit.

"What was the victim like?" asked Barker. "Is he well known in Montecito, well liked, sociable, established here?"

"I never met him," said Johnny, "but yes. I'm told he is well liked, active in our community, a resident for over twenty-five years. Some have said he's a charming guy with a warm heart. They said you could always count on him for a contribution to the police union fund, the Catholic Church, or whatever charitable organization was raising money. His wife and daughter are well known here too, although now he and his wife are in the middle of a divorce."

"And you, Judge. Did you know him?".

"I was in a fraternity with Tom at U.S.C. We kept in contact over the years."

"What was he like at college?"

"That was years ago. But he was sociable, like Johnny says. Sometimes I had the feeling it was all an act. Like we never saw what the real Tom Flanders was thinking underneath. Maybe that's why we were never close."

"That's crap and you know it, Judge. You rich S.C. frat guys only think about two things, booze and sex."

The Judge shrugged, "If you say so, Barker. I've got to be going guys. I'll let you two have fun."

The Judge stood up, gazed down at the short Mr. Barker in his fancy grey suit, much as you'd gaze at an insect on the floor, then walked out.

CHAPTER 14

Buck Jennings was in his office in Houston, in the middle of budgeting the PAC money required to grease the skids for selection of a replacement Undersecretary in charge of Nuclear Energy. The President was already in his pocket, thanks to a clandestine understanding with the President's Chief of Staff. But the senators were a separate issue and an expensive one. It was like herding cats, but all very doable as long as you had the budget. The money would be used to support the next cycle of re-election campaigns of certain key members of the Senate Committee who would approve the appointment.

It galled him to spend the money again after spending it once already to get Tom Flanders appointed Chair. *The tricky bastard. Double-crossed us as soon as he got his appointment sealed up, leaving a bitter taste in everyone's mouth.*

Buck's telephone rang and he picked it up, breaking his face into its big smile, acting out the theory that people could sense if you were happy and if you were smiling when they spoke to you over the phone. "This is Buck," he said in his best happy voice.

It was his trusted partner in Montecito.

"Yes. I understand." Buck said softly into the phone. Then, "What? What did you say? He's still breathing? Shit…shit…shit. Christ, I'm just in the process of arranging the appointment of his successor."

"A coma? Is he going to come out of the coma? Wake up? Look, I need to know if Flanders is going to show up in his office tomorrow morning, or next week, or some time and say 'The Undersecretary in charge of Nuclear Energy is back.'"

"God damn it, I know there are no guarantees. I'm fucking asking you what you think. What's your best guess? That's what you're liberally paid for."

"I see. Just a matter of time? He won't be showing up anywhere ever again. Can you guarantee that? I don't give a shit, money's no object. Okay. That's better. I understand where we are. It sounds all very salvageable. Keep me in the loop on everything."

He slammed his phone down in disgust. "Damn incompetents," he muttered. Why was everything going wrong this week? His karma was shitty.

CHAPTER 15

Iris McGinnes peered out from her doorway at the Judge and Blaine, standing tall at five foot eight, long blond hair parted in the middle and stringing down either side of her face, hippy style, almost to her waist. She was trying to gauge how much trouble she might be in. Her brown eyes were intelligent, narrowed now, cagey, suspicious. Her white face and large sensitive mouth contrasted with the black long-sleeve top and black jeans she wore. She looked all of her twenty-four years, and there was no doubt she was Irish. But, the Judge noted, she was also not the young woman Flanders had kept naked pictures of in the back of his filing cabinet.

There were dark circles under her eyes, suggesting grief, or perhaps just lack of sleep.

"Yes? Can I help you?" The hint of a Boston accent lingered in her voice.

"I'm an old friend of Tom Flanders, Iris. Tom might have mentioned me, the Judge; I'm his old fraternity buddy from U.S.C. Tom asked for my help. And this is my partner, Blaine Forbes."

She brought a small hand out from her oversized sweater with its long sleeves and tentatively shook the Judge's hand. "Come in. I was making some tea. Would you like some?"

It was a modest condo, furnished in thrift store modern, with a small living area, a tiny galley kitchen, and a closed door suggesting a tiny bedroom at the back. Bright yellow curtains in the kitchen were the only thing hinting at the personality of the occupant. She directed them to an overstuffed sofa, once bright paisley, but now wearing tired, faded colors, and they sat.

She squeezed into her tiny kitchen, bustled around a bit, and emerged carrying three mugs in one hand, a teapot in her other, and a box of green tea bags under one arm. She leaned down to dump them all on top of the low stool in front of the sofa which served as her coffee table, poured water into the three mugs, slid two of them around to the Judge and Blaine, and then the box of tea bags. She settled on a stiff-looking wood chair facing them, took a big breath, and then said, "Okay."

"What is your relationship with Tom, Ms. McGinnes?" asked Blaine, jumping in with his usual bluntness.

A shadow fled across Iris's face, quickly hidden.

"Since you're here, you already know our relationship, sir. We're lovers."

"We're sorry about what happened to Tom, Iris," said the Judge.

Had you seen him recently, Judge, before he got shot? Before this coma thing?"

"No. Tom had received a threatening letter which he was particularly concerned about, a death threat really, and asked me to look into the matter. But I was too late to stop him from being shot."

"He showed it to me Judge. Told me you might help. It's so unreal. It seems like he isn't really in a coma, that any moment he'll come striding through my door."

Iris pulled out a Kleenex she had stuffed up one sweater sleeve and dabbed at one eye.

"When did your affair start?" asked Blaine. "Before he split with his wife?"

"We've been together for almost two years Mr. Forbes, long before he separated from the Ding Bat."

"He left his wife for you?" Blaine's voice was carefully flat so as not to convey any judgment.

"Tom never did anything for anyone but himself. He left his wife for whatever reason. He supports me because he likes the sex. The Ding Bat never made him happy in bed. She's just an undersized prune. Spent all her time criticizing him, that is, when she wasn't out spending his money. She was a real spender. Besides, she had her own secret affair going."

"How do you know that?"

"My friend, Jerry, saw them together on Venice Beach."

"Did Tom help you with this condo?" Blaine asked, again a direct, uncomfortable question.

The Judge watched Iris lean further back in her chair, away from Blaine. The Judge wondered if Blaine was just oblivious to Iris's feelings, or so focused on the case he couldn't wait to nurse answers out of her. Or perhaps he was showing off for the Judge.

"Initially, yes. Tom bought me this place. It's not much. But I've never had anything before. For me, it's a palace. My place. But since the divorce started everything's been tied up; so my allowance has been reduced. He used to help me with utilities, the H.O.A., taxes, but he stopped that weeks ago. Just my monthly expense money now. And maybe a dinner out after we fuck if he's in the mood. It's truly been tough."

"Does Tom's wife know?" asked the Judge, softly, quietly.

"We don't… I didn't think so. I tried to be careful, discreet. Tom said the property settlement negotiations were tough enough, without bringing in any extraneous issue. But Tom loved to go out for dinner. Before the divorce mess, we went out a lot. And, well, Montecito is a small village, people talk."

"Did you see the threatening letter?"

"Yes, Judge." She took a sip of her tea. "Tell me Judge, when did you find out about…about the shooting?"

"I got here just today. I had a trial to finish up. I sent Blaine ahead to talk to Tom. Blaine was at the house when Tom was shot."

"You were there, Mr. Forbes…when… when Tom was shot?"

"Yes."

She glared at Blaine then, her small hand springing out a sharp finger, a dagger, which she jabbed in the air at Blaine. "You just stood and watched my Tom get shot?"

"There was nothing I could do," said Blaine. "I was lucky I wasn't hit. The bullet whizzed past my chest."

"Too bad you couldn't have moved over a little, taken the bullet instead," she whispered with venom.

Blaine leaned back into the sofa, away from the naked ferocity he saw in her eyes now.

"Do you know anybody, Iris, who might want Tom dead?" asked the Judge.

"No, Judge."

"No one hated him, or strongly disliked him?"

"No…well…he was a strong personality; I suppose there are lots of people he rubbed the wrong way, people who didn't like him."

"Anybody specific?" asked Blaine.

"His wife, Bitsy. She was really angry about the divorce. I guess there were other people. But he didn't deserve this. To be shot in the chest and now lingering between life and death in a coma…shit!"

Iris turned to the Judge again. "Catch him, Judge. Find the guy that did this to Tom. Kill him, or at least make him pay for a very long time. Tom is my lucky star. He's going to support me a lot more once he's better."

"Do you love Tom?" asked Blaine.

"Love is a hard thing to define, isn't it? I was very fond of Tom at the start. He is charming, and so worldly, and of course very rich. And he has wonderful and amusing stories to tell about D.C., and his travels, and his hunting of wild animals. When does fondness turn to love, Mr. Forbes? And when does it turn to something darker…dependency perhaps? I could have loved Tom I think. But our relationship didn't progress that way."

"How did it progress?"

"He has supported me financially. Has paid me four thousand a month to be available for him. He's created his vision of a 'taken care of world for Iris' and put me in the middle of his vision. In some ways, it's been all very dazzling."

"And in other ways?" asked the Judge.

"Once he had me like that, totally dependent financially, he changed."

"How so?"

"I don't know. I guess he's more critical of what I do, and what I say. Guess he has the right to be since he's funding me. I wish we cuddled more like we did at the beginning. The sex is still good, but sometimes he comes for sex and then just leaves after. Kind of a 'slam-bang thank you ma'am' sort of thing. That can leave me feeling a little empty. Hell, I don't know. Sex is different for a man, not like it is for a woman. We women need more time to feel close, romantic, connected, I think. Not like an overused sex toy.

Sometimes he comes over in a bad mood, all strung out. He can become emotionally abusive then, tearing me down verbally, and once even physically. I keep hoping things will go back to the way we started. Besides, I can't afford to dump him. I can't let go of his financial support. I'm trapped in the dependency he's carefully woven me into."

"How did he physically mistreat you?"

"Two months ago he was angry with me about something, grabbed my arm and squeezed real hard, till I cried. It hurt like hell. Left a bad bruise. I had to cover up my arm. That's why I started wearing this old sweater. The bruises are gone now, but I guess I still feel naked without the sweater. He also now likes to pretend to suffocate me a little during sex. Guess that's all the rage. I don't know.

Anyway, he's kind of mean to me occasionally, but I think he needs me, loves me in his own way. And of course, I really need the money."

"Did you call the police, walk out on him, or maybe threaten him after he hurt your arm?" asked Blaine.

"I did the same thing as any other red-blooded American girl would do." Iris's chin came up, her eyes flared at Blaine. "I added another lover." Iris sat back in her chair, proud of herself, watching to see if Blaine was shocked. He certainly looked surprised.

"Who is he?"

"Jerry Martel. A bit younger than me, a surfer dude from the Montecito beach community, only twenty-one, built. Plumbing like a horse. He was wonderful. It was partly getting even with Tom, but I quite fell for Jerry. He was broke of course. But he was a lot of fun. We had a great time spending Tom's money. He was attentive, affectionate, focused on me, and sympathetic. It was almost like having a puppy, but with privileges. And the sex was awesome."

"Did Tom know about it?"

"Not at first, but he found out somehow."

"How do you know Tom found out?"

"Cause Tom came over here about two weeks ago and we had a big fight about it. That's how. Then he fuckin' went to Jerry and scared the shit out of him. Told Jerry he couldn't see me anymore or Tom would have Jerry beat up, have both legs broken so he would never surf again. Jerry is big, but he's just a tall boy at heart. He was scared spitless. He told me goodbye, left Montecito, went down to L.A., to Venice Beach. Said he couldn't risk seeing me again."

"Tom didn't stop the money?"

"No. But look where I am now. What the fuck am I supposed to do? Jerry's gone. And Tom's in a bloody coma, maybe going to die. I've got nobody. Tom didn't deserve to be shot. Destroyed my only source of serious income. Shot in his own home, shot by a monster; while you," she stabbed a finger again at Blaine, "the man sent to protect him, just stood around and sucked your thumb."

She began to whimper then. Thrusting a Kleenex across her face from her sweater sleeve, she stood with her head bowed, and made a dash for the privacy of her bedroom, muttering through the tissue they could let themselves out.

It was unclear whether she was sniffling about Tom's condition, about the loss of her boyfriend Jerry, or about the loss of Tom's money.

CHAPTER 16

Blaine drove the Mini, with the Judge squeezed uncomfortably into the passenger seat. Sometimes Blaine experienced a certain perverse pleasure in watching the Judge suffer in the cramped Mini, though he'd never admit it. Sort of payback for the Judge lording his forty years of experience and instinct honed to a fine edge over Blaine.

Blaine stopped at the signal on the main road running through the Village of Montecito. He was still chaffing at the anger Iris McGinnes had directed at him.

He glanced out the rolled-down window and found himself staring at a young brunette who had pulled up in a red Mustang convertible with its top down. He absently admired her profile. Perhaps she felt the energy of his gaze. She suddenly turned her head to look at him, their eyes locking for seconds.

And Blaine lost his breath. There was no other way to put it. Young, early twenties, in her tennis outfit, white, with sweat marks here and there. Big blue eyes, soft cheerful lips, and an open face that hinted of sweetness and curiosity. It was the face of someone he'd never seen before yet had always known. Known in a dream? In a former life? Perhaps a future wife? Maybe a partnered spirit he'd traveled the world with before and would do so again.

Blaine smiled at her with a natural affection he couldn't control, couldn't hide. It was like he'd suddenly found home, where he belonged, the only partner that made him complete.

She smiled back at him… then winked.

The light changed and she made a left turn, roaring away, leaving him there in the Mini, transfixed. The honking horns behind him and the Judge's tap on his knee brought him back to reality. By then her red Mustang had sailed down the side road and disappeared into winding lanes and greenery which made Montecito so enchanting.

"Gone! Christ! Gone."

CHAPTER 17

Back at the hotel, in Blaine's room, the Judge set up his computer, and they inserted the SD card Blaine had found on the underside of Flanders' desk. It was a video file that began with static and grey color for the first 30 seconds. It had been filmed in an office, a secret recording of a meeting between Flanders and another man. Apparently, the other person had no clue Flanders was recording their meeting. The camera must have been on his lapel or perhaps his tie clip.

Flanders leaned over the front of the man's desk so the video flashed on the desk sign on the massive desk behind which the other man sat. It read, 'Senator Franklin Ross.'

After an exchange of pleasantries, the two men got right to the point.

"You want to be appointed Undersecretary in charge of Nuclear Energy, right?"

"Yes."

"You know you have to be appointed by the President, and then survive a Senate Committee investigation, review and approval?"

"Yes."

"That no stone of your personal life is going to be left unturned as a result?"

"Yes."

"Are you prepared to pay the price for my support to accomplish this?"

"Yes."

"And you understand the price. You will continue your efforts to stifle use of atomic power in this country in favor or oil and gas, and perhaps coal and green energies?"

"Yes."

"You know how this works," said the Senator. "One hand washes the other. My oil and gas lobbyists have very well-funded PACs. Their PACs will lavishly support election campaigns I specify, as long as I can ensure that the Undersecretary in charge of Nuclear Energy tamps down on any effort to expand use of atomic energy in this country. I'm relying on you to uphold my side of this bargain, in exchange for which I'll provide the political capital to make you Undersecretary."

"I understand."

"To pull this off it's going to require lots of money from Oil and Gas. You go back on your word here and it could be very dangerous for you. You understand that?"

"Yes, sir."

"Okay then. It's a deal. Just follow the notes I've given you when you go before my Committee for your confirmation of appointment. I'll arrange for your appointment to be rubber-stamped."

The Senator stood up and leaned across his desk to shake Flanders' hand.

The video ended there.

CHAPTER 18

The Law Office of J. Edgar Travis was on the second story, up old stairs at the side of one of the Montecito storefronts. The Judge huffed and puffed his way up narrow steps that were way too small to be to code, feeling at the top as though he'd climbed the mainmast on a fighting galleon. He paused at the top to slow his pulse and find his breath. As he did so, a small door next to him, the first door in the long hall on the second floor, opened suddenly, and a stout gentleman came flying out. He looked about eighty, with flushed cheeks, watery blue eyes, thick glasses, and only a few strands of silver hair pasted down on his head. He was dressed in a dark suit that was a little too loose, and wore a white dress shirt with a long narrow tie of a style the Judge hadn't seen in years.

Sharp blue eyes behind his coke bottle glasses flashed, sizing up the Judge in one look.

"If you have shortness of breath young fellow, you should pause a little after every two steps."

"Yes," said the Judge. "You may be right."

"I own the building. I don't need some middle-aged attorney falling down my steps. It'd be Hell with my insurance rates."

"How'd you know I'm an attorney?"

"Son, you got it written all over you. Probably a good one too, and perhaps reasonably honest; but that last part's only a guess. I've got to get to the City Clerk's Office and file something before they close."

"Are you J. Edgar Travis?"

"Was, last time I looked. You hoping to visit with me?"

"Yes."

"Well, tell you what. Why don't you walk along with me over to the City Clerk's? Not too far. And we can chat. That way I won't have to bill you for my time right off."

The Judge smiled and nodded. This was his kind of crusty old lawyer.

"I'm helping Johnny Marks and his department investigate the shooting of Tom Flanders. Happened close by here."

"At his home. I read about it. Tragic. Never fails to surprise me how violent the human animal can be. If we just did a better job of expressing ourselves, listened better, and sprinkled on a little more tolerance for different views, we'd be in a lot better place."

"Yes. You're right. Anyway, I understand Mr. Flanders is one of your clients."

"Yes. He is. How'd you know that? I can't discuss the affairs of my clients, young man."

"But your client is now in a coma and may well die."

"Yes. I know. They called me from the hospital. But I expect that even if he dies, I still owe a fiduciary duty to his estate and his heirs. And right now, he's not technically competent, but he's not dead."

"Tom and his wife are separated, divorce papers filed. He told his wife he was going to see his attorney and change his will so that all his separate property, the bulk of their shared estate, would no longer go to her. I'm just wondering if that's right."

"Hmmm. I can't disclose any confidential information about what's in the will. But since the wife has already told you, I guess I can confirm a little. Yes, I was instructed by Tom to make certain changes in his will."

"And did Tom get in to sign the amendment before he was shot?"

"You're pushing a little too far, son. I'm not sure I can disclose that."

"It may be critical to catching the person responsible for shooting Tom."

The old attorney stopped in his tracks, carefully looked around, satisfied, muttered in a low voice:

"No. The poor bastard had an appointment to come in the very next morning. Tom's old will still stands as of now. But I can't chit-chat about it further. You'll have to excuse me. I have to walk a lot faster than you seem able to, son, to keep up my pulse, and make it to the Clerk's Office before they close. Good day to you."

CHAPTER 19

Blaine and the Judge were sitting with Johnny Marks on the patio of the Pierre Lafond restaurant amongst colorful umbrellas and potted plants, the Judge and Johnny enjoying lattes, Blaine gobbling down a full breakfast. The Judge marveled at how much his young partner could eat.

"Where are you from originally, Judge?" asked Johnny.

"I grew up in the San Gabriel Valley, just outside Los Angeles. Back then we thought we were the only valley; no one had ever heard of the San Fernando Valley. There were Hispanic and Chinese and Japanese farmers, and of course white folk of all sorts. And we all got along just fine. As kids, we'd heard there were black people, but none of us had ever seen one. It was rural, agricultural, and relaxed. An idyllic time. What about you, Johnny? Where'd you grow up?"

"Houston, Judge. Hot, steamy Houston. When I turned twenty-one I left for good, ended up in California." Johnny smiled. I became a policeman in your missing San Fernando Valley."

A small man came onto the patio, eyed the handful of people there, spotted Johnny, and made his way over to their table.

He stood no more than five foot three, with a tanned face, tanned hands, and tanned chest exposed at the top of his white dress shirt with its extra-large collar, one button too many unbuttoned. He had silver hair, a million-dollar smile showing perfect teeth, bushy eyebrows carefully manicured, and tight brown eyes. The stretch marks at the corners of his eyes, the tension in his skin and the thinness of his upper eyelids suggested extensive face work.

Johnny leaped up from his chair to grasp the man's hand, shaking it with both of his.

"Mr. mayor," Johnny said, "so nice to see you."

"It's not a social visit, Johnny. It's about this damn shooting. The locals are all stirred up and the shopkeepers are bleating that they're going to lose a ton of business over the negative publicity."

The mayor turned to the Judge and stuck out his hand to shake. "Hi, I'm Alan Danzer. I'm the Honorary mayor of Montecito. We aren't technically incorporated as a city but rather an unincorporated area of Santa Barbara County, so we can't legally have a real mayor. But folks were kind enough to get together and designate me the Honorary mayor."

"You need no introduction, mayor," said Johnny. "Gentlemen, I'm sure you recognized Alan, the host of the longest-running game show on TV ever, 'You Bet Your Cash'."

"That was before streaming, Johnny. Anyway, nice to meet you two." Danzer reached across a loaded plate of eggs, pancakes, hash browns and bacon to give Blaine's hand a shake.

Then he turned and said, "So, you're the Judge, the famous private detective."

"I don't know how famous," said the Judge modestly, still managing to look smug, his feathers puffing. "This is my partner, Blaine Forbes, who is enjoying his breakfast."

Blaine paused to look up and nod, a fork full of hash browns midway toward his mouth. "Ours is a busy profession, sir. Got to grab food whenever you can," Blaine muttered.

"Are you enjoying Montecito, Judge?" asked Danzer.

"I am. It's very relaxing here. How did this place come to be?"

"Well, that's a story and a half, Judge. Its full name was El Montecito, an archaic use of the Spanish word for woodland or countryside. Its first inhabitants after the Indians were retiring soldiers of the Santa Barbara Presidio in the 1780s, given land far from town to live on as a part of their pension."

"Did the lower and higher villages of Montecito develop then?"

"Yes. As the Spanish population increased, the area along today's East Valley Road near Montecito Creek began to develop rooming houses, an inn, grocery stores, dance halls, and saloons. It was a rough and ready town. Spain yielded California to Mexico in 1821, and Mexico yielded California to the United States in 1848. After that, a trickle of American farmers looking for inexpensive arable land joined land speculators to take up land grants offered by the Common Council of Santa Barbara for a few dollars an acre."

"When did Montecito become an enclave for the wealthy?"

"Actually, very early. By 1890, well-heeled Easterners began to arrive, building elegant Victorian-style homes and estates as winter residences. And Montecito became a 'Name'. Land speculation and subdivision increased, and in the 1920s a second wave of newcomers settled in, erecting homes in the new style of Mediterranean and Spanish Revival. Montecito became a destination for the rich and famous and has maintained that reputation ever since."

"Well, it seems a great place to just kick back and relax."

"It is exactly that," said Danzer. "And I'm sorry to disturb your relaxation and your breakfast gentlemen, but I must. It's absolutely critical, Johnny, that we put this Flanders case to bed quickly, arrest the perp and be done with it. It's been a tough year already for our business community, what with the coming recession. We can't afford to take any more negative publicity. You understand?"

"I understand," said Johnny.

"We'll do the best we can, Mr. mayor," said the Judge more cautiously.

They watched Danzer depart, weaving his way across the crowded patio, bending here and there to shake a hand or pat a shoulder as he went. He seemed to know everybody.

"So, Johnny, Blaine tells me the next-door neighbor showed up on the adjacent driveway after the police arrived the night of Flanders' death. What's his story?"

"Ted Olson?"

"Yes."

"Ted's a bachelor; lives alone. Lived in his house for over twenty-five years. I heard he built it himself. On the night in question, he arrived home during the police search around the outside of Flanders' house. Their houses are close and share adjacent driveways divided by a thin hedge. He came tearing though the hedge and scared the hell out of the sergeant standing guard at the top of Flanders' driveway. Demanded to know what happened. Asked if Flanders was okay."

"How'd your guys handle it?'

"We didn't tell him much. Sent him back through his hedge with an officer, who entered his house and searched to be sure it was safe before the guy went in. He seemed relieved to have the support."

"So, he wasn't home when Flanders was shot?"

"No. He was in a grocery store buying groceries."

"Did the store check-out guy remember him?"

"No. But it's a big popular store with lots of customers and lines at the registers. And the check-out kid was new."

"And this Ted Olson didn't see or hear anything unusual before he left home?"

"No."

"And on his return?"

"Oh yeah. He did. A whole lot of police cars, flashing lights and police tramping through the bushes in the dark."

The Judge could feel Johnny smiling at the Judge's stupid question. But the Judge knew there were no stupid questions, only stupid answers.

CHAPTER 20

As they walked across the street from the breakfast joint to the Mini Cooper, Blaine said, "Okay, Judge. Where do we go now? Any ideas?"

"I'm still puzzled by the attitude of this neighbor, this Olson. When we met him, he didn't seem nearly as excited, worried, or anxious as I would be if my next-door neighbor was shot by a sniper. I think we need to talk a little further with Mr. Ted Olson."

The Judge crammed his way into the Mini with difficulty, even though he'd basically skipped breakfast. Trying to lose weight was so damn discouraging.

Blaine roared the car, tearing around curves and sliding with barely a stop at stop signs, until they were back on Barker Pass Road, and at the foot of the twin driveways going up the hill. The left, Olson's, was perfectly maintained, no potholes, sporting a coat of new slurry for looks. Blaine roared up Olson's driveway.

Or at least he tried to.

The Mini coughed once mid-hill then just decided to stop, a silent protest no doubt for accumulated abuse. Blaine slammed on the brakes so they didn't roll backward down the driveway and across the street, likely into the middle of a neighbor's lawn. The Judge noted he was grinding his teeth again. Not an uncommon occurrence when Blaine was driving.

But Blaine tried to appear nonchalant, pedaling the gas with firm determination several times and then hitting the starter button confidently. The poor car coughed once, twice, shaking the Judge in his seat, then began inching its way further up the hill at a snail's pace, refusing to produce any additional speed out of pure malice.

They hit the plateau at the top of the drive, the Mini still barely moving, and then the car died again with a cough, smoke belching from its tailpipe.

Olson's front door flew open and he came striding out, attracted by the commotion. The Judge opened his door, put a death grip on the outside rim of the car's top with one hand, and hoisted himself out of the Mini and away from it, his jaw set in a chiseled grimace of distaste.

"Hello, Mr. Olson," the Judge yelled across the driveway, "delighted to see you again."

"Well, well, what a surprise," said Olson. "It's Charlie Chan and number one son in our neighborhood again." He produced a warm smile that took some of the sting out of his sarcasm, and motioned them across his driveway toward his front door.

They trooped over and followed Olson through his antique front door, rounded at the top, framed with black metal bars and brass stars, looking like it belonged in the Inquisition of a few centuries before…perhaps it did.

The house was California Colonial, which meant it had a red tile roof and sweeping balconies here and there on its second floor so one could play Romeo and Juliet, but modern conveniences like sliding glass doors and large windows unfettered by bars.

They walked into a great room soaring two stories high with hardwood walls festooned with the stuffed heads of various creatures. There were framed pictures documenting hunts he'd been on and kills he'd made, and even a couple of trophies from African hunting clubs. A second-level balcony ran along one side of the great room, likely serving as the gallery for the de rigueur four guest bedrooms with ensuite bathrooms and the master with lavish features. The stairs for the second story were hidden somewhere, either behind the adjacent library to the right, or more likely behind the dining room and adjacent kitchen to the left, both of which peeked out from the two sides of the great room. It was all quite grand and had the smell of money, lots and lots of money.

Olson settled himself on a large sofa, heavily upholstered, its frame of old dark wood heavily carved with Spanish swirls, and directed them to the matching sofa across a coffee table built from an old carved Mexican door, its top covered with glass.

"As you know, we are investigating the shooting of your neighbor, Tom Flanders. How well did you know Mr. Flanders?" asked the Judge.

"Not well."

"How long have you been in this house?" asked Blaine.

"Years and years."

"We understand Flanders moved into his house about the same time."

"Yes."

"So, you've lived next door to each other for years and years, and share almost a common driveway, but you don't know each other well?"

"That's about it."

"Do you have some specific reason to dislike Mr. Flanders?"

"He's an asshole."

"How do you know he's an asshole if you don't know him?"

"I just know."

"Is there some bad blood over something with your neighbor?" asked Blaine.

"I don't have to tell you that. Ask Flanders."

"We would. But he's in a coma."

"Oh well."

"We're trying to determine who shot him. I see you have a gun case over there. Is there a twenty-two rifle in the case?"

"Yes. The police just returned it. They checked it out I guess, ran ballistics, gave it a clean bill of health."

"Do you own another twenty-two rifle?"

"No."

"Well, here's the deal," said the Judge. "You were on the scene. You live next door. And apparently you have reason to dislike Flanders. You can see how it looks."

"No. I can't see how it looks. I was shopping down at Pavilions when it happened. I wasn't even here."

"Can you prove it?" asked Blaine.

"I can if I have to."

"Okay. Let's say you have to."

"What time was Flanders shot?"

"Seven o' five."

Olson gave a big sigh, stood up, meandered into the kitchen and pulled a trash can out from under the sink. He rummaged through it for a minute, pulled out a shopping receipt tape, studied it, then marched back into the big room and threw the Pavilions receipt down on the coffee table by Blaine.

"The receipt shows me paying for my groceries at seven o' nine," said Olson.

Blaine spread the receipt out on the coffee table and took a picture of it with his cell.

"Okay," said the Judge. "We agree you weren't here. But tell us about the feud between you and Olson, just so we have a complete picture."

"You really want to know?"

"We really do."

Olson smiled, but it was a mean smile all the same. "I had Flanders' wife as my girlfriend before he met her, and we carried on our sexual liaison under his nose right up to the week before their wedding. After the ceremony, Tom found out about it somehow and made quite a scene. I think that's when he began abusing his wife. Anyway, that was twenty-five years ago. We haven't spoken since. Now, if you two will excuse me, I have work to do." He walked ahead of them on light feet and saw them out the fancy carved door.

"We kind 'of got the bum's rush, Judge," said Blaine as they crawled into the Mini.

"We certainly did," said the Judge. "Will this car make it on this driveway?"

"Oh sure, Judge. It's downhill."

"Okay. Let's head into Santa Barbara and see if we can talk to Flanders' wife and daughter."

CHAPTER 21

Blaine drove the Judge down a quiet street in Santa Barbara with manicured lawns, a mixture of bungalows and newer houses, all small; three bedrooms or under, on small lots with close lot lines. Hardly the style of homes in Montecito on their one-acre lots, but the cars parked on driveways and on the street were all newer, middle to upper-priced vehicles, even some Teslas, their cords snaking from the driveway into garages for connection.

Number 1245 was older, more bungalow style, with a driveway and two-door garage on one side and a brick walk on the other leading up to a small porch and the front door.

One garage door was closed, the other one open enough to reveal a red vehicle with a soft black top. The top was down.

They parked and got out of the Mini, Blaine leading, apparently determined to be more forceful in their investigation. They cut across the lawn to intersect with the brick walk, and Blaine strode up onto the little porch and punched the small black button at the side to ring the doorbell. A buzzer sounded inside, reminiscent of an angry bee.

There was the sound of high heels ponying across a wooden floor, then the door opened a crack to expose one blue eye that examined them suspiciously.

Satisfied with what the eye saw, the door swung wide, and Blaine lost all composure, his mouth dropping open.

The Judge spotted the change instantly and pushed in front of Blaine to say, "How do you do, Miss? You're Miss Flanders?"

"Yes."

The girl was pretty in a collegiate sort of way, thin and willowy, with porcelain white skin, a turned-up Irish nose giving her a pixy look, large blue eyes, dark eyebrows, dark brown hair, and a few freckles peppering her nose. She had a generous mouth displaying a wide smile, and bright red lipstick that matched her red pullover sweater, worn over a white blouse and a pleated ivory skirt. Her red pumps were color-coordinated with her lipstick. Looking at her, the Judge realized he'd seen her before. She was the girl in the red Mustang with its top down, who Blaine had been ogling at the stoplight in the Village.

"We're helping Captain Johnny Marks and his Sheriff's Department investigate the shooting of your dad, Miss Flanders. We are hoping you and your mother can assist in our investigation by answering a few questions. They call me the Judge, because I was one for a number of years, and this is my partner, Blaine Forbes."

The Judge turned to sneak a peek at Blaine, now behind him, more composed but very red in the face. He was standing bolt upright, not his usual slouch, and had pasted a smile on his face broader than the stern of the Titanic.

"The name's Laura. Surely you don't think I had anything to do with my dad's shooting, Mr. …ah…Judge?"

"No. Nothing like that."

"Oh. Okay. Well…why don't you come in?"

The Judge stepped into a small living room, followed by Blaine. The room was crammed with large expensive-looking antique furniture and even a piano. Likely furniture originally belonging to Tom's big Montecito home, taken when mother and daughter moved out.

"Have a seat," said Laura, pointing to an antique sofa dressed in 'turn of the last century' brocade.

The Judge settled on the sofa, sinking into his seat on deep springs and padding. The room was so crowded the Judge had the feeling he was sitting in a furniture store crammed with samples. Blaine took an overstuffed chair to the Judge's right, and Laura plopped down on a matching sofa across from the Judge, then slid down to its end, closer to Blaine, eyeing him, recognition sliding across her face.

Blaine leaned forward in his seat, saying, "We're sorry to disturb you, Laura. But there is a shooter running around and we want to stop him before he hurts someone else. We wouldn't intrude on your privacy otherwise." Blaine bracketed her face with his honest blue eyes and produced his best boyish look. The Judge was always amazed at the way Blaine could turn his amazing charm on and off as though it was on a switch.

It worked. Laura blushed slightly, unwound her arms from across her chest, and eyed Blaine with new interest. "I don't know what to tell you, Mr. Forbes, I want to help of course."

"Just call me Blaine, Laura."

"Is your mother home?" asked the Judge.

"Not right now. She's out with her friends at her gun club."

"She shoots then?"

"She's just taken it up. Kind of stupid if you ask me. They shoot clay pigeons. Now she lives alone I guess she wants to feel safe and able to fend for herself."

"You don't live here then?" asked Blaine.

"I have a condo with a roommate on the other side of town."

"A boyfriend?" probed Blaine.

The Judge gave Blaine a sharp look. It wasn't an appropriate question. It was none of Blaine's business. A slight color came to Laura face and her chin came up. "A girlfriend, Mr. Forbes."

"How is your dad doing?" asked the Judge.

"Tom's still in a coma. They're hoping he'll come out of it soon. Otherwise, it'll look pretty grim."

"Can you tell us a little about your dad, Laura?" asked Blaine.

"Well, for one thing, Tom is an absolute bastard. He probably deserved to be shot."

"Oh?"

"You don't get along with your father then?" asked the Judge.

"No, I don't. I hate Tom."

"I understand your dad is the Undersecretary in charge of Nuclear Energy for the country. He must be very busy. Probably not a lot of time for family?"

"You got it. Doesn't give a shit about us. And this Undersecretary gig, what a racket that is."

"How so?"

"Tom's been in the pocket of the Oil and Gas Industry for years. He sold out early after becoming an atomic energy scientist. Became a paid consultant for Oil and Gas, and a principal speaker about the dangers in using atomic power as a source of energy. He's been lavishly paid for speaking gigs around the world; given free trips to exotic places, women, gifts, tickets, stipends, payments for technical reports published under his name that someone else ghostwrote. None of that shit he really believes. Tom says, 'You've got to lean in toward where the money is.'

He let it slip once he was clearing over five hundred thousand a year from these activities, compensation for being the oil and gas donkey and bad-mouthing atomic energy.

Then they turned around and got him appointed Undersecretary for Nuclear Energy for the country. What a joke. Now they can really screw the use of atomic energy into the ground."

"Who are they?"

"Lobbyists for oil and gas companies, some electric utilities…oh, and manufacturers of generators, I think. The companies all try to keep their hands clean by using lobbyist go-betweens. They greased the skids on the Congressional Committee so Tom got the Undersecretary job. And of course they'll get their pound of flesh out of him for that."

"What were all the articles and speeches about?" asked Blaine.

"All about how unsafe atomic power was in any form. How we need to rely on oil, gas, coal, and green energy, as sole sources for our power in this country."

"But when I talked to him, Laura, he was all excited about using compact molten salt atomic plants for energy."

"If that's true, there must be a money play for Tom somewhere in that. Everything he does is carefully calculated. Tom'll double-cross the devil for a nickel. That's how he's built."

"I can understand you might not approve of the way he makes his money, Laura," said the Judge. "But you said you hate him. Hate sounds like there are more personal reasons involved. Why do you hate Tom?"

"For what he did to Mom."

"What was that?" the Judge asked softly.

She kept her eyes on the Judge, eyes aflame now. "He emotionally, verbally and physically abused her all their married life."

"Physically?"

"Yes. Do you know what it feels like to be a woman and have your husband put his big meaty hands on your arm, then squeeze as hard as he can, bruising you to the bone, enough so you scream in agony and beg him to stop? Only to have it happen again, and again, again, until it became almost a daily occurrence. Leaving welts, swelling, ugly black bruising. Perpetual layers of pain in your arm as you move through the rest of your day, knowing he'd likely be back at night to abuse you some more. My father is an ugly, mean bastard, and deserves whatever he gets."

"That sounds difficult."

"You have no idea. Only now, since they've been separated for two months, has mom started to wear short-sleeved blouses and sleeveless cocktail dresses again. Years and years of keeping her arms covered, hiding her shame, the bruises he gave."

Blaine asked, "Can you think of anyone specific who might have a reason to want your dad dead?"

"It's probably a big club, Blaine. Tom isn't a kind person."

"Who comes to mind first, Laura?"

"I suppose Dr. Emma Broadwell, the person Tom was competing with for the Undersecretary job.

She was very jealous according to Tom. She thought she'd sewn up the Undersecretary position for herself. Then Tom waltzes in and grabs the job out from under her. She was really angry. Tom said she called him a lot of evil names. Even threatened him, said he'd end up in jail because of his various conflicts of interest."

"Anyone else?"

"The neighbor next door didn't like him much."

"Ted Olson?"

"Yes. I guess they'd had words about where the property line was or something when Mom and Dad first moved in. Before my time.

Oh, and I was over there two weeks ago to pick up some of my clothes. When I walked in Dad was on his cell, shouting at his business partner, Lance Kelly."

"Could you tell what it was about?"

Something about some Complex Atomic Solutions company. Sounded like Kelly was desperate to sell their shares but Dad wouldn't agree. The list goes on and on."

"What about your mom?" asked the Judge.

"Like I said, he treated her like shit. If he dies and hasn't changed his will she stands to inherit the house, the stocks, the whole mess. But she wouldn't hurt a fly. It's not in her character. She's a turn the other cheeker."

"Anyone else?"

"My impression is some people in the oil and gas industries weren't very happy when the first thing Tom did after becoming Secretary for Nuclear Energy was to promote some new kind of atomic power. And of course, there's me. I have strong reasons to dislike him because of what he did to my mom and me."

"Is your mother seeing anybody new?" asked the Judge.

"As a matter of fact, I think she might be. But if she is, she's playing it pretty cagey. I haven't met him yet. She's been going out a lot in the evenings of late. But she doesn't talk to me about her love life."

"Do you have a boyfriend?" asked Blaine.

"Me? No way. Had a boyfriend in high school, but I dumped him when I went to college. I'm barely twenty-four. I've been busy with my school. Going to be a veterinarian. I prefer animals. They're a lot more reliable than people. Guess you think that's strange, Blaine. But it's the way I feel."

"I can understand that," said Blaine. "I don't have a girlfriend. Just never found the right person who felt right…like a soul mate."

"Errr…yes…" said the Judge. "Well, I think it's time we get out of Miss Flanders' hair, Blaine. I'm sure she has things to do."

"I suppose we should," said Blaine with a lack of conviction. "Here, Laura, here's my card. If you think of anything else, or maybe if you just want to talk to someone about stuff, need a sounding board, I'm available. Do give me a call. That's my direct line. We'll be in town for several days, and I'm always looking for an interesting dinner companion. I live just down the road in L.A., and I'm up here a lot."

There were Blaine's bright blue eyes again, his soft smile, and this time Laura got all the teeth too, perfectly matched white ivory setting off his irrepressible grin.

The Judge gave a big sigh as he hoisted himself up off the sofa and headed for the door, dragging a reluctant Blaine behind him by sheer force of personality.

CHAPTER 22

Johnny Marks called a meeting for 1:30 in his office to go over what leads existed on Flanders' shooter. Blaine and the Judge were a little late, getting a scowl from Craig Barker, Mr. FBI. Barker had dragged a metal chair with an actual cushion on it from the lobby and was seated in the corner of the room facing Johnny's desk, back to the wall, tapping his foot impatiently.

"Okay, guys. What do we know?" asked Johnny. "I can report Flanders is still alive and still in a coma. The doctors say he'll either come out of it over the next week, or if not, then likely never.

We found no casing where the shooter lay and fired, so the shooter must have taken it with him. The area where the shooter lay was swept clean with an adjacent branch snapped from a bush. He left it absolutely clean. There was a report of a gardener's truck parked on the street below the Flanders house at the time of the shooting, but its description doesn't match Minato's. And a similar gardener's truck was stolen forty-five minutes before from a location three-quarters of a mile away and then abandoned in a vacant lot perhaps minutes after the shooting. Nobody saw anything. That's about all I've got so far."

"We've visited Flanders' mistress," said Blaine, "and the neighbor, and Flanders' pretty daughter. The neighbor, Ted Olson, was away shopping at the local market when the shot was fired. The mistress, Iris McGinnes, was abused by Flanders and has lots of issues, but is dependent on his money. Money which will dry up if Flanders doesn't recover. She seems an unlikely candidate for shooting him."

"Iris had a second, secret boyfriend, a Jerry Martel," said the Judge. "Flanders found out about him, separated them, and threatened to break the boy's legs. The young man took the threat seriously, dumped Iris and moved down South to Venice Beach.

And there's Flanders' gardener, Minato. Lost his family in Hiroshima. Hates all politicians with a vengeance. And particularly Tom Flanders, because he's cheap and because he's an atomic power guy. But Minato still works for Flanders as the gardener. A strange bird. I suppose he's a possible suspect, would know where to lift someone else's gardener's truck, knows the lay of the land.

There's a business partner of Tom's in Virgina, Lance Kelly, who could be a suspect or a source of information on others who might have a motive. And some political illwill around D.C. connected with Flanders' actions as the Undersecretary for Nuclear Affairs. That's about all we've got."

"What about the bullet, Craig?" asked Johnny. "Has the FBI identified the type of gun used?

"We're working on it. Don't have anything yet."

CHAPTER 23

The Marksman liked his life. It was a storybook life: high pay, risky, romantic, adventuresome, and challenging, as each minor detail had to be carefully orchestrated. And he took pride in his profession. When he'd first started, he'd often wonder why someone wanted their target dead, wondered who was hiring him, wondered if his victim had a wife, kids, insurance, a standing in the community, wondered what the person felt in that instant he was erased from the earth. Was the kill for money, for jealousy, for power, to protect someone's position? Those were the usual reasons.

But after five years at it he didn't wonder anymore. He did the job he was hired anonymously to do and collected the second half of his fee through his business drop. He enjoyed the surveillance, the planning, the setup, the act, the withdrawal, and the sweeping clear of any evidence of his passing in the sand. He was only a silhouette, a brief shadow. He'd diverted the course of life for over fifty humans. He was paid handsomely for each kill and lived handsomely off his fees. It was like playing a high-stakes game of monopoly, a game he always won.

The Marksman settled in at the antique French desk in his living room and began to write checks. Way too many checks. Not really enough cash in his accounts to cover his lifestyle. Business had been slow this year. The Flanders assignment had been the first hit job to come along in a while. Course it had been easy; close by, and a person he already owed a little visit to.

But Flanders wasn't even dead. Well, at least not quite. In a coma or something. His client would bitch and moan about that, try to shortchange him on the second installment of his fee. That's where his secret weapon came in handy.

His services were offered over the Dark Web with the assurance of complete anonymity. They had no idea who he was, and he had no idea who they were…. Except that he did.

He knew precisely who his clients were. He had a very private and specialized app, a Crawler, on his Dark Web site. When he was contacted there, it automatically crawled out through the Web, following the signal back, sifting information, searching, searching, penetrating layer after layer of subterfuge, until his crawler reported back who was communicating with him, or at least enough information that it wasn't difficult to figure out his client's name, address and telephone number. He'd made a computer file with the legal name, contact info, and address of each client he had taken on. He added to his file "The Who?": who the client wished killed. "The Why?": Why did the client want the target's life terminated? What had the target done to client? The price he charged for the job, and the terms for payment. He had cards on each client going back to the beginning; five years' worth. Just a little insurance in case it was ever needed.

If his current client declined to pay the second half for the job, he'd wave the information he had on the client in their face, describing what might happen if the client tried to welsh. One couldn't be too careful. He wasn't exactly a contractor who could file a lien on the house he'd worked on to enforce payment. But he had his own methods to assure payment. He'd had to resort to his SD card information twice before. It'd worked like a charm. His second payment came immediately in both cases. He smiled at the thought.

He wondered if a little more advertising was needed over the Dark Web. Wondered if his current client would pay the second half of his payment, even though the target was only in a coma, not dead. If his client tried to back out of payment of the second half of his fee, the Marksman knew he needed only threaten to list the story of the murder contract with local press and connect his client's name and reason for contracting a kill. It would shake the money out of any tree, he was sure.

CHAPTER 24

Blaine took a deep breath to buck up his nerve, then picked up the phone to dial. He felt like a teenager in high school.

High school had been terrible. He'd been terribly shy, with good reason. His nose and ears had grown ahead of everything else; he'd been overly skinny and overly clumsy, frequently tripping over his own feet. His forehead and cheeks had been dotted with acne in red patches he found difficult to resist scratching. He also sweated a lot, leaving his roll-on deodorant pretty much useless by lunch.

Anyway, to hell with that. Now he was a full-fledged detective, and the junior partner of one of the most controversial private investigators in the U.S.

He took a deep breath and plunged ahead, willing his finger to press the numbers. The call was picked up practically instantly after the first ring. He wasn't prepared for that. He gasped, likely sounding like an obscene caller or something, and then managed in what he hoped was a normal voice to ask. "Is Laura available?"

"This is Laura." The voice was cautious.

"Oh. Hi, Laura. This is Blaine Forbes. I was there this afternoon and met you with my partner, the Judge, to ask some questions about your dad."

"Yes."

"And…and…we saw each other earlier at the intersection in town. You were driving a Mustang convertible with your top down, in your tennis duds, and I…well, I was driving another car.”

“That silly little Cooper with all the dents and dirt. You’re too tall for your Cooper, and your partner, the Judge…well, he looked like he would need a can opener to get out.” She giggled at her own joke. “He didn’t look happy.”

“Oh, he always looks like that. It’s his judicial face. You have to ignore that. He’s got quite a big heart underneath.”

Laura’s rollicking voice turned formal. “So, what can I do for you, Mr. Forbes?”

“Well…ah…it was so nice seeing you again this afternoon…I mean in spite of the circumstances and stuff. I wondered if you’d like to have dinner sometime?” These last words came out in a rush; Blaine couldn’t help himself. He poured a big smile into his cell phone.

There was silence. His heart fell. She must be appalled…

And then her voice came back, with its rollicking tone.

“You mean like a date? A dinner date with you? Yes, yes…I think I’d like to, but it would have to be a Dutch treat.”

“Oh, great.” Blaine gushed, relieved.

“When?” she asked.

“Tonight, tomorrow night, next month, whenever you’re free.”

“I could do tonight. Where would we go?”

“Anywhere you’d like to go. Anywhere.”

“Okay. Why don’t we go to Bouchon? I’ll call and make a reservation. Shall I meet you there, or do you want to pick me up?”

"I'll pick you up." Blaine was genuinely beaming now, and he suspected it could be felt over the connection.

"In the Mini?"

"Don't worry, I'll get it washed." He could feel her smiling now, gently teasing.

"Don't worry about it, Blaine. I've ridden in worse. Why don't you pick me up at six? I'll give you my address. I live in a townhouse with my roommate in Santa Barbara proper."

"Done." Blaine scribbled down the address she gave him. "See you then." Blaine hung up the call, set his cell down, and rubbed his hands together in anticipation. She actually remembered him and everything. "Wow!"

Blaine went out and unloaded the Mini. It was surprising how many hamburger wrappers, French fry boxes, napkins, and whatnot the tiny car could collect in the course of a week or so. Then he took it to the local Santa Barbara car wash and let the hands scrub it inside and out. He produced a can of polish and personally went to work on some of the scratches and dings, blending the paint until they looked better. The Judge would be proud of him. He got in to drive off and sniffed suspiciously. It still smelt of old French fries and ketchup. *Damn.*

He went back into the car wash counter and eyed the various cans of smells available to make the Mini smell better. It was a hard choice. He didn't want something cloying or unmanly, but then again it had to be strong enough to overcome the existing odor. He gave up trying to make a choice and bought both Evergreen Forest and New Car Smell, opening them, tucking them under the front seat and hoping for the best. He drove off smelling like a newly minted evergreen forest.

CHAPTER 25

Blaine parked the Mini across the street from Laura's townhome in Santa Barbara. He was a little early, it was only five forty-five. The Mini had never looked or smelt so good since the first day he bought it from its former owner. He sat in the car for fourteen minutes, nervously playing with the knot in his canary yellow tie, then sorting through his music list, wondering what sort of music Laura liked. He hoped it wasn't rap. He couldn't stand rap and had only one rap song in his music library, *Wishing Well* by Juice WRLD, which he supposed could be played over and over, but it would jangle everyone's nerves after the third play.

He slowly got out of the car, straightened his frame to stiff upright, much as a prisoner does before facing the firing squad, then marched across the street, over the lawn, and up onto the porch of the house. It was a two-story townhome, newer, but small. As he reached for the doorbell, the door suddenly opened and there she stood, her blue eyes staring at him with that rollicking look that made it seem like everything was fun.

"I watched you sitting in your little car across the street and was wondering when you were going to come over, Blaine. It looked like you were going to camp out there forever."

"Oh…well…I didn't want to be too early." He let his eyes drift down to see the rest of her, a simple white blouse, one button too many unbuttoned, exposing a lovely amount of beautiful golden tanned skin, no hint of a bra, and dark jeans that emphasized her slim figure, long legs and flat stomach. Her long brunette hair was combed back and woven like a mare's tail into a long ponytail stretching down her back, exposing generous ears and hinting at erogenous zones. He told himself to stop thinking like that and focus on the conversation. She wore leather boots that looked well-loved and comfortable, bringing her head barely above his shoulder; a small matching rectangle purse, also well-used and loved, was slung over her shoulder.

She said, "Let's go. You can stare at me more over a glass of wine," slinging her arm through his and marching him off the porch and over the recently sprinkled lawn toward the Mini, ignoring the steppingstone path to the right and getting the tips of Blaine's Florsheims wet.

They settled into a back table at Bouchon, the last two-person table at the end of the row, squeezed up against wood paneling with barely any room between tables, and no privacy. It was 6:30 and the joint was already full. They sipped wine for a while before ordering and somehow managed to use up three hours in conversation and dining that went by so quickly it seemed like twenty minutes. She was so easy to talk to, happily chatting about herself, her past, her present, and her future. Listening intently when Blaine spoke, looking into his eyes, asking perceptive questions which Blaine found himself often having to pause to think to answer.

"So how old are you, Blaine?"

"Twenty-eight."

"You know I'm only twenty-four."

"Yes."

"Do you think you're too old for me?"

"No. Do you?"

"No." She smiled. "Do you think I'm too young for you?"

"No," he said. She smiled again. That was the right answer.

"After all Blaine, you were only four when I was born. Have you ever been married?"

"No."

"Come close?"

"Yes."

"What happened?"

"She died."

"Oh. I'm so sorry."

"It's okay."

"Was it like with us? Were you attracted to her like you're attracted to me?"

"No. It wasn't….not like us. She was a friend. We were solving a case together. She came along for the ride, and we became a team. We slept together at some point, and it became an affair. And from there we grew closer and closer until she suddenly got sick and died."

"Oh my God. It must have been awful."

"It was."

"But it's different with us?"

"I fell in love with you the instant you looked at me from your Mustang convertible at that stop sign."

"You knew then, Blaine?" Laura's eyes got wide.

"Yes."

"I guess somehow, I knew there was something special too. It was the way you looked at me or something. You made me feel flushed. Alive. Wanted."

She leaned across the small table, then, to kiss him on the tip of his nose, then bounced back into her seat, leaving him stunned.

"I want to see more of you, Laura…a lot more. Tomorrow. All week. All the time. We've started something here. I want to finish it. Follow it to its end, or maybe find it has no end."

After dinner, he drove her back and parked across the street again from her townhouse. But they both wanted more time together. She invited him in for a drink and he agreed, surprised at how wobbly he was from their libations. She was wobbly too, and they clung together, making a zig-zag pattern across the street and small lawn to her tiny porch, where she fumbled with the keys. "My roommate isn't in or I'd just ring the bell," she explained.

She took him upstairs to her tiny bedroom, saying she wasn't ready to share him with her roommate if Judy came home early from her trip, and they stretched out on her queen bed. Laura produced a bottle of vanilla vodka, and they sipped at it, whiling away more time. A small clock beside her bed read two a.m. Finally, she said, "I think I'd better go to bed. I'm feeling woozy."

"I am, too," Blaine confided. "I don't think I'm up to driving. Perhaps I can just stay here."

"Here? Where?"

"Perhaps I could stretch out on Judy's bed for a while, till I'm feeling better?"

"Oh no. You can't sleep there. Judy might come home."

"Well, I could sleep here with you, in your bed."

"But we don't know each other 'that' well, Blaine. That doesn't work."

"I'm way too smashed to drive. Let's give it a try."

Laura looked doubtful.

"Come on, Laura. I won't do anything you don't want me to do. I'm safe."

Blaine took his shoes off while Laura watched.

"You don't want me to get hurt, do you?"

Blaine took off his shirt.

"No. Of course not. But don't you think it's a little soon?"

"Naw, we won't do anything. It's just I can't walk straight right now."

Blaine took off his pants and underwear and slid under the covers.

"Kay, Blaine. I don't want you hurt. But understand, I'm not doing anything."

Laura took off her boots and slid into the queen bed beside him, fully dressed in her jeans and blouse. They cuddled together briefly then both collapsed into deep sleep.

CHAPTER 26

Blaine struggled to get his eyes open. He finally got little slits open to see the bedroom, but the pain behind his eyes was too much, and he quickly shut them down. It was still early morning, he could tell by the light, and God his head hurt. He gritted his teeth and tried again, managing to get them both open, rising on one elbow and looking around. Laura was beside him in the queen bed, softly purring in her sleep, fully dressed except for her boots.

He had no clothes on at all. He'd slept nude, she'd slept fully dressed. He remembered now. It was the only way she reluctantly agreed to sleep with him on their first date. But thank God he'd not tried to drive home. He supposed he could have taken an Uber, but where was the fun in that?

With agonizing slowness, he got up and dressed. His shoes were the hardest part. Then he carefully maneuvered himself down the steep staircase and into her little kitchen, desperately looking for coffee. Instant coffee, canister coffee for her Keurig, ground coffee for the filtered coffee pot sitting in a corner, anything would do. He went through all the high cupboards above the counter. No coffee. He couldn't bring himself to lower his head to the cupboards below. He'd tried, and he'd thought his head would come right off.

He finally gave up, staggered back up to her bedroom, and collapsed on the bed beside her, fully dressed, letting his shoes stick out. It woke her. She looked at him through blurry eyes, then smiled a big smile. It was good.

"Need coffee in worst way," he muttered. "Looked downstairs but couldn't find any."

"Okay, Babe. I have some. It's a little hard to find. Let me make some for you."

He nodded his consent, then thankfully drifted off to sleep.

He didn't know how long it was, but he was suddenly disturbed awake by a commotion. Laura was screeching in a high voice from the bottom of the stairs. "Come back, Robert. I said you can't go up there. No. No. Robert! Come back right now. No. Don't."

His eyes fluttered open, making them hurt again. A man bounded through the door of the bedroom and stood over Blaine, hands on his hips. "What the fuck you doing in my girlfriend's bed!" he snarled.

Robert was very angry and very tall, his face twisted in shock and rage. Blaine thought he might be a dead man.

Laura bounded around the corner after the man, pulling him away from the bed, her voice almost a wail. "Blaine was just leaving, weren't you Blaine? Nothing happened."

Blaine struggled and managed to get out of the bed and stand. But his head hurt awfully, and he was a little dizzy.

"Hello. I was just leaving. Looks like you two have some things to talk about," Blaine muttered, pushing past the boyfriend, and starting down the stairs. "I'll call you later, Laura. Remember, we have a date for lunch today." Blaine made his way through the living room and out the small townhome, hoping the cool morning air would stop the pain in his head.

Blaine drove slowly back to his hotel. The pain in his head had not subsided. He'd really binged last night, a clear mistake. It was eight in the morning. He crammed two aspirin from the glove compartment into his mouth and chewed them. They tasted awful. He hoped the Hell they worked.

But there was another feeling in him too. A new feeling he hadn't experienced before. It felt like a piece of him was missing, had been carried off by a beautiful brunette with rollicking blue eyes, leaving him only half a person now he wasn't with her. He'd never felt like this before. It was…amazing!

CHAPTER 27

His wake-up call came at eleven, jangling him out of a deep sleep. The aspirin and the additional sleep had worked. He felt like a new man, his mojo back.

He called Laura's cell but there was no answer. He left a message saying he would be over about 12:30 to pick her up for lunch as they'd agreed. He waited a half hour and called her again. Again, she didn't answer. Was she going to dump him to soothe the feelings of this Robert guy? He didn't know. But by God he wasn't going to play dead. He'd force the issue.

He drove the Mini the fifteen minutes over to her townhome, bounded onto her little porch, and rang her bell. Nothing happened. He rang it again, longer this time.

The door suddenly opened, but it was Robert standing there, his face still contorted with anger. "She doesn't want to see you," Robert said.

"But we have a lunch date."

"She doesn't want to have lunch with you."

"Well, if Laura wants to cancel our date, she, of course, can. But she's the one that has to see me and tell me, Bud. Not you."

"Just a minute." Robert slammed the door in his face.

Blaine waited and waited. Five minutes went by and nothing. Blaine rang the bell again, leaning on it this time. Thirty seconds later the door opened. This time it was Laura. She was flushed, her blue eyes sparked with anger.

"I'm sorry Blaine. I do want to have lunch with you. Just give me another couple of minutes, would you please?"

Blaine nodded, and the door closed. Another five minutes went by. Blaine decided enough was enough. He rang the bell again, leaning on it for a good 30 seconds.

The door opened and Laura stood there again. "I'm sorry Blaine. Robert and I are having a bit of a difficult discussion. Why don't you come in?" Blaine followed her inside and closed the door behind him.

Laura seated herself in the middle of the small dining table. Robert sat at its end, looking unhappy. Blaine could see Robert clearly now. He was perhaps twenty-two or twenty-three, but his pouting made him look like a kid. He was a couple of inches shorter than Blaine, and skinny. He looked like a nerd, perhaps an engineer.

Blaine decided to take a John Wayne approach, choosing to lean nonchalantly against one of the walls, towering over the two seated people, rather than sitting. Robert called him on it, "Can't you just sit? You look threatening."

"No. I like it here," said Blaine.

"Robert was just leaving, Blaine, and then if you give me a couple of minutes to change, we're off to lunch."

"Laura, I want to talk to you privately for just two minutes. You owe me that."

Laura sighed. "Blaine, I'm sorry, can you just wait two more minutes outside, please. And I'm certain we'll be done."

"Sure." Blaine sauntered back across the room and out the front door again, into the sun. He walked off the porch, across the lawn and over to the Mini to lean against the car, figuring he'd give Robert a graceful exit.

Two minutes later the door opened again and Robert bolted out, slamming the door behind him. He walked across the lawn and over to Blaine.

"She doesn't know what she's doing. I think she's hung over. I'm her boyfriend," said Robert. "Just who are you anyway, an old friend or something?"

"No. We just met, we went out to dinner and now we're going to lunch. Nothing else happened."

"So why do you want to take her to lunch? You trying to date her? Push me out."

"Actually," said Blaine, "I'm looking for a wife. I think I'm going to marry her."

Robert's jaw dropped open but no words came. He just kind of gasped air for a couple of seconds, then spun on his heel and marched off to his car parked further along the street.

Blaine walked back across the lawn, up onto the porch, and rang the bell again. This time the door opened immediately; a dainty hand reached out to grab Blaine and haul him inside, and the door was firmly shut again. Laura stood on tiptoes to throw her arms around him and give him a wet kiss.

CHAPTER 28

Dr. Emma Broadwell looked like a cat that had swallowed the cream, her green eyes glowing, a real smile spread across her face, the first real smile in a long time. She marched down the government office corridor with a strutting cat's style, a tall lean woman with attitude, her bright green business suit and green eyes shining against the grey walls.

Broadwell's assistant, Murray, trotted along beside her like a small terrier, trying to keep up on legs much too short. Murray was small, round, and viewed the world through coke bottle glasses, but he was very good with details. Murray carried an armful of notes for Broadwell's schedule. Meetings, appointments with the powerful, lunches, dinners, speeches, podcasts, talk shows, the life of a busy power broker in D.C.

She was flitting from meeting to meeting today, half the meetings with oil and gas lobbyists who would have their clients write checks to PACs supporting one of the Senators Emma chose to designate. The other half of the meetings were to nail down exactly who those lucky Senators would be. She was lining up support for a second effort to become Undersecretary of Energy for Nuclear Energy, now that Ugly Tom Flanders was incapacitated. She was determined to become the Atomic Energy Undersecretary and enjoy the largesse her oil and gas friends were only too glad to provide to steer the country away from the use of atomic energy. It was truly a wonderful system, and she knew how to work it like the showgirl she was. And so glad to be rid of Ugly Tom Flanders, the last impediment to her reaching the goal.

Murray suggested they fly out to California to visit Tom Flanders in the hospital. She snorted in disgust. Murray was always quick to try to spend her money on boondoggle trips. He particularly loved to go to California, a stupid desert ruined by too much water, too many trees, and too many people. A place where her nose always ran from all the pollen.

Ugly Tom Flanders was a mean little bastard. As practical as she was in selling power and prestige for money, Flanders had somehow outfoxed her in contriving to steal her appointment. He'd been a pain in her butt for a long time with his maneuvering. But then he'd really gone off the rails, bleating about his small atomic plants, trying to push atomic power back into the mainstream as a source of power, biting the very hands that had fed him, those that had helped him become Undersecretary. He'd played a dangerous game. He'd gotten what he deserved.

She ducked into Frank Ross's Senate Office. He was out of town, but she had special privileges and could use the office. His chubby little Hispanic office secretary smiled and waved from behind her desk, but Emma knew she was actually grinding her teeth. The secretary didn't approve of Emma, nor of Emma's cozy relationship with her boss. Bed hopping was an honored profession in D.C amongst the powerful and the want to be's, but the secretary didn't understand that. It was way above her pay grade.

Emma deposited Murray in the waiting room and waltzed past the secretary and into Frank's office, throwing her voice over her shoulder to say, "I'm expecting Buck. Show him right in."

Five minutes later the door to Frank's office opened and Buck Jennings stepped in, sliding his Stetson off his head and looking very much the old cowboy he was.

"I'd say it was nice to see you, Buck, but it looks like you let everything get screwed up out in Montecito."

Buck Jennings slid a chair up to the overhang of Frank's big desk and sat down. "I wouldn't say that, Emma. Our mutual friend is at least currently incapacitated, unable to serve as Undersecretary. We'll push to have him quickly replaced." Buck produced his famous smile.

"I'm not impressed, Buck. I swear that asshole has nine lives. Dead is dead. A coma is ambiguous and incomplete. When exactly are you going to push the Senate Committee into dumping Flanders and appointing me Undersecretary in his place?"

"All in good time, Emma. All in good time. I know you have Frank in your pocket, or more specifically your pants. But I have to line up the Senate Committee Chair and some additional members, so we'll have the necessary votes."

"I've got a lot of them in my pocket already, Buck. They're chomping at the bit, waiting for your PACs to make good on the offers I've made. They want to see the cash, Buck. See it splashed around on their election campaigns."

"Okay. Let's let nature take its course from here. See what happens with this coma thing. Give it a week or two."

"That's bull shit, Buck, and you know it. Our deal wasn't for me to wait around for perhaps weeks to see what happened. I want to move against Flanders and move now, while he's vulnerable. Next week, let's call back the Senate Committee to consider a replacement Undersecretary, given Flanders' incapacity. And at the beginning of the week you have your PACs begin to make good on their commitments."

"I recommend we go slow, Emma. There's an investigation into the Flanders' shooting in Montecito. This may not be the best time to lean on our committee members."

"Fuck that. I want to move now. You and your oil and gas friends have made certain commitments to Senator Ross and to me. I'm ready to perform on my end. Wipe proposals for new atomic energy models right off the planet. But I can't do it unless I'm Undersecretary. And I won't do it if you don't quickly, and I mean real quickly, get me that title."

"Okay. Okay. Let me talk to my partner in Montecito. See what can be done to move things along."

CHAPTER 29

The Judge and Blaine rendezvoused at three and drove back to Bitsy Flanders' house.

Bitsy opened the door on the second ring and invited them in. The Judge was surprised to see she wasn't bitsy at all, standing at least five foot seven. She wore a polite smile, reflected in grey-blue eyes, and held her chin high, perhaps an indication of a life of challenge. She was a platinum blonde, with high cheekbones, a chiseled face, and an aristocratic look. The years had left a few lines, but she was still a beautiful woman. She must have been a head-turner when she was younger. She was slim, skinny really, with a scrawny neck and a modest bust, packaged in a light brown military-style shirt with double flap pockets and light brown Chino pants.

She shooed them into her living room toward one of the matched embroidered sofas, Blaine craning his neck the whole way, hoping for a glimpse of Laura. Bitsy sat down opposite them.

"You wanted to talk about my soon-to-be ex-husband, Tom, I believe. The one who's now in a coma," said Bitsy, diving right into the topic. There was a slight hint of satisfaction in her voice as she said the word 'coma'.

"Why do they call you Bitsy?" asked the Judge.

She smiled. "When I joined the sorority at U.S.C I had the flattest chest of any of the girls so they gave me that nickname. When I was pregnant with Laura the problem solved itself, but the name just kind of stuck."

"You and Tom are not on the best of terms I guess," said the Judge.

Bitsy smiled, showing white teeth that looked sharp and aggressive. "No. Twenty-odd years of physical abuse doesn't create great friends. Now we're in the middle of this divorce and property settlement negotiations and the bastard goes and gets himself shot. Probably did it was deliberately just to slow the process down. Dumb-fuck bastard."

"What happens if he doesn't come out of his coma?" asked Blaine.

"At some point, I am told I can get a court order and have him disconnected. I'd pull out the plug right now myself if I could, but I'm not allowed." Bitsy displayed her teeth again. Her smile was ferret-like now.

"I understand you're in a gun club, Mrs. Flanders," said the Judge. "Do you own a rifle? Like maybe a twenty-two caliber rifle?"

"I do. It's in the gun case over there. I can shoot it too. I practice at my gun club; I plan to go hunting when it's open season."

"Was it open season on your husband?" asked Blaine.

"Apparently it was. Couldn't happen to a nicer guy. The police came, carted my gun away, and then returned it. No match I guess with the bullet that hit Tom."

"There's a rumor you've taken a lover since Tom filed divorce papers. Is that true? Mind telling us who it is?" asked Blaine.

"The answer to your first question is yes. And to your second question, it's none of your damn business."

"This is an attempted murder investigation, Mrs. Flanders. And we need you to answer our questions."

"I don't have to answer shit, young man. And particularly not to you two...private dicks. You're not even peace officers. But I am not telling the police or anyone. I do have a special friend, I admit. He is quite prominent in this community. It would not do him good politically to have his name bandied about. He's asked me not to disclose our relationship publicly, and I have promised not to do so. So there." Bitsy folded her arms across her chest, indicating she'd say no more.

"Do you know anyone who might have wanted your husband dead?" asked the Judge.

"How about everyone, Judge? Tom was a mean, conniving asshole with lots of enemies over a lifetime of screwing people over. There are any number of people who'd like to see him dead."

"Like who?" asked Blaine.

"The gal he outmaneuvered to be appointed the Undersecretary for Atomic Energy, Broadgate or Broadwell or something. The oil and gas companies he screwed over by turning his back on oil and gas after he was appointed. Laura overheard him screaming at his dodgy business partner, Lance Kelly, so they must have had a falling out. On a personal level, his mistress who he probably mistreats like he mistreated me. The gardener, Minato, who Tom routinely abused and insulted, something of an anti-atomic freak I believe. Likely anyone else with whom he's had any significant social or business contact."

"What about you?" asked Blaine. "You admit that you hate him. He was about to sign a new estate plan that would cut you out of his estate. The shot just missed his heart I understand. If the shot had killed him, you'd be sitting pretty. You'd inherit his entire estate."

"Hah…of course. I did hate Tom's guts. I put up with his crap for years because of our daughter."

"And the money."

"All right, and the money. What a waste of all those years, when I should have been looking for someone else who would love me and be kind to me. Yes, it could have been me, but it wasn't. And I don't like being accused by some young puppy barely out of school." Bitsy looked daggers at Blaine. "I think you two had better leave now." She slid up from her sofa and scooted them through the living room and out the front door, slamming the door behind them.

"Well, Judge," said Blaine. "That went well."

The Judge shrugged. "We're not in the business of making friends, Blaine."

CHAPTER 30

The Marksman's fingers shook with anger as he typed his message over the Dark Web, responding to the imprudent message from his client seeking to delay payment of the second installment of his fee until Tom Flanders was actually dead.

"I've done what I was hired to do. Flanders is no longer able to serve as Undersecretary of Atomic Energy. He'll not be out promoting small-size atomic energy anymore, even if he comes out of his coma and survives. He has no ability to oversee his affairs, no way to continue his career. He'll be an old frozen relic if he lives, worse off than if he'd died.

He sent his message with a slash of his forefinger on the return key, breathing heavily.

His response came back immediately.

"As we like to say, no tickee, no laundry my friend. We'll wait and see."

The Marksman tried again, this time more forcefully.

"You think you're anonymous, but you're not. I know exactly who you are, where you are, and why you wanted Flanders dead. You don't trifle with a professional. You could find yourself the object of my next job. Make my second payment immediately or I guarantee you'll be very, very sorry!"

The Marksman waited and waited and waited, staring at his dark screen. There was no response. The client had gone offline. *Goddamnbloodysonofabitch!*

CHAPTER 31

They gathered again in Johnny Marks' tiny office: Craig Barker from the FBI, the Judge, Blaine.

"What about the bullet, Craig?" asked Johnny. "Has the FBI identified the type of gun used?

"Oh, we've done far more than that," said Craig, a smug look on his face. "First, the bullet was a twenty-two caliber. Shot down a rifled barrel for precision, so we can infer a twenty-two rifle is likely the murder weapon. Flanders' wound seems to indicate an overly powerful charge, suggesting the perp packs his own ammo. And it was an almost perfect shot, through the glass, right past Blaine's protruding belly, and into Flanders' chest, barely missing his heart. Whoever pulled the trigger was a real marksman."

"Anything else?" asked Johnny.

"Oh, yes. See, Johnny, you get the FBI involved, you get real, sophisticated detectives on your case. Years of experience, honed intuition, backed by the sophistication of the FBI labs and computers. We're not amateurs dancing around for publicity." Craig threw a disgusted look at the Judge. "You guys are all on the wrong track."

"Okay, Fancy Pants," said the Judge, "Cut the grandstanding and tell us what you got?"

"Well. I ran the crime details through our database as well as INTERPOL."

"And?"

"There's been a series of killings over the last five years, assassinations if you want, here in the U.S. and in Europe. No one victim related to another. Nothing in common except the manner of the killing. A twenty-two rifle, a sniper setup, the victim shot in the chest, a super loaded twenty-two round suspected, the killer's perch swept clean, the shell casing carried off. No perp ever arrested or charged, or even identified as a person of interest."

"A contract killer," said the Judge.

"What's that mean for the case?" asked Blaine.

"It means we're looking for two people, Blaine. The contract killer who pulled the trigger, and the person who hired him."

CHAPTER 32

Pavilions Market was a large box store, set down on a large parking lot filled with cars. Blaine entered the crowded store and admired the big produce section with its fresh fruits and vegetables stacked high, backed by a large deli counter running along the wall and serviced by three people. Shoppers darted this way and that with stainless steel carts, provoking smiling exchanges at the corners of rows where mini traffic jams developed. Some carts were loaded to the gills with expensive-looking tins, cans, cheeses, wrapped protein from the butcher, and wines, a testimonial to the wealth of Montecito residents. Others not so much. A few shoppers sheepishly carried green plastic baskets on their arms filled with store brands.

Blaine turned to a young man with a broom and asked to see the manager. He was shown to a tall skinny fellow, mid-forties, in jeans and blue-striped business shirt, partially covered by a brown apron. All smiles. Mr. Friendly. The captain of this money-making machine for the chain that owned the store. Blaine showed his credentials, explained he was working with the police, specifically Johnny Marks, and asked about Ted Olson.

"Yes. The police came and asked the same question. We have so many customers and we're so busy, it's really impossible to keep track of specific shoppers."

Blaine showed the manager a copy of Ted Olson's receipt.

"Yep. That's us. The guy was definitely here paying his bill at the time stamped on the receipt. But nobody would remember him among the lines of people who check out."

"Which register was it?" asked Blaine.

"Let me see the receipt again." The manager bought out reading glasses to reexamine the receipt. "Register two. The second one in line."

"Do you have cameras and video on where you check out?"

"We do. Everybody does. Shoplifting is a huge problem in our industry."

"Do you still have the tapes for this particular night?"

The manager nodded. "Come with me."

He led Blaine to the back of the store, through an 'Employees Only' door, past cold storage, and up grimy looking stairs to a balcony of offices running the length of the rear of the building. He ducked into one marked 'Security' on the door, where a large heavy-set man in a grey uniform lapped over the arms of an office chair, watching video feeds of check-out activity below. "This is Sam. He can pull up the tapes for you. I've got to get back on my floor."

Sam reached over to spin a second rolling office chair over beside him, extended a meaty paw to shake hands, and said, "What do you want to see?"

"Here's a copy of the store's receipt. Can you pull up the video for this exact transaction? It went through register two."

"I think so. Sit down. It'll take a while."

Blaine didn't realize he'd drifted off, until Sam gently shook his shoulder. The video of the exact transaction was up on the screen.

"Can I get a copy of the video of that transaction?" asked Blaine.

"I guess so, as long as the boss says it's okay."

The video showed the buyer purchasing wine, cheese, crackers, likely a wrapped steak, and grapes, from a very young-looking checker, hardly old enough to shave. But the customer was a small Asian man, Chinese, middle-aged. It wasn't Ted Olson buying the groceries.

"Can you give me a snapshot of that man, Sam?"

"Sure, but even better I can tell you who he is."

"Who?"

"Jimmy Lo. He owns the local dry cleaners. His shop is in the center of the Village, on Coast Village Road. He also has a side business renting P.O. Boxes."

"Thanks, man," muttered Blaine, snapping up the photo off the printer and heading for the door.

CHAPTER 33

Blaine drove the Mini with difficulty up the steep drive adjacent to Flanders' house, and the Judge scrambled out the passenger side, waving his hands about to disburse the fumes from the little car's effort. Blaine got out and they walked up the faux red adobe pavers to the small porch. They stepped over an Amazon delivery package there, and Blaine pushed the doorbell button in the wall, setting off a cascade of church bells inside. They waited. Nothing happened. Blaine pushed the button again. More bells…. Nothing happened.

"Guess Ted Olson's not home, Judge," said Blaine.

"But look Blaine, his car's over there." The Judge pointed to the Mercedes with its top down, sitting in the shade of a tree at the back of the driveway.

Blaine shrugged. "Guess he doesn't want to see us."

Blaine reached over out of curiosity and pushed on the tall wrought iron handle to the front door. The door slid open noiselessly on well-oiled hinges, exposing a part of the hall with its matching fake red adobe pavers, and a small slice of the living room.

"In for a penny, in for a pound," muttered Blaine, stepping inside and shouting out in a deep voice, "Hello. Anybody home? Hello…hello. Here to talk to Ted. Ted, are you here?"

The Judge reluctantly followed Blaine in, wondering if they were going to be shot.

Turning the corner from the hall to the great room, the Judge ran into Blaine's back, Blaine having skidded to a stop at the edge of the great room, staring at the back of the overstuffed chair that was part of the center grouping of furniture. One arm hung languidly over the arm of the chair, the hand pointing to the floor. The arm was covered with blood, as was the floor beneath, where the blood pooled and then ran under the chair.

The Judge put a hand on Blaine's shoulder to steady him, and said, "You stay here a minute. Keep a look out."

The Judge walked around to the front of the overstuffed chair. The beautiful brocade of the chair was now covered with red, and bits of flesh. What was left of Ted Olson was there, most of the upper half of his skull blown away, A shotgun was slung down across his chest, still clutched in his other hand with one finger on its trigger. It looked like he'd eaten his shotgun.

"Is that Olson?" called out Blaine.

"Yes," sighed Judge, "it used to be. You check the upstairs, Blaine, and I'll take the rooms on this level. See if anyone else is here. Be careful."

Blaine dashed up the stairs at the end of the library and then moved cautiously along the balcony overlooking the great room, opening doors and checking rooms. Sixty seconds later he called down from the balcony, "No one up here, Judge."

"Nor down here. If someone else was involved, they're long gone."

Blaine came back downstairs to take a closer look at Olson. "You think he killed himself, Judge? Or you think he had help?"

"Hard to tell, Blaine. If Olson had help, they were very artful in the way they arranged the body and the shotgun. It would have been someone with significant experience in such matters. We'll have to let police forensics decide."

Satisfied that there was no one else in the house, they began to search for some clue as to how this had happened. Blaine took the upstairs and the Judge took the down. After a while, Blaine called the Judge back upstairs to a second bedroom that was set up as an office. The room was paneled in pine, with a tongue and groove floor covered by a large oriental carpet in green and purple hues. In one corner at an angle facing the room was an antique desk of considerable heft. Its drawers were all pulled out, upside down on the floor, their contents scattered about the room and the surface of the desk. Someone had been desperately looking for something and in a hurry.

"Think they found what they were looking for?" asked Blaine.

"I doubt it, Blaine. The search has the feel of someone in a panic."

"Which means someone else was here and perhaps Olson was murdered."

"I agree, Blaine. The Amazon delivery at the front door may have spooked them."

Blaine picked up a picture frame from the floor which likely had stood on the desk, its glass shattered from its fall. It was a picture of Olson from perhaps twenty-plus years before, standing with his arm around the waist of a petite but beautiful woman in front of the Olson house. The woman was smiling and staring up at Olson. She looked vaguely familiar to Blaine.

The Judge looked over Blaine's shoulder. "That's Flanders' wife by God," said the Judge. "a much younger Bitsy Flanders."

"There's nothing much else up here, Judge. Some mail, unpaid bills, and stuff."

"Let me see."

Blaine handed over a stack of recent bills, which the Judge rifled through.

"What about this P.O. Box bill, Blaine? Olson had a P.O. Box, but by this bill, it appears he held one under a different name: 'Alan Cain' at this address. That's a little suspicious. Wait a minute. Didn't you tell me the guy whose supermarket receipts Olson stole to embellish his alibi operated a dry cleaners store with a P.O. Box sideline?"

"Yes."

"Was his name Jimmy Lo per chance?"

"Yes."

"This P.O. Box bill is from Jimmy Lo Dry Cleaning. Olson had a P.O. Box in Jimmy's dry-cleaning shop. Maybe Olson had Jimmy manufacturer an alibi for him."

"Jesus, you may be right, Judge."

"There's nothing much downstairs Blaine. See anything else to look at?"

"I was just thinking the bedroom closets are funny in here, Judge."

"How so?"

"Well, for one thing, they are unusually deep in both bedrooms."

"So, the guy liked deep closets."

"And they are back-to-back. I mean the closet in one room is back-to-back with the closet in the other room."

"So?"

"Closets are usually alternated when they're built into a common wall for two bedrooms."

"What do you mean?"

"The first closet in the first bedroom will be cut into the common wall and run halfway across that wall from the door. The closet in the second bedroom will cut into the wall, starting at the middle of the wall and run from the middle of the wall to the back corner of the wall. They are inset that way to preserve space."

"And?"

"Here the closets in each bedroom are set into the wall back-to-back and go deep into the wall. And their interiors each run deep, but their widths only go half along the bedroom wall and then stop."

"Yes. So?"

"It means there is enormous empty space inside the common wall between the bedrooms, from the middle of the common wall all the way over to its exterior corner. There is empty space in the wall twice the depth of the two closets, running from the wall's mid-point, back to its corner."

The Judge's eyes narrowed. "A secret room."

"Maybe."

The Judge thumped on the wall. It provided a satisfyingly empty sound. "Go in the other bedroom and see if you can find a latch or something. I'll look here," said the Judge.

In the other room, Blaine leaned against the wall, and it slid into the space behind perhaps an inch. He then placed both hands spread flat on the wall and pushed sideways. The wall became a sliding door, sliding easily on oiled wheels a quarter of the way toward the center of the wall, opening up a second hidden sliding panel. "Judge, Judge! I've found it! In here!"

The Judge came running as Blaine slid the interior door open to expose a small room tucked between the walls, perhaps eight feet deep and running halfway along the wall of the bedroom for eight feet. It was paneled in polished dark wood; spots in the ceiling automatically switched on to light the space. Across the width of it ran a desk, with file drawers, a swivel chair, and two computer screens that also automatically powered on. The opposite wall had peg board, and lodged there was an AK 47 rifle, a Savage model 110 medium-heavy rifle with a fluted barrel, a Glock 40 pistol, and a .22 rifle with a polished cherrywood stock. Boxes of ammo were stacked along the bottom of the wall.

Blaine's mouth dropped open in amazement. The Judge went immediately to the computers and toggled some keys. Nothing. They were locked out.

"Time to call the police," said the Judge.

Blaine nodded, retrieved his cell from his back pocket, and dialed Detective Johnny Marks. Half an hour later they sat on a lawn bench outside the Olson house while the police swarmed like disturbed ants inside and out and Johnny strutted around like a majordomo, giving orders to his crew.

CHAPTER 34

The Judge and Blaine finally extracted themselves from the onsite police interrogation at Olson's house, coasted the Mini down the long driveway to Barker Pass Road, pulled around the corner, and then pulled over for a private chat.

"Where next, Partner?" asked the Judge.

"Well, we now know that Olson was not the one at the supermarket and was likely busy at the time shooting Flanders. But what about Jimmy Lo, who took his place, and the P.O. Box that Olson kept at Jimmy Lo's under an assumed name?"

"Let's go, Blaine."

The Chinese Laundry was crushed between an Italian eatery and a toiletries shop in the middle of a retail strip in the lower Montecito Village. It consisted of a single glass door and an adjacent window, through which a zillion clothes could be seen hanging on a convoluted double-high conveyor belt that nosed up and down and around like a roller coaster. The small plaque on the inside of the closed door said "Closed", even though it was the middle of the day.

Blaine knocked on the door while the Judge stood behind him to watch for movement through the window. There was none. Blaine then pounded on the door with a heavy fist, making it rattle. Still nothing happened. Blaine tried the door. It was locked.

"Maybe around back," whispered the Judge.

They walked the full length of the Italian eatery, down its side, and around to the back. The second exterior door, belonging to the dry cleaners, was closed, but when Blaine tried the knob it opened. The place had a musty smell, a combination of dry-cleaning fluid, dampness, and something else that raised the hairs on the back of Blaine's neck.

They eased in through the back door, pushing plastic-shrouded clothes aside where the belt swooped down low in front of them. There was a beat-up white counter running most of the width of the storefront, and a side wall with perhaps fifty little brass mailboxes mounted there, the windows on most of the boxes black staring across the room, empty

One box was open, its little door hanging from one hinge, likely a victim of somebody's hammer and crowbar. A beat-up desk on the other side of the small room had been searched, its drawers pulled out, their contents dumped on top of the desk. The cash register on top of the counter had its cash drawer standing open, the cash gone.

That third smell was more intense toward the front of the shop… the smell of blood and innards. On the floor inside the counter, which was open, no shelves, lay a body in a white coat, covered in red. Someone had stuffed a small Asian man there, his head leering out, patterned with what looked like repeated blows to the head with a hammer. The Judge checked for a pulse. There was none.

There was a small leather book lying on the floor near the stowed body. Blaine picked it up and thumbed through it. "It's a list of the owners of the P.O. Boxes, Judge."

"Who had box forty-two, the broken one?" asked the Judge.

"Alan Cain."

"Alias Ted Olson."

"So how do you think it pieces together, Judge?"

"I think our Mr. Ted Olson was a professional assassin. He killed Flanders under a contract from someone else."

"Okay, then what happened?"

"I think there was maybe a down payment and a second payment for the job, and whoever hired Olson didn't want to make the second payment."

"Because Flanders was only in a coma, not dead."

"Right. But Olson pressed his contract client for the second payment, maybe threatened him a little. Who knows."

"And the guy that made the contract wasn't having any of that," said Blaine. "So, he came to town and shot Olson in his home."

"Yes. And there must be something that ties the person who contracted the kill to the Flanders murder."

"Hence the desperate search for that piece of evidence," finished Blaine.

"Right. Whoever it was tore Olson's place apart looking for anything that might connect them to the assassination attempt."

"You think they found it there, Judge?"

"My hunch is they didn't. They searched Olson's home for it, then panicked when the Amazon delivery guy showed up, and left in a hurry."

"But maybe they saw the same receipt we saw Judge, for the P.O. Box. Or maybe that's how Olson's killer and Olson originally communicated. The killer came here, tortured this man for Olson's box number, killed him, and forced open Olson's box."

"That's the way I see it, Blaine. But our killer didn't find what he was looking for in Olson's box. So he tore this place apart, still looking for something."

"Damn."

"Let's assume our hypothesis is correct, Blaine. And you're Olson. Where would you hide dirt on the people who had hired you."

"Gosh, Judge. We searched Olson's house. And his secret room, and now his P.O. Box. I don't know."

"Think, Blaine. I'm out of fresh ideas. Where would you hide secret files?"

"If it were me? I guess…guess…I know. I'd buy myself an old sport coat, put a jump drive in its pockets, give it to my collaborator dry cleaning guy, and have it roll around and around the conveyor belt forever, sort of in plain sight."

"Excellent idea, Blaine. Let's turn on the computer for the conveyor belt and see what we find."

Blaine turned on the old industrial dry-cleaning computer next to the cash register, which didn't need a password, and typed in 'Ted Olson'. The computer buzzed and fizzled a bit and then spit out on its screen. 'No client record.'

"Well, it was a good idea," sighed Blaine.

"Try the name the P.O. Box was taken out in," said the Judge.

Blaine dutifully typed in 'Alan Caine'. There was more buzzing and fizzling, and suddenly the conveyer belt came alive, shuffling up down and around its roller coaster track at 20 miles an hour, finally stopping at a disreputable-looking sport coat. Blaine reached up, unhooked the coat from the belt, and rummaged through its pockets.

"Nothing, Judge. Damn."

"Feel in the material Blaine. Are there any lumps or hard spots?"

"Here, under the armpit. There's something in the lining. Damn, there's some kind of little pocket sewed in on the inside of the left armpit."

Blaine turned the coat inside out and unsnapped a little flap high up on the inside of the jacket to uncover a small pocket. He reached in with two fingers and extracted a small cloth bag containing five micro SD cards. "Damn, we're a good team, Judge."

The Judge smiled. "All right, let's call Johnny again. And Blaine, you still have your laptop in your trunk?"

"Yeah."

"Let's make a copy of these cards while we have them."

Johnny arrived five minutes after the field team he'd sent to secure the crime scene, his FBI guy in tow. Barker said in a deliberately loud voice so the Judge and Blaine as well as the entire team could hear, "This is exactly what I told you, Johnny. These amateurs come in and muck up the entire crime scene for us. What a God Damn Cluster Fuck! Jesus, I hate these pompous amateur detectives. Do you guys have to mess up every crime scene you find?"

'We didn't touch the body," said Blaine. "And look what we found." Blaine shook the bag of SD cards under Johnny's nose. Johnny's eyes widened. He snatched the bag from Blaine and stuck it in a plastic evidence bag, then into his coat pocket, looking a little wolfish now he had perhaps valuable evidence. "Hope you guys didn't open the bag, mess up any prints," he muttered.

"Make sure I get a copy of everything, Johnny," said Barker.

"Me too," said the Judge.

"Sure. As for you two," Johnny nodded at the Judge and Blaine, "Well done. I just wish you'd stop leaving a trail of bodies around Montecito as you prowl around my town."

CHAPTER 35

Blaine nursed the Mini around an extensive traffic jam in the middle of Santa Barbara. One car had apparently stalled out in the major intersection and another car hit it. He didn't want to be late to meet Laura, but he was going to be. They had agreed to have dinner at a restaurant called The Lark. Laura had said she had errands so she would meet him there.

And now Blaine was running late…of course he was running late. Damn it, he was always late. He slid the Mini into the parking lot, swerved a little cockeyed into a space, and leaped out of the car as it was almost still rolling, dashing for the restaurant entrance.

He stepped disheveled through the entrance, and scanned the restaurant. Outside, from a patio festooned with heating lamps, in one of its darker corners, blue eyes locked on his. And suddenly everything was okay. He felt himself relax, pure joy seeping into his features. She was here. There she was. God, he needed to be close.

He made a beeline for her; it was like she was the only person in the restaurant. She was all he could see. She stood as he got close, then stepped around the little table to throw her arms around him, pressing her body tight, raising on tippy-toes to give him a long wet kiss.

They stood together like that for an eternity, then she patted him on the shoulder to let go and sit down. She whispered her toes were hurting.

They huddled over the little table and talked and talked. Two hours and several rounds of drinks flew by.

They shared childhood stories, how and where they grew up, the quiet victories and resounding defeats, siblings, best friends, pets, parents, their first dance, their first car and learning to drive. They had a mutual passion for boats, particularly sailboats, now that Blaine had learned to swim and had been taking sailing lessons. They spoke in soft melodic tones, but they communicated in other ways too. The way they looked into each other's eyes as they spoke and listened, the way they reached for the other's hand as crossroads in lives were revealed and explained. They giggled together over amusing stories from their pasts, and made light of painful times and things they felt compelled to share.

Waiters came to take drink orders, then food orders, then dessert orders, and finally the bill. They ordered without thinking, randomly, oblivious to the restaurant, the staff, the other patrons, and the food they ate mechanically. Finally, the proprietor came over to whisper he was sorry but they were closing in five minutes.

"So, do you hold to the third-date rule, Blaine?"

"What's that?"

"My college friends claimed there is a third date rule. That a nice girl doesn't sleep with someone right away, but if the guy is interested enough to ask her out on a date twice, then it is okay if she wants to sleep with him on the third date. The invitation for a third date proves he's seriously interested in her."

"This is our third date, Laura."

"Oh, does a lunch date count?"

"I don't know, I'm not sure I've got a grasp on the rules. Either way, I don't think it applies to us, Laura."

"Oh." Laura looked a little disappointed.

"I'm already in love with you, Laura. I want to be with you forever. Sex is part of that, but what I feel for you is so much more. I want to be close to you all the time, sleep with you in our common bed all the time, wake up, wipe the sleep from your eyes, and see you. Dance with you under the moon, share every part of my life with you, hold you on tough days, boast to you on successful days, commiserate with you on failed days, share every experience with you life can provide."

"Oh." Laura's eyes broke into that rollicking look Blaine so loved. "Good. To hell with rules. Let's go to your place and cuddle and whatever. See what a third date can really mean."

They car tagged to the Ritz-Carlton Bacara, sped through the lobby, skipping the bar, and headed up to Blaine's room. Laura took a flying lunge onto the queen bed, rolled over on her back spread eagle, and watched him with her rollicking eyes, waiting to see what he would do.

"Are you sure?" Blaine asked. "We don't have to start so soon."

"Be quiet before I change my mind, Blaine. Come here and be close. You're the most interesting man I've ever met."

He jumped onto the bed beside her, rolled to her side, and reached up one sleeve to tickle her under an arm. "Eeek," she screamed, then burst into a spasm of giggles, trying to push his fingers way. They tussled a little and then leaned into another long kiss that sent fire through Blaine's loins. Suddenly it was a race to see who could get out of their clothes first; it was something of a tie.

They held each other close for a long while, relishing the feel, the scent, the warmth, the aura of the other. Then they joined together as only a man and a woman can, rolling around the bed in a rising level of passion until suddenly Laura collapsed in climax accompanied by a small series of cries and gasps, her legs and torso shaking. Blaine came immediately. Then he held her that way, inside, never wanting to leave. Joined, they drifted off to sleep.

Morning didn't break through the blackout curtains, but when the maid rapped on their door around eleven seeking to clean the room Blaine struggled out of a sound sleep to find Laura, her head on his chest, arms and legs wrapped around him, purring softly in her sleep. He tried to untangle himself to answer the maid, but Laura's arms and legs only tightened, refusing to release him. The maid used her master key to open the door a smidge, stuck her head around the corner, took one look at the scattered clothes, underwear, the two heads in the bed, and scurried away, closing the door behind her.

CHAPTER 36

It was two in the morning. The sleepy Mark/Westcliff Hospital was just that. Sleepy. A janitor and two intensive care nurses were around, of course, but no one took a second look at the man that slowly walked into the ICU and down its long corridor toward a specific room. His face seemed familiar; he looked like he belonged.

He strode into Flanders's room in the ICU and softly closed the door. There was no change in Flanders's condition. He was still in his coma.

The man went to Flanders's bedside, studied the room for a minute. Some sycophant lackey had sent a fruit basket encased in cellophane, that was now turning a grimacing black, adorned with ballons also on their last legs. The man half-grinned to himself, toggled off 'Alarm Sound' on the vitals monitor, and hit the one-minute alarm pause on the ventilator. Grabbing a balloon, he uncoupled the ventilator tubing in front of Flanders and stuck the half-filled balloon on the end of the connector instead. One final deep groan death rattled out of Flander's husk.

Then the man casually opened the door and strolled out of the long silent hospital corridor. Just another check on just another patient. No one noticed the way he side-stepped spots in the hall, avoiding the hospital's video cameras.

Thirty minutes later, a bit late actually, the veteran nurse assigned to Flanders made her way over to do her last set of rounds. She paused at the doorway, her eyes widened abruptly. A "Get Well Soon!" balloon inflated and deflated itself, bobbing away over Flanders cyan-blue face. The vitals monitor flashed brightly, alarms silent, ventilator humming along merrily.

"Ah, Shit." she said quietly to herself. This was all really bad. Bad for the hospital. Bad for her, particularly since she was a half hour late checking on her patient.

She stood in thought for a while, then looked out the door to the corridor and nursing stations. No one was around. She marched over, slipped the balloon off the ventilator tubing, dropped it to the floor, and recoupled the tubing. Then she toggled the alarm switch for sound 'on' and made a dash out of the room for her station as the alarm went off and all Hell broke loose in the ICU.

CHAPTER 37

The Judge had asked Blaine to find the homeless guy who'd slapped the poster on the Mini's passenger window on the Judge's trip from the airport and follow the poster back to its source. Meanwhile, the Judge went off lollygagging with Johnny.

Blaine chafed a bit at his assignment, having thought they had a 50-50 partnership, but had to admit it was a lead that needed to be followed, especially since they had just received word that Flanders had died. According to the Judge, his cause of death was too timely, suspiciously so.

He didn't find the homeless man near the off-ramp they'd come off from the airport, but after trying at two other off-ramps, Blaine found the man on a surface street leading into the lower Montecito Village near the town's official off-ramp.

Blaine rolled down his window and motioned the man over; he came scrambling.

"Hi, boss. Going to donate a little green so I can get a sandwich?"

"I might, if you've got the information I need."

"I'm all ears."

"You posted a paper on my windshield the other day about atomic energy."

The man raised his hands, palms out, as in self-defense. "I didn't mean noth'n by it. Honest. The sheet and glue comes right off. I'm sorry if I offended you."

"Why'd you do it?"

"Amy pays me twenty-five cents a poster."

"Amy who?"

"Amy Clark. She passed them out to a bunch of us at the camp."

"Where's your camp?"

The man looked around, wanting the suggested money but careful not to be seen giving information to the enemy. Finally. he blurted out, "Along the tracks."

Blaine gave his outstretched palm a twenty-dollar bill. The man's hand closed around the bill with desperation and he was gone, shuffling off at a fast pace.

Blaine drove to the railroad tracks that paralleled the 101 Freeway and spotted the encampment. It was a sizable camp of perhaps 100 people, some with tents, some with makeshift plastic protection, but it was all still a sad affair. These were the cast-offs, the people society no longer needed, or wanted, and people deemed too broken to fix. It was a poor reflection of the values of the richest country in the world.

Blaine walked around piles of trash at the camp's beginning and mused about the things people collected in shopping carts or neat piles outside their plastic shelters. Piles of stuff discarded by others, mostly useless to the current owners, but nonetheless handfuls of possessions they laid claim to, the only stuff these people possessed. Perhaps that was the point; they still owned a few possessions, things they called their own. Perhaps this flotsam from society gave them a bit of solace. Blaine approached one of the men sitting in the shade of a tree at the start of the camp.

"Hello, sir. I'm looking for Amy Clark. Can you direct me?"

The man looked at him dully for a moment, then nodded and pointed to the second tent in, not bothering to speak.

Blaine nodded a thank you and approached the second tent, his voice ringing out. "Hello…hello…Amy Clark…looking for Amy Clark."

A small head was thrust out between the flaps of the tent, and then the entire animal. She was about thirty, dirty brown hair, dressed in an ill-fitting castoff blue dress, contrasting with her beat-up combat boots.

"Yes." She gave Blaine a toothy grin.

"Hi. My name's Blaine Forbes. I'm trying to track down the source of these anti-atomic energy posters that cars are being tagged with."

"Why? You a cop? You here to make trouble?"

"No no. I just need a little information. Are you the one handing out the posters, paying a quarter a tag?"

"What if I am? They're not for rich people like you."

"I'm just wondering why, and where the money's coming from?"

"You a reporter?" Amy's eye lit up with hope.

"I am sometimes," Blaine fudged.

"Well, it's a fair deal. They give me fifty cents for each poster tagged to a car. I split it with my friends that help fifty-fifty. That's all there is to it."

"Who's 'they'?"

"The Activists for Gay Rights."

"They have an office in Santa Barbara?"

"Certainly do. In Downtown Santa Barbara."

"I'd love to talk to them. Who do you deal with there?"

"Nancy something. But don't tell anyone I told you. You'll screw up my deal."

"Promise I won't."

Blaine returned to the Mini and googled The Activists for Gay Rights. They existed alright, Blaine drove to the field office address. It turned out to be a small little cottage, converted to business use, with a lawn in front, a small porch, and an old front door painted a bright red, with a small window in it.

When Blaine knocked, the little window opened and a pair of brown eyes barely reaching the bottom of the little window peered up at him. Then the door swung open.

"Are you Nancy?"

"I am, good-looking. Come on in. What can I do for you?'

She was mid-twenties, the age when you volunteer for people-help projects. She wore a white blouse and grey silk pants over low heel pumps, saddle leather and new. Her clothes bespoke money, and plenty of it. She had the finished look of a college girl from a rich liberal family, going in to slay dragons.

"I'm Blaine Forbes. Interested in the anti-atomic energy posters you're paying people to post."

"It's not illegal, Bud. There's something called freedom of speech in this country."

"I didn't say otherwise. Why are you so against the use of atomic energy?"

"It's an awful power source. It results in huge nuclear waste, nuclear weapon proliferation, and nuclear accidents. Just consider the waste issue. Radioactive nuclear waste must be managed for thousands of years. And remember, nuclear power plants create fissile material that can be used for dirty bombs. As more countries build nuclear plants, the risk of nuclear weapons increases four-fold."

"But…"

"No buts, every clear-thinking American should be against the building of distributive nuclear plants in every city in our country."

"How far would you go to stop the building of nuclear plants?"

"What do you mean?"

"Would you go to the extreme of, say, sending a threatening letter to the Undersecretary for Nuclear Energy?"

Nancy blinked. "I was just making some tea, Mr. Forbes. Would you like some?"

"Yes, that'd be great."

"Sit down on the sofa over there and let me fix us up."

Blaine collapsed onto the sofa, sinking almost to the floor, and wondered if he'd be able to get up. Nancy dashed around the corner to the small galley kitchen and he heard her bustling, then the sound of the kettle being filled and plunged onto the stove burner. It got quiet. After a few minutes, the whistle on the kettle went off and continued to whistle. Blaine let it go for about thirty seconds, then called to the kitchen to ask if Nancy needed some help. When there was no answer, he somehow hoisted himself up out of the sofa and stumbled into the little kitchen around the corner to see if there was a problem.

There was no problem. Nancy was just gone, the back door still open exposing her escape route. "Damn…damn…damn…" he muttered. He felt like a sucker. He supposed that's because he was.

CHAPTER 38

Blaine went back to his car, and looked up The Activists for Gay Rights on the California Secretary of State's website. It was there, a nonprofit properly chartered with the State of California. It named the agent for service of process as one Barry Minski, with a different address but still in the City of Santa Barbara. Blaine drove over to the address and parked in metered parking across from the office building, which claimed by its sign to be the newest, best-located, and swankiest office location in the entire City of Santa Barbara. Blaine suspected it was also the most expensive office building in the city. These people certainly had money.

Blaine went back to the California Secretary of State website to look up the most current filed financial report for The Activists for Gay Rights. He studied the organization's numbers for a minute, then left the Mini and entered the office building, taking the elevator to the penthouse floor.

Double walnut doors across from the elevator on the sixteenth floor proclaimed 'The Activists for Gay Rights' on a brass plate. Blaine pushed one of the double doors and entered. A small buzzer went off deep in the interior of the space, a door opened somewhere, and a grey-suited man swung around a corner and into the lobby to greet Blaine. He was tall and slender, early thirties, his grey suit cut to fit him to a T. One finger of the hand he extended to shake Blaine's was studded with a large emerald ring; his nails were immaculate and sported a clear polish, and he wore an antiseptic look on his face. Blaine immediately disliked him.

"I'm Barry Minski. We don't have many visitors here. How can I help you?"

"Are you the Executive for The Activists for Gay Rights?"

"I'm the Managing Director."

"Great. I was hoping you might be able to tell me why a charitable organization named to help with gay rights is sponsoring anti-atomic energy propaganda and utilizing the homeless to distribute it."

"And who are you that's asking?"

"An investigator."

"Investigating us? Oh my. Well, you see, we have friends in Washington D.C. who are charitable organizations, and they sometimes ask us to help by supplying people on the ground for various campaigns they run. It's hard to raise money for charitable organizations these days, everybody seems broke or disinterested in contributing their time or money to worthy causes. So, we have to help our charitable friends scrape by with their campaigns."

"And being compensated for the help?"

"Err…yes."

"I looked at your last filed Annual Report, Mr. Minsky. Looks like for last year the Managing Director's salary consumed about sixty percent of all money raised for that year by the non-profit."

Minsky stiffened. "This organization requires a Managing Director with special skills. People like me don't come cheap."

"Another thirty percent was consumed in expenses, like this office space, clerical staff and the no doubt fancy car you drive. That left a paltry ten percent to spend on charitable purposes. What sort of special skills do you have, Mr. Minsky?"

"The ability to tap into charitable contributions made by industry."

"Which industry?"

"Energy. Companies that provide stable energy to the country, not a one-way ticket to nuclear fallout."

"Why are energy companies concerned about gay rights?"

"They're not. But they're seriously concerned about the risks associated with the spread of atomic energy. We provide grass-roots feet on the ground campaigns to get their message out around the country."

"Their message being?"

"Don't tinker with atomic energy. You'll get burned."

"Do they know you are using the homeless, at fifty cents a throw, to get your message out?"

"Hey. If it works, it works. We got the message to you, didn't we? We're left to our own means as to how we distribute the message."

"Which company, specifically, funds your organization?"

"I don't know. We rely on an individual in D.C., sort of a broker, who collects contributions from companies in the industry and then pays us to undertake campaigns."

"Is the broker legit? What's his name?"

"Jennings is a long-time power broker and player in D.C., originally was a Senator for Texas, been a lobbyist for years. He's the real McCoy. Certainly legit!"

"Tell me about the threatening letter you send to Tom Flanders."

"What…what…what are you talking about? Who are you?"

"A private investigator, helping the police to find the person who shot Tom Flanders in the chest. He's subsequently died so it's now murder."

"I had nothing to do with anyone getting shot."

"You know Tom Flanders?"

"No."

"But you sent the letter didn't you? You drafted and sent a threatening letter to a Federal official."

"Well..." Minsky's voice was choked and low, hardly auditable. But then he rallied.

"What if I did? So what. It was just a joke. I meant the man no harm. Never met him. Just a prank. A foolish effort to get Flanders to stop pursuing new and dangerous atomic energy inventions."

"It's a violation of Federal Law to threaten a Federal Official. Did you know that?"

"I wouldn't call the letter threatening. In fact, I believe it was meant merely to be a warning to its recipient. And I didn't create its content. It was dictated to me. I had it typed up and delivered was all."

"Why did you write it?"

"Someone said it'd be useful if I did."

"Who?"

"My guy in D.C. The lobbyist."

"Why?"

"I don't know the details. We got paid five grand to act as the scribe, type up the letter, and have it delivered to a specified address."

"You said your lobbyist's name was Jenning's something?"

"That's right."

"I'd like your lobbyist's address."

Barry fumbled with his phone, then rattled off a street address in D.C. "Thanks," said Blaine. "That's all I need for now, but we may have further questions later."

Blaine spun around to the door and marched out, leaving Barry gasping for air.

CHAPTER 39

Blaine was bummed again. His arrangement with the Judge was supposed to be a partnership. So, how come he got all the dull assignments? He wanted to stay in town and see Laura Flanders some more. But no. He was the one designated to go to Virgina and then D.C. while the Judge got to stay and swan around Montecito. Life was so unfair.

He brooded about it part of the way east on the plane as he researched Complex Atomic Solutions, using the internet in tandem with the contents of the unmarked file folder the Judge had found in Flanders' office. Complex Atomic Solutions was owned in part by Tom Flanders and his business partner, Lance Kelly. Together they held 40 percent of its common stock, almost enough to control the company, given the propensity of small shareholders not to vote. It was a private company, but there was a lot of information available if you knew where to look, and thanks to the Judge, Blaine had a few extra pieces of the puzzle. pieces that Flanders had kept for his own private record.

Finally, his research through, he nodded off into a deep sleep that included dreams about Laura. The flight attendant shook him awake to tell him they were at the gate and he was the last passenger left on the plane.

He muddled his way through the airport and taxied out to the small town of Littlesburg, Virgina. Complex Atomic Solutions turned out to be set up on a sprawling parklike property, surrounded by high walls, which included labs, warehouses, manufacturing facilities, and one small office building. Security was tight at the gate manned by two armed guards, but Blaine had called ahead, and his credentials and pass were waiting for him.

A gopher-type young man was assigned to guide him around, answer questions, and primarily keep an eye on him. The guard sternly warned that Blaine was not to go anywhere without his guide, and that his guide knew the limited areas in which Blaine would be permitted.

"Welcome to Littlesburg, Virgina, Mr. Forbes. I'm George French," said the gopher, solidly pumping Blaine's hand.

Blaine asked, "What is it exactly that your company does, George?"

"Generally, we manufacture nuclear reactor components for U.S. Naval submarines and aircraft carriers and other nuclear and non-nuclear research and development companies, and make components associated with such devices."

"And at this location?"

"Here in Virgina we principally manufacture naval nuclear reactors for submarines and aircraft carriers. We also provide office space for several independent consultants who work closely with us in advancing our business. I believe it's one of our consultants you want to see."

"Yes. A Mr. Lance Kelly."

"Lance Kelly's office is right this way."

"Do you also manufacturer compact molten salt reactors?" asked Blaine.

"We do. Not many people know about those. They're still pretty top secret. I'm not supposed to give details. But this is a great company to work for. There's a rumor we're going to be acquired by a venture capital company with lots of money to invest in us. And they've allowed employees like me, who own some shares, to exchange our shares into the new company's shares. I'm going to make a ton of money when this deal goes through."

"How many shares do you own?"

"I bought five thousand shares at a dollar a share, had to use my college fund money, but I'm certain it's going to be worth it. And my mom, she bought the same, used her birthday money she's saved up for years. Maybe we'll take a trip together when we cash in." George's eyes were dancing now. "Right this way, sir, up the back stairs. Mr. Kelly's office is right up here."

Blaine was led up some rickety stairs along the exterior side wall of one of the warehouses to a second floor, and to a door at the top leading into a long hall. George tromped down the hall to the end, Blaine in tow, to a door containing small brass letters announcing: Kelly & Associates.

Blaine pushed the door open and walked into a reception room done up like the Captain's quarters in a frigate in the days of sailing ships, with tongue and groove wood ceilings and walls, portholes mounted over its windows, an antique cannon resting against one wall next to a mock gun port, and an assortment of artifacts mounted on the walls at various spots around the room. Blaine felt like he was in a museum.

A middle-aged woman sat at an antique French desk, also wood, and looked up at him as he entered, her glasses sliding from her nose to hang from a cord wrapped around her neck.

"Can I help you, sir?" she inquired in a high tweedy voice.

"I'm here to see Lance Kelly," said Blaine.

"Got an appointment?" Her face lapsed into a bulldog look, the keeper of the gate protecting the king from the barbarians.

"Yes."

She looked disappointed.

"I'm Blaine Forbes." Blaine said, lowering his voice and putting some gravel in it, imitating the Judge.

"Oh…oh…let me just buzz and see." She put her ear to her phone, hit two keys, and spoke softly into the phone.

Thirty seconds later a door behind her opened and the great man himself, Lance Kelly, came bounding out. "Come back to my office, please, Mr. Forbes. Don't mind Helga, she's a little brusque sometimes, but she has a good heart."

Kelly was all oily smiles, reminding Blaine of a used car salesman. He wore a plaid designer shirt with a very large collar, open, contrasting to his chicken-like white scrawny neck. The shirt pocket sprouted a clutch of pencils and pens, implying he might be an engineer, but he wasn't. The plaque behind his desk proclaimed he was a licensed Investment Adviser. Blaine wouldn't have trusted him to invest a dime.

"What can I do for you, Mr. Forbes?"

"You can call me Blaine. And I'm investigating the death of Tom Flanders."

"Whoa, wow…I heard about that. A lovely guy, so I understand. Hardly knew him myself, but by reputation."

"That's funny," said Blaine. "Since we've found evidence you and Tom are sort of business partners with respect to your joint holdings in Complex Atomic Solutions."

152

"Oh, well, yes. But we own our stock separately. We're not a partnership. We've each made an investment in this small company."

"Complex Atomic Solutions doesn't look small, standing here on the inside, looking around, Kelly."

"Well…no. I suppose not. If you look at it that way."

"I understand you had something of a sensational argument with Flanders about a tender offer for this company."

"Yes, well, Tom was a hard-headed S.O.B. sometimes."

"Tell me about the dispute."

"Well… see… I'm kind of in a jam. I need to sell my position in this company, and I need the cash to pay off a private debt. We had a generous tender offer, a tax-free exchange. Get us out clean with great liquidity. But Tom refused to go forward with the deal."

"You two together hold controlling shares in this company?"

"Yes. Well, close. Twenty percent each. I set up the deal. We each bought one million shares of common stock at one cent a share. Well, I actually bought two million shares, Tom arranged the financing, and then we transferred Tom's one million over to him."

"That sounds like a pretty cheap price."

"Well…I only negotiate good deals."

"If the tender offer goes through, what would you each get for your one million shares?"

"Five million shares of the new company."

"Tom would get the same?"

"Sure."

"Restricted stock?"

"Err…well…registered actually."

"Worth how much a share?'

"Well, who knows? Always a risk when you try to sell shares where there is no public market." Kelly smiled his used car salesman smile.

"I heard there was an underwriter who was going to take the company public," said Blaine, making a calculated guess.

"Oh, that. Well, there was a letter of intent. Course not really binding. Lots of outs. You know."

"At what price were they going to take the company public?"

"Err…maybe a dollar a share." Kelly smiled haplessly.

"So, you and Tom would have each netted five million from your penny stock investment?"

"Err…something like that I suppose. Anyway, it would have gotten me out from under my debt, but Tom wouldn't consent to the merger."

"Did the company have to get approval from the Department of Energy for its new compact molten salt atomic plant?"

"Yes." Kelly's voice was a whisper now.

"And Tom was the Undersecretary for Nuclear Affairs?"

"Yes."

"And did he give approval as Undersecretary of Atomic Energy for the compact atomic design, or did he recuse himself?"

"He approved it," Kelly whispered.

"And this is after you bought the two million shares, one-half of which were secretly assigned to Tom?"

"Yes…you're a quick study, Blaine."

"Isn't that a conflict of interest? Or maybe even a bribe?"

"You shouldn't throw loose words like that around. You could get yourself sued."

"Why wouldn't Tom sell?"

"It was stupid. Stupid reasons."

"Like?"

"First, Tom didn't want to lose the company. He thought the tender offer was just a shell game to bury the science of compact atomic power plants. Thought the offer came indirectly from oil and gas interests who would simply bury the company and its technology."

"Was that true?"

"I'm not sure…maybe."

"So, what did you say?"

"Who cares, says I. A dollar is a dollar, good anywhere. But Tom said no, he didn't want this molten salt project buried."

"Who was the interest behind the buyer?"

"An underwriting firm was the front. It was hard to tell who was really behind the offer."

"And the second reason?"

"Tom was in the middle of a divorce and negotiating a property settlement through the divorce attorneys. No one knew Tom and I shared this almost controlling interest in Complex. I suspect he didn't list his interest on his financial statement in the divorce proceeding. And even if he did, at a penny a share it was nothing. Nothing to get anybody excited about."

"Like the ex-wife and her attorney?"

"Ah…yes."

"But with a tender offer announcement and a public listing of the shares on NASDAQ in connection with a public offering at ten dollars a share, it would be impossible to miss." Said Blaine.

"I guess something like that. But I desperately need the cash from the merger deal and still do. If I can't figure a way to raise it, and quickly, I'm toast."

"What happens now?"

"It's likely that under his current will, Tom's shares will go to his wife. I sure hope she'll play ball."

"How much do you owe? Who's the debt owed to?

Kelly muttered something unintelligible.

"What?" asked Blaine sharply.

Kelly sighed, said in a low voice, "A very unforgiving lender."

"A bank?" asked Blaine.

"Private."

"How private?"

"I'm not going to say any more. But I'll talk to them. I'm hoping they understand you can't get blood from a turnip. If they can only give me a little more time, even with their exorbitant interest rates, I can pay them off in full."

"Did they know Flanders was holding up your only way to pay off the debt?"

"Yeah. I had to tell them something. I explained about Flanders, how he was making it impossible for me to get liquid on my position in Complex Atomic."

"You think this lender had something to do with Flanders' death?"

"What? No…I mean I don't think they'd…oh my God, shit, you may be right."

"Who are they?" snarled Blaine. "Spit it out. Who's the lender?"

"The Chicago Mob," said Kelly very softly, fear creeping into his voice.

"Do you think they arranged to have Tom killed so you could get liquid and pay off your debt?"

"They can't have…I mean they wouldn't have dared to…I mean…oh my God…I don't know anything anymore." Kelly's face lost all of its color.

"Please leave now, Mr. Forbes. I don't want to talk about this anymore. Leave me alone!"

CHAPTER 40

B.K. Carpenter, an old friend of the Judge's, sat across the table from Blaine at Segreto, a speakeasy bar and lounge in D.C., accessible through a secret door and down a set of stairs, underneath a Pizza Shop on 9th Street. Betsy was wolfing down her second martini and stuffing the last of a pizza into her mouth. It was the most expensive pizza Blaine had ever ordered. He wondered if the Judge would be the one with heartburn when he saw Blaine's expense account.

They'd shared a bucket of fancy French fries, dowsed in LeBlanc Ardenne Champagne Vinegar, coated in cage-free goose fat from France, truffle oil, and shaved black summer truffles from Italy. The fries had disappeared quickly, leaving Blaine regretting he'd been too slow to claim his half. Betsy certainly knew how to eat, quickly and with gusto, particularly when she had a buyer. Blaine had to admire the ability to chew so fast and hold a rapid-fire conversation at the same time. She was an eating machine. Or perhaps just broke and starving.

Betsy looked across the table at Blaine now with her watery blue eyes, preparing to educate Blaine on how politics *really* worked in the United States.

She had blonde stringy hair that long ago had lost its luster from too many dye jobs, a pink complexion that was blushed now from her cocktails and wore tight yellow high-waisted yoga pants that were not the best look for a mature woman. Her yellow-striped blouse was one button too unbuttoned, displaying a lot of cleavage and parts of her matching yellow bra. She was a one-off for sure. But the Judge said she knew everybody and everything that was happening in D.C. and now that the food was dispensed with, she began the lesson.

"Let me start by explaining Washington, Blaine."

"Okay."

"Lots of places are about money, or prestige, or old money status, how much acreage you control, or how famous you are as an actor or sports jock. Village life centers around these things and makes the wheels go round, creating a pecking order in village society that everyone understands and kowtows to."

"And Washington D.C.?"

"D.C is about none of those things. It's exclusively about only one thing."

"What, if not money?"

"Power! The pecking order here is all about how much power you have; and how much more power you're going to acquire. And if you hit a brick wall on your climb for power, it becomes how close you are to someone else who has more power than you, or is getting more power than you. And how you can be seen with that person and in the know about their thinking, so their power rubs off on you. The town is all about a climb to power. The power junkies who make this town swirl are not interested in your money or your pedigree. It's only about your power."

"I understand, kind of. I really wanted to talk about Tom Flanders. The deceased Undersecretary for Atomic Energy in the Energy Department. Did he have power?"

"Oh yes. Very much so. Poor Tom. I knew him well."

"How well."

"Well, let me tell you the story of Flanders. Tom came to this town broke but credentialed thirty years ago and set up shop as a scientist. He was a lovely young man back then, all starry-eyed and principled. Grand ideas about atomic power as the future of energy in this country. But over thirty years…hell, within thirty weeks…this town will grind your principles and dreams out of you. You can't make a living here on your principles."

"So, what happened to Tom?"

"He bounced around for a while and starved. Then Tom became practical. Gave up his effort to support atomic energy development and sold out to the monied special interests that want to keep things just as they are, with no atomic power on the menu."

"Okay, so he got disillusioned. Kind of sold out."

"He did. And that changed him, twisted him somehow. His old friends drifted away, missing the old Tom, and new friends filled in the vacuum. Friends playing the system, seeking more of the power that makes D.C. run. Soon he was employed by the oil and gas industries, the electric companies, the manufacturers of big generators, and more recently, the green energy scammers. He was the darling of this base, spreading the word on the dangers of atomic energy, and how we must keep the genie in the bottle."

"So, he made his living being anti-atomic energy?"

"Very much so. He was an entertaining spokesperson, lots of wit and a bit of Irish charm. Well-liked by those who employed him and admired by those who listened to his carefully orchestrated presentations that aimed to tamp down any exploration of the use of atomic energy.

But his message, honed over many years, was so different from his original ideals and beliefs, I think it ate at him. He knew he'd sold out, lost his integrity, become just another huckster for money. It made him depressed and a little mean. We all loved the old Tom. I didn't spend much time with the new Tom. He wasn't fun anymore."

"How'd he get the Atomic Energy Commission position if he was against atomic energy development?" asked Blaine.

"Oh, that. That job was bought and paid for so he could go around the country and further tamp down any thought of using atomic energy. The votes of the members on the House committee responsible for appointing the Atomic Energy Undersecretary were all bought and paid for."

"You mean like bribes?"

"Shh. We never use that word in D.C. in polite conversation. But of course, that's exactly how it's done. In the end, money controls all votes. So, only the large corporations and the super-rich control what is really done in D.C., except in election years when different calculations have some sway."

"But what about government by the consent of the governed?" Blaine protested weakly.

"The Supreme Court on a five to four vote in 2010, turned that philosophy upside down. Now we are a country controlled by special interests funded by large corporations and the wealthy. And our representatives for the most part are bought and paid for, and dance as they're told to dance."

"What did the Supreme Court say?"

"They held that corporations and other outside groups can spend 'unlimited money' on elections. So-called 'Independent Expenditure Only Committees', or Political Action Committees, can raise unlimited money from one or more donors to spend on supporting any politician's election campaign they choose. Campaigns are very expensive, even more expensive since the Supreme Court's ruling.

As Jessie Unruh, a famous California legislator and political kingpin, said years ago, 'Money is the mother's milk of politics'. The current system gives the ones with money special access and influence over the political process. They essentially dominate what our Congressional representatives and other elected officials decide to do.

Our elected representatives know they cannot stay in office without PAC money to bolster their campaigns. So, they politely accept the benefit of the money, spent of course so…independently…through the PACs, to get them re-elected, and they listen very carefully to what the PACs want done, and vote accordingly. Quite a Democracy, hey?"

"So, Flanders sold himself?"

"Yes. But he was a rare case. He manipulated a deal to become Undersecretary for Atomic Energy in the D.O.E. on his promise to squash any new atomic energy technology wanting to come to market. It cost the Oil and Gas PACs a pretty penny in PAC disbursements to certain senators to make Tom the Undersecretary.

Then, once Undersecretary, Tom reneged on the deal he made. He turned around and floated a new form of compact atomic energy, even managed to have the Army give the company that invented it a large and lucrative government contract for the new atomic energy design. He essentially double-crossed the oil and gas industry.

Tom must have had some side deal so rich he believed he'd never have to work again. Because he would have never worked again in D.C. after so blatantly biting the hand that thought it was feeding him."

"And then he got shot," said Blaine.

"You said it was an assassination?"

"We believe so. A contract for hire killing."

"Surprise, surprise. Actually, that wasn't as big a surprise to a lot of people as you might think. The system is in play and well-established. It's not wise to double-cross it."

"You think the special interests arranged it?"

Betsy spread her hands in a classic shrug of 'I don't know'. "You're the detective, Blaine. I'm just a lowly campaign consultant."

CHAPTER 41

Lance Kelly settled into the small booth, all padded red leather, and reached over to shake hands with Buck Jennings. Code Red of 18th Street was a noisy bar, but Buck had picked an out-of-the-way table in the back. Lance did a double take at the large tree seemingly growing in the middle of the bar, all strung with lights, then slid around the table close to Buck so they were huddled together privately.

"So, what is the plan here, Buck? My shares will be worth five million dollars if the combined company goes on NASDAQ."

"The plan is for you to take a better deal, Kelly," said Buck. "My people will fund the entire tax-free exchange and make it happen, but only if it doesn't go public. They want Complex Atomic Solutions to disappear, go away, stop making small box atomic reactors. They will pay you double what you'd have realized from selling your shares over NASDAQ. Double! Your payment dumped into your offshore account. Untraceable. Pay taxes on it or don't, as you see fit. But Complex Atomic Solutions has to quietly disappear into the night."

"What about the minority shareholders? What will they get?"

"Nothing. They own shares in a private company now. The proposed combined company will stay private. No liquidity. No side market. The other shareholders can paper their bathrooms with their certificates for all I care. Do you really give a shit?"

"No. I guess not. To Hell with them. Just so I get my cash. But I and Flanders' widow together only own forty percent of the outstanding stock. We don't own control. We'll need a part of the independent shareholders owning at least another eleven percent to swing shareholders' approval for the deal."

"Of course…of course. And we'll get it. We'll do a nice, polished circular offering explaining how wonderful the combined company will be, how it will have access to more capital to expand, how it will have the benefit of more experienced management, and so on. They'll be chomping at the bit to see the deal approved and done."

"You won't tell the other shareholders the combined company won't go public, won't expand operations?"

"I'll handle that part. Explain there's always a chance we might go public, but we have no current plans. And there's always the chance the combined entity might be acquired for public stock by a public company. After all, anything can happen in business." Buck turned on his big smile. "Here, I've brought you a draft of the circular offering for the deal, and it says pretty much that."

"And what do you get out of the deal, Buck?"

"A cash payment in an offshore account, just like you. My Oil and Gas friends have been screaming for a way to torpedo your damn Complex Atomic Solutions Company, and its box car size reactors, and I have provided the solution. But what do you care, Kelly? I learned long ago not to worry about how many chips the player beside me is accumulating, and to focus solely on how many chips I'm getting. Nobody gets hurt and it all works out just the way our industry guys want."

"What about the widow? Will she play ball?" asked Kelly.

"I'm sure she will. She needs cash as much as anyone. I'm going to fly out to talk to her soon. Flanders' assets are held in what was an Inter-Vivos Trust which is now permanent. And it's my understanding she is the sole trustee and the sole beneficiary under the will he was going to change but never got a chance to. I need to get out this week and visit with her. The estates will need money to pay estate taxes. I don't think she'll be a problem. I'll need you, as a significant shareholder, to write a nice letter endorsing the merger."

"Done. You'll have it in your email in the morning."

"Great, Kelly. Thanks for driving up. It's a pleasure doing business with you." They formally shook hands and then Buck slid into the bar crowd and disappeared, leaving Kelly with the bill.

CHAPTER 42

Blaine cooled his heels in Senator Franklin Ross's waiting room for a half hour, then turned to the other waiting occupant in the room. "Senator Ross must be very busy. Have you been waiting long?"

The other man had a dusty look, although he was clean. Perhaps it was his scuffed boots. Perhaps he just belonged on a horse, not on a crappy metal chair in this crappy little office. The man was of medium height, with bronze skin that looked permanently tanned. Intelligent dark eyes that seemed to look so deeply into Blaine that Blaine felt the hairs on the back of his neck rise. Blaine felt like he was being measured for a suit. Then the man smiled at Blaine. It was a warm glow of a smile, spreading across the man's face, pulling Blaine in, making him suddenly feel relaxed, calm, perhaps even loved. What an amazing smile.

"Frank is a very important Senator these days, many irons in the fire. I expect he'll see us shortly," said the man.

"Are you working on one of those irons in the fire, a project for Frank?"

"As a matter of fact I am. I'm helping him determine who he should bring forward to fill a vacancy in the government."

"Are you a headhunter?"

"Oh my goodness no. I'm a lobbyist." The man turned on his radiant smile again for an instant.

"I'm Blaine Forbes." Blaine stuck out his hand. "I'm working on an article for the Wall Street Journal about campaign finance."

"Buck. Buck Jennings," said the man, leaning over to give a firm handshake.

Blaine struggled not to let the shock show on his face. It could not be a coincidence that the lobbyist who paid for a threatening letter to be sent to Flanders was cooling his heels in the office of the Senator in Flanders' blackmail insurance video.

Blaine produced his boyish grin, no match for Buck's smile, and engaged in a bit of flattering and self-deprecating small talk before making his ask.

"Perhaps we could grab a drink later this afternoon and you could share your perspective for my article."

"It's possible…in fact, let's do it. Tell you what. Let's meet at the Jack Rose at four, my favorite bar underneath an Italian pizza kitchen. It's in Georgetown."

After a few more minutes of idle chat, the door to an inner sanctum staff office opened and a secretary's hand beckoned Buck from his chair and in.

So, I wait some more, thought Blaine to himself.

Twenty minutes later the secretary appeared in the staff door again and beckoned Blaine in. Blaine's new friend must have exited through a side door as he was not in the office and didn't pass through the waiting room.

The Junior Senator from Missouri was all smiles as he hurried around his desk to shake Blaine's hand. Blaine had the feeling everyone Franklin met was deemed a potential campaign contributor until proven otherwise. "What can I do for you, Mr. Forbes? That's a very distinguished name you carry. How can I help?"

Franklin looked his forty-five years and then some. He had a red flushed face and watery grey eyes that nervously darted everywhere but never quite looked at you. But his handshake was firm, complemented by his other hand out-reached to pat Blaine's shoulder. Like he was the coach, and Blaine was part of his little league team.

"I'm doing a story for the Wall Street Journal," lied Blaine.

Franklin straightened up like he'd been hit by a bolt, his smile spreading wider, hope for free publicity filling his eyes. "Yes. Of course. How can I help?"

"I understand you're the Chair of the Senate Committee which confirms the appointment of the Undersecretary of the Office of Atomic Energy?"

"Yes."

"And you introduced the motion to approve Tom Flanders as the Undersecretary of the Office of Atomic Energy?"

"Well, yes." Ross took a tentative sip of what looked like very hot coffee, "Quite a qualified guy. There was nobody else of his experience and expertise in the running."

"And you heard what happened to Flanders?"

"Yes…well…that was awful. Shot in a home robbery or something. Just horrid. But I understand he's still alive. How is he?"

"Actually, he's dead."

"Oh my God…no. No, I hadn't heard that."

"Flanders had something of a record as an outspoken advocate for the oil and gas industry when he came before your committee. He advised extreme caution about extending the use of atomic energy to supplement the country's power needs, did he not?"

"Yes. That was my impression. And quite right too. We can't be too cautious in trying out new methods when it involves atomic energy. One mistake and territory the size of a state could become uninhabitable for a thousand years."

"I was looking at some fund-raising reports prior to our meeting, and I saw that the oil and gas industry contributes liberally to your election campaign."

"Yes. Well, they have been quite generous, it's true, I guess we see eye to eye on many aspects of government policy."

"Did the oil and gas lobbyists make contributions to your campaign in exchange for your support of Flanders for Undersecretary of the Office of Atomic Energy?"

"Well, no. It doesn't work like that."

"How does it work?"

"The money was not a quid pro quo. They didn't hand me a check and tell me to vote for Flanders. We don't operate that way. We don't vote lockstep with those who make campaign contributions. If you contribute to my campaign and I take a different position from ones you advocate, then you may decide not to donate to me again. But you can't ask for your money back or threaten me because you donated and I didn't do what you wanted. The only incentive I have to side with you, aside from your incredibly persuasive intellectual arguments, is that you may donate to my campaign again.

And of course, all money I receive is tracked. My campaign is required to disclose who gave me money. And lobbyists are required to disclose they gave money to me too, and they are required to disclose who pays them to lobby. And the money is limited, at least for direct contributions to my campaign. There is a limit to how much each individual and business can give to a single campaign."

Franklin smiled, confident he'd checked all the boxes and put any issue to rest. It sounded like a canned speech, trotted out any time the touchy part of campaign contributions was broached.

"I understand your position, Senator. But you have to admit it all sounds a bit shady. They pay into your campaign, and you are incentivized to approve their man for Atomic Energy Undersecretary. And I understand the Oil and Gas PACs also contributed quite heavily, supposedly independently, to your election campaign, and to the election campaigns of certain fellow committee members."

"It's all quite legal, and the American way, sir." Franklin sounded a bit huffy now. "Why are you so interested in Flanders?"

"You see, Senator, it's like this. Flanders was a long-standing advocate for not expanding the use of atomic power but rather continuing our reliance on hydrocarbons for energy. And then suddenly, he wasn't. Suddenly, he was gung-ho for compact atomic power to replace energy for the grid."

"Isn't he allowed to change his mind? It was obviously no skin off Franklin's back."

"Sure. But the facts are he was pro-oil and gas leading up to his appointment. Oil and gas paid a lot of money to you and others to put him in a position of power in the Office of Atomic Energy so he could maintain this no-atomics policy. Then Pow! As soon as he's Undersecretary, he double-crosses oil and gas and completely reverses his position, coming out for small configuration atomic plants. And now, suddenly he's shot; the victim of a contract for-hire murder."

Franklin put his hands up, flat, the classic gesture of *'wasn't me'*. Then he looked at his watch, indicating Blaine's interview with the great man was about over.

CHAPTER 43

"Just one more question, Senator."

The Senator's eyebrows furled; he actually looked quite goat-like, thought Blaine as he dug his cell phone out of his pocket.

"I don't think I want my picture taken with you, young man."

"Oh, this isn't about taking pictures. It's just this videotape I wanted you to see and hear. I thought you'd enjoy it since you're prominently featured."

Blaine hit the play button and turned the cell around, putting it under the Senator's nose. It was an interesting play of shifting expressions across the Senator's face as he watched, starting with astonishment and ending with a look of horror as the Senator's words rolled through, *'I'm relying on you to uphold my side of this bargain, in exchange for which I'll provide the political capital to make you Under Secretary.'* Then: *'To pull this off is going to require lots of money from Oil and Gas. You go back on your word here and it could be very dangerous for you. You understand?'*

The Senator suddenly stood up, coffee cup in hand, then clumsily spilled the entire cup all over Blaine's cell. "Oh, sorry. Clumsy me. Send me a bill and I'll pay for a new cell phone."

"It's okay, Senator, it's only a copy. Do you think your words were a threat, perhaps a motive for attempted murder since Flanders did go back on his word, did come out pushing for new atomic energy technology?"

"That's ridiculous. Absurd! It was just a practicality I was warning him about."

"I see."

"What are you going to do with that video?"

"Oh, that. I sent the original to the New York Times this morning."

"You snotty little bastard! Get out. Get out of my office. Never come back."

Franklin Ross opened up a sheaf of papers on this desk, pretending to read them, ignoring his own shaking hands, as he also ignored Blaine as he got up and walked to the door. Senator Franklin Ross was clearly in a true rage.

CHAPTER 44

The Jack Rose Dining Saloon proved to be a crowded and noisy bar even at four in the afternoon, but Buck scooped Blaine up and ushered him into an elevator and up to the Balcony Room which was mostly empty and quiet.

"Well, son. How'd you get along with Franklin?" asked Buck

"Not so well. We had a disagreement over what it means to sell your vote."

"Oh tisk tisk, son. That's the way the business moves in D.C. Everything is for sale, it's always a matter of price."

"You said you were a lobbyist. Who do you lobby for?"

"Mostly oil and gas interests."

"Are you the one who bought Tom Flanders a seat as Undersecretary of the Office of Atomic Energy?"

Buck looked startled, his face draining of color. He recovered quickly, pasting on his wonderful smile again and leaning in for warmth. But his eyes narrowed to almost slits.

"Son, you know better than to ask a question like that. Votes aren't allowed to be bought. As lobbyists all we can do is lobby, set forth our positions with rigor and specificity, marshal our arguments and the advantages which attach to the legislative result we advocate, and hope for the best." Buck's smile got even wider.

"You must think I'm stupid, Buck. I played something for Senator Ross today, a video of his making a deal to use his political capital to get Tom Flanders appointed Undersecretary for Atomic Energy, and explaining how big PAC money would be used to buy votes of Senators on the confirmation committee to assure that result."

"Did you hear my name mentioned?"

"No."

Buck sat back in his chair, visible relief spreading across his face.

"But Oil and Gas interests were mentioned. That's where the PAC money ultimately came from. And that's you, isn't it? Aren't you the key lobbyist for Oil and Gas? Weren't you part of this deal?"

"Well, I am a primary guy for Oil and Gas, although there are others, but I hope you're not accusing me of being part of a vote-buying scheme?"

"Oh, I'm sure there's no evidence, nothing in writing. But isn't that how you do business? Your PAC agrees to donate money to advertising campaigns to elect a representative, and the representatives then vote a straight oil and gas ticket on all matters affecting oil and gas. Everybody knows what side their bread is buttered on…and buttered well."

"Well, since the Supreme Court…"

"I know all about the Supreme Court decision in the Citizens United ruling and the resulting rise of PACs. But that doesn't make it right. And since Congress is compromised, they're the last body that would move to adopt legislation changing this ridiculous system. The end result is the people with money control everything."

"And so it's always been. It's the way of the world."

"What happened to one man, one vote?"

"That's always been a high-sounding philosophy, but always a myth. It never works. There's no such thing in the U.S. Money decides everything."

"Aren't you ashamed to be a part of it?"

"No. It's how I make my money, a lot of money, and about which I'm perfectly happy. And you know, Blaine, I'd be a little careful of spouting words like you're doing about the unfairness of our system. It's an entrenched system, understood by all its players, and protected by our government. You could get hurt."

"That how you threatened Tom Flanders, with those kinds of words? I saw the letter Tom Flanders was threatened with, and I know you dictated it."

Buck's mouth dropped, but no words came. He slammed his jaw shut with a crunch. His countenance went from shock to fear in an instant, his eyes darting around the bar to see if they were being recorded.

"Only Tom wouldn't play ball, would he?" continued Blaine. "He had his own pet atomic project he wanted to promote and he gave your cartel the finger. So, you put out a murder contract out on Tom."

Buck's smile was gone. His face was turning bright pink and his eyes were bulging now. Blaine could see he was holding his tongue with great difficulty.

"I've said enough, sir," Buck managed "I can't say it's been a pleasure. Good day." Buck stood up stiffly from his seat, turned, and marched from the room. Blaine discovered he'd been left with the check.

He turned the facts over in his mind. His instinct was that Senator Ross had no hand in the shooting of Flanders. But Ross was certainly an accomplice to something more than just mere political horse trading with Flanders and the Oil and Gas Industry. And Buck

Jennings was at the center of it all. Was Jennings the perp who contracted to kill Flanders?

CHAPTER 45

Buck stopped at the bar downstairs for shot of whisky, straight up. It didn't help. He grabbed a cab and headed for his office and a secure telephone. He rushed past his secretary's desk without a word, and into his office, slamming the door behind him with a crash.

His fingers trembled as he tried to dial his secure phone line, making it difficult to input his partner's Montecito number. He finally got it right on the third try.

The phone rang four times and then went to voice mail. He dialed the number again, cursing his partner for not picking up. This time he got a voice on the other end.

Buck yelled, "You son of a bitch. This deal has all gone to shit. We're all going to hang."

"What's the problem, Buck?" The voice was calm, reassuring.

"It's not a problem. It's a God Damn Cluster Fuck. This kid, this smart-alec asshole detective, knows everything. He knows I drafted the threatening letter to Flanders; he knows I bought votes to make Flanders Undersecretary for Nuclear Energy, he knows I bribed Senator Ross. He even knows I'm involved somehow with you and your initiation of that contract over the Dark Web."

"What's the kid's name?"

"Blaine Forbes…I googled him; he's part of a P.I. outfit run by someone who calls himself the Judge."

"Okay. We can't be talking like this over the telephone, no matter how secure your end is. It's just not wise. You'd better hop a plane out here to Santa Barbara. We need to meet and plan out our damage control, and I mean tomorrow."

"Okay. I'll fly out tomorrow. I'll send you a time to pick me up once I've booked a flight"

"Good."

The line went dead.

CHAPTER 46

The Judge was packing up at the Hotel Bacara, preparing to move to cheaper digs down the road in Summerland, to a suite motel recommended by Johnny. There was a soft tap on his door as he zipped up his suitcase. Puzzled, he went to the door and peeked through the small hole to see who was knocking. But whoever they were, they'd put their thumb close to the hole on their side. All he could see was the pad of their thumb. Then he recognized the soft giggle on the other side of the door. He swung the door open quickly, startling the person standing there, who he grabbed, hauled into his room, threw his arms around and planted a big kiss on. It was Katy, his wife.

"Oh Judge, she whispered, "you're so romantic when you're surprised." She was grinning from ear to ear…and so was he.

Katy was tall, 5' 8", slender, all arms and legs. She had long brown hair, twisted together today into a ponytail that bobbed behind her. She had small delicate features and smile lines. Her nose was a bit long and narrow, but in that it matched her head, more oblong than round, but all very delicate. Her face was pale white, as though never in the sun. And she had the most extraordinary eyes, vivid blue like the Caribbean, large and intelligent, with long lashes.

They'd been married for ten years and she'd produced them a son. Perhaps there were a few more lines now, a bit of grey in her hair, and sometimes circles under her eyes when she hadn't gotten her beauty rest. But when the Judge looked at her, she was the same as ten years before when she'd burst into his life and stolen his heart. She was twenty years younger than him, and the Judge, feeling old, had taken to calling her the "Kid". From the Judge's perspective that's what she was. But the Judge loved her dearly, and she was devoted to him.

"I didn't expect to see you this week, Kid."

"I know. But I missed you, I got lonely. I had a nightmare last night that you'd been shot. I mean it's possible. You get wound up in silly cases and forget about your personal safety. Anyway, I dropped Ralphie and the dog at my parents' house, and then just kept driving. I wanted to be beside you, sleep next to you…you know…"

"I do. I'm the same. I've missed you so much."

"Why are you packing?"

"Guess you came at the wrong time, Katy. I'm moving to cheaper digs, a full suite in a motel down in Summerland. This place is too expensive for our budget."

"A suite you say? Sounds delicious. Guess you're going to have to take me to Summerland. A mini-vacation."

"With pleasure, Kid. But first I'm going to buy you a super brunch." The Judge tucked his arm inside hers and marched her out of the room, heading for the elevators and brunch on the patio.

Over brunch, Katy whispered, "Judge, you've got oodles of money. I don't care as long as I'm with you. But you can certainly afford to keep us here if you want."

"You know how I am, Katy. I grew up poor, I was poor for a long time, so now I'm frugal."

"Frugal? Hah! You're still poor, Judge. You still act poor, think poor, feel poor. Your money, what is it? It's like a security blanket you wear. You wrap it around you, clutch at it, obsess about it, work at growing it, and complain when I want to spend a little of it on something extravagant. You're like an old maid with your money."

"I suppose I am. I swore, when I was six and my mother had me going door to door around the block in San Gabriel selling Christmas cards to make my own allowance, I'd never be poor again like I felt then."

"And yet the irony is that with all your money, you still feel poor."

The Judge smiled, "You're right. I guess that's why I have you, Katy. My spender wife."

"Humph."

The Judge felt pain as the toe of Katy's shoe hit his shin under the table in a mild kick. He now realized why women liked heels with pointy toes.

"Where's Blaine?"

"Blaine flew back east to Virgina to meet Kelly, the business partner, and then some people in D.C. He's on the way back. I think he's anxious to get back. He's dating the daughter of Tom Flanders."

"No way."

"Way. He's quite taken with her. Her name's Laura.

"Blaine wears his heart on his sleeve. I wish he'd find a real quality girl and settle down." Blaine was Katy's younger cousin, and she'd introduced Blaine to the Judge originally in the hope he would keep the Judge out of harm's way. It hadn't worked very well, and now she had to worry about both of them.

"So, okay Judge. Tell me about this case you and Blaine have been working on."

The Judge described the shooting of Tom Flanders; how it turned out to be a murder-for-hire job; how Blaine had discovered how the threatening letter had come into existence; how they'd decided Ted Olson was most likely the assassin but were too late, finding him murdered in his house; how Flanders has succumbed to his wounds, how Flanders and his business partner Kelly were at cross purposes, giving Kelly strong financial incentive to see Flanders out of the picture; about Flanders' mistress and the mistress's other boyfriend; about Flanders' divorce proceedings and his wife's secret boyfriend; about Laura, Flanders' daughter who Blaine was gaga about; about the embittered gardener and the aggrieved celebrity mayor; about Buck Jennings, the lobbyist, and Ross, the Junior Senator from Missouri."

"Well, it sounds like a collection of real characters, Judge."

"You've got that right."

"There's one particularly shadowy figure, isn't there? An unknown quantity."

"Who would that be?"

"The mysterious boyfriend of the almost ex-wife…Bitsy."

Katy was right of course. She had an unerring instinct to pick out the odd piece and ask where it fit. The Judge often thought Katy was the better detective.

The Judge grabbed his suitcase from his room and settled up with the hotel. They climbed into Katy's Tesla, which the Judge was not allowed to drive, and headed down Highway 101, the Judge affectionately resting one paw on Katy's thigh, happy to be beside her again.

CHAPTER 47

They squeezed into Johnny's office for a meeting. The Judge, mayor Alan Danzer, Mr. FBI Craig Barker, and of course, Johnny, squashed behind his desk. Blaine, still in the Dulles Airport, was conferenced in on the Judge's cell.

"Let's start with what we know," said Johnny. "We know the shooter was Ted Olson, we know Olson was a contract-for-hire killer, we know that someone hired Olson to kill Flanders; we suspect that person killed Olson so Olson couldn't disclose the name of that person. We think he killed Jimmy Lo too, and ransacked his dry cleaner and P.O. Boxes, looking for incriminating evidence. So, we're looking for a person not merely making a contract for someone else to kill, but also a person who is prepared to kill himself. Get his hands dirty. Is that what we're saying?"

The others nodded.

Blaine added, "And we hope there is evidence which identifies that second killer. Maybe in the encoded files left in Olson's coat at the Chinese Laundry."

"So, who do we have as suspects?" asked Johnny.

"There's Minato, the gardener," said Barker.

"Yes," said Blaine. "Minato was acting strange the next day in the garden. And his family and friends were all killed at Hiroshima. He called Flanders an arrogant prick. He didn't like Flanders as an employer and definitely believed Flanders was cavalier about the dangers of using atomic energy."

"There's Lance Kelly, the business partner," said Johnny. "According to Mr. Forbes, he was desperate to sell the stock in Complex Atomic Solutions to pay off his mob debts. Said it was a matter of life or death…his! That's got to be a strong motive. And if he's been dealing with the Mob, you've got to wonder about his morals. Seems like he'd do anything."

Danzer said, "There's this Senator. This Frank…what's his name?" said Danzer.

"Franklin Ross," said Blaine.

"Yes, Ross. Politicians are all ruthless and untrustworthy. The higher the office, the more ruthless and the more untrustworthy. I know. I was one." Danzer smiled. "According to Blaine, Flanders double-crossed the Senator and switched loyalties once appointed Undersecretary for Atomic Energy, changed from pro-oil and gas to pro-atomic energy. Jeopardizing the Senator's PAC money."

"What about the wife?" asked Barker. "Estranged from her husband, being screwed by divorce attorneys over the property settlement. Attorneys are vultures." Barker punctuated this by stabbing at the Judge with a pointed finger. Then he went on. "The wife was a victim of abuse from Flanders all those years. In our experience," Barker puffed himself up a little like a small bird puffing its feathers, "thirteen percent of the time the perpetrator of a murder is a family member."

"Or perhaps the wife's mysterious boyfriend," said the Judge.

"Or the daughter," said Johnny. "Hated her dad. Disassociates from even being related to him by referring to him as 'Tom'. Didn't seem the least upset he was in a coma. Said he deserved to be shot."

"Oh no. I'm sure it wasn't Laura!" said Blaine.

The other men looked at each other, and the Judge rolled his eyes. All of this had the flavor of the older boys laughing behind the younger kid's back, but Johnny couldn't resist saying it out loud, even going so far as to lean closer to the Judge's phone.

"We got to get all the possibilities out on the table," he said. "We can't allow ourselves to be cock-blinded."

"What about the lobbyist, Buck Jennings," said Blaine, redirecting. "It was his money that went down the drain when Flanders double-crossed the Oil and Gas Lobby."

"Or the new lady vying for appointment to Undersecretary for Atomic Energy, Dr. Emma Broadwell," said Danzer. " From what you learned, Blaine, she and Flanders were bitter rivals for years. She schemed to become Atomic Energy Undersecretary, then Flanders outmaneuvered her and got the appointment. Now he's dead and she's got a free path forward to the job she wanted."

"What about Flanders' mistress, Iris McGinnes, or her surf-boy lover?" asked Barker. "McGinnes was abused, just like all the other women in Flanders' life. And Flanders found out about the boyfriend and threatened him. Told the boyfriend to stay away from Iris McGinnes or Flanders would ruin his life."

The Judge thought about Alan Danzer's ex-wife, and the snapshots of her that Flanders kept in his filing cabinet, but he decided it would be impolitic to add one of the members of their informal committee to the suspect list while he was in the room. "Let's face it gentlemen," he said. "We've got lots of motive, lots of people who hated my old college chum, but we've got no evidence tying any of them to Ted Olson, the hired assassin.”

The others in the room glumly looked at each other. “He’s right,” said Johnny. “We can speculate all day about motive and who hated Flanders the most, but the fact is that everybody seems to have hated Flanders, and we’ve got no evidence tying anybody to Olson’s contract.”

“Well, that just won’t wash Johnny,” Danzer said. “The town’s in hysteria, the press is all over this, painting an awful picture of Montecito. We’ve got to catch the responsible party and shut this case down before more damage is done to our community. Johnny, you’d better have a suspect arrested within the next forty-eight hours, or the Santa Barbara Sheriff is going to replace you with someone who can. And the same goes for you, Craig, Mr. FBI. Prove up or shut up, or I’ll spend my political capital to get a competent FBI replacement who produces results.”

Danzer pushed his way between bodies and stomped from the room.

CHAPTER 48

Buck got off the airplane and waded his way through the Santa Barbara Terminal, dodging the baggage claim and ending out on the street in the pickup area. He crawled into the waiting car and it sped off, out of the airport, turning north. The driver suggested Starbucks, and pulled off highway 101 almost immediately, leaving the car and returning with two steaming venti lattes and two ham and cheese croissants.

Buck nervously gulped his latte, ignoring that it was too hot, hoping it would wake him up and dissipate some of his anxiety. Then he attacked his croissant, so much better than airplane food. He rocked his head from side to side, trying to get a sudden kink out of his neck, and moved his seat back and down a little, stretching his legs, trying to find some position of comfort. He hated long airplane flights, even sitting in first class.

He focused on the highway, noting the scenery and the signs, then turned to his companion to ask, "Where the hell we going? I thought we were going down to Montecito for dinner."

"Oh yeah Buck. Sorry. I've got a quick stop to make up here, then we'll zip back." His companion glanced at Buck, the hint of a strange look on his face, quickly covered.

"It's been ten minutes. This must be a hell of an errand," said Buck.

"But quite a necessary one, Buck. How long have we known each other? It's been a lot of years."

"Yeah. We go all the way back to the old days in Houston, before it changed and became so snotty. You were my brother's best friend."

"How is Rex doing. I haven't heard from him in years, Buck."

"We lost him. Practically the last casualty in Afghanistan."

"Oh. I didn't know. I'm sorry."

"Yeah, life happens."

"We used to have great times in Houston, Buck. You, Rex and me."

"I remember," said Buck. "We've all had a great ride in life. You ever miss Houston? The humidity, the heat, the excitement of the storms coming in off the gulf, those hot women?"

"No, my friend. I prefer the cool air, the ocean breezes, the quiet, and the hint of eucalyptus in the air that is Montecito. I made a good life here and I enjoy it."

"I can understand that."

"You know Buck, after all the years and all the times, and all the friends who've come and gone and all the experiences and all the women, I guess you're about the oldest friend I've got."

"Thank you for that." Buck flashed his famous smile.

"Yeah, I think there's really nothing that could come between us… well except perhaps only one thing." Buck's partner turned his head to look at Buck as he drove.

"What's that?"

"Self-preservation."

Those two words hung there in the air between them in the small car as though chiseled in ice, bringing the temperature down to 'chill'.

"The trouble with you Buck is that fantastic smile of yours. You've always been able to con people with it, hide behind it, flash it, and swing it around like a matador's cape directing adverse attention elsewhere, away from you. It's been a fantastic gift you've used for real self-benefit, but it's prevented you from ever taking a stand, being strong, or even ruthless when required. Behind your golden smile, you're soft, easily panicked, unreliable."

"What are you talking about?"

"I'm talking about taking this little ride. Not something I'm happy to take. But you brought me into the middle of this mess. In fairness, I agreed because it served both our interests.

But now it's all blown up in our faces. And you're panicking. I can tell. I could hear it in your voice over the phone, smell it on you when you got into the car. You're waffling. Next thing I know you'll be flashing your golden smile and trying to cop a deal. We can't have that."

"What are you saying?"

"I'm talking about the heavy dose of fentanyl I put in your latte. I'm afraid it's bon voyage for you, partner. Perhaps if there's a Hell, we'll meet again there."

Buck opened his mouth to speak but his voice caught in his throat. His body had been growing more and more limp, he had thought from the long airplane ride. But now his breathing was more and more shallow; it felt like he was barely supporting his lungs. He looked at his hands. They were cold, clammy, bluish purple. He couldn't seem to get enough oxygen. He started choking, then it changed to almost gurgling.

"They call that the Fentanyl Death Rattle, Buck. It won't be long now, old friend."

The car interior started to spin around in a circle in front of Buck's eyes, slowly at first, then faster and faster, turning to grey dots, then all grey, then nothing…

CHAPTER 49

The Judge was driving Blaine's Mini. Katy had taken her Tesla off for shopping and then had headed for Summerland and the suite at the hotel. She was no doubt there already, settled into the comfortable bed and asleep.

This had left the Judge with the Mini to drive up to the Santa Barbara Airport to retrieve Blaine. For some reason, the Mini smelled like a Christmas tree lot engaged in a losing battle with a fast-food drive-thru. He so much wanted to hold his nose while he drove, but driving required two hands: the left for the steering wheel and the right alternating between the steering wheel and the stick shift. Surprisingly, the car had been washed recently, and the trash was removed from all the seats, though the ghosts still lingered. Blaine must have been cruising around town with Flanders' daughter. Nothing else but puppy love could account for Blaine attempting to be fastidious about his miniature mobile garbage truck.

Anyway, it was embarrassing to be driving the Mini, all slouched down in the driver's seat so he could see under the top of the windshield. The only saving grace was it was late at night and no one could really see him. Blaine was arriving at midnight on his late flight out of D.C. Blaine could drive his own damn car on the way back, and the Judge need only contend with getting himself in and out of the passenger side.

Only, of course, the Judge was early, and the flight was late. The Judge lingered outside against the arrival hall, pacing up and down, until finally Blaine came out with his rollaboard, spotted the Judge, and waved cheerfully.

"You drive," muttered the Judge, extracting the keys from his pocket with their assemblage of boy scout knife, mini flashlight, medical I.D. tag, and Irish shamrock in a bright green which read, 'Luck to everyone who carries me', and plopping them into Blaine's hand. The Judge proceeded around the car to fold himself into the passenger side like a nervous audience member folding himself into a magician's magic box.

As Blaine drove them out of the airport, the Judge directed Blaine south on Highway 101. "We have a limited budget on this case, Blaine. We have to be frugal. I checked us out of the Ritz-Carlton Bacara, and into an inexpensive motel in Summerland."

"Aw, Judge. I was just getting used to the ambiance of the Bacara."

"I'll bet you were. With no funds in your own pocket to cover the freight. Oh, and Katy's here. She came up this afternoon to see what was going on. Couldn't resist."

"Great. Always good to see my Cous." The Judge knew Blaine had a soft spot in his heart for his cousin.

The Mini sped through the night, one headlight blinking off periodically, demanding attention from Blaine, who ignored it. The other beam was constant, a single beam like a single yellow eye, trying without success to penetrate the fog that had crept over the highway from the sea and now blanketed the land, snuffing out the distance.

At the Judge's direction, Blaine pulled the Mini off the freeway at the Summerland offramp and coasted down the hill and into the motel parking lot. The lot was dark and damp, the tall lot security light having long since turned itself off. The Judge directed Blaine to their assigned space. Blaine pulled in, turned off the engine, and started to open his door, automatically lighting up the compartment. The Judge began to untangle himself from his seatbelt before squeezing out the passenger door of the Mini. The Judge was thinking about the king-size bed with the fresh sheets and Katy's warm body to cuddle against.

There was a sudden flash through the mist, lower and brighter than the occasional flicker of lightning overhead that worked its way through the fog. There was a metallic bark, like a rifle, and a concurrent crash as Blaine's entire driver's side window exploded into a spider web of glass, tumbling down into his lap and over his knees as a second slug slid past Blaine's forehead and smashed a hole into the Mini's dash.

"Christ…duck!" screamed the Judge, trying to squeeze his bulk pretzel-like below the windows and into the foot well of the Mini.

A second rifle report heralded another slug streaming an inch above the Judge's spine as he tried to hump himself mostly below the Mini's windows.

"Christ, Blaine…get out of the car. We're sitting ducks here."

The Judge managed to find the door handle, opened his door, and plunged his rolled body out of the car and onto the asphalt like a roly-poly bug dumped from a jar.

Blaine got out of his side of the car onto his hands and knees as a third slug buried itself into the inside panel of his open door, causing Blaine to yelp with fear. Blaine scooted crab-like on all fours around the car to the Judge's side and the two hunkered down for a moment as another shot streamed in just barely above their heads.

"We've got to move, Blaine. Let's make for the front door of the motel. On the count of three….one…two…three."

They bolted together across the three car spaces and ran through the reception office's glass door, which shattered behind them as another slug punctuated their retreat.

The Judge screamed to Blaine to kill the lights, as another bullet sailed close to the Judge's head, leaving pain, like a bee sting.

Blaine dived over the reception counter and killed the lights to the lobby and reception, putting them in pitch black, no longer lighted silhouettes. It went quiet for thirty seconds.

Then the motel manager, an elderly rotund Hispanic lady, came padding into the reception area in her pajamas and flicked the light back on, muttering in Spanish something that sounded a lot like "What the fuck?"

Another bullet whizzed through the glassless front door and drilled itself into the night manager's flank, exiting her expansive posterior and continuing its forward motion, missing Blaine's head by barely an inch. She let go a blood-curdling scream and fell to the floor, flopping around like an injured duck

Blaine rose up above the bar again and dived for the wall switch ramming his head into the wall this time, but managing to turn the light off once more.

"Call nine-one-one, Blaine," yelled the Judge. "I'll try to reach Johnny."

Blaine produced his cell from his pocket and dialed 9-1-1. The Judge dialed Johnny, who picked up immediately.

"What's up?"

"We're under attack, Johnny. Taking fire."

"Where are you?"

"At our motel in Summerland."

"Did you call nine-one-one?"

"Yes."

"How soon did they say they'd be there?"

"Twelve minutes," Blaine screeched over to the Judge.

"Okay, I'm just coming to the roundabout in Montecito; I'll be there in fifteen. Hang tight."

The Judge felt something trickling down his cheek and put his hand there. His cheek was warm, wet and sticky, and so was his hair. He pulled his hand away but couldn't see what it was.

The firing had stopped. There were no visible targets, and the Judge hoped to keep it that way. Three minutes later there was the sound of a vehicle careening down the backside of the nearby hill, its lights out, not visible in the fog.

Then it got eerily quiet.

The spell was broken as three cop cars came screaming into the parking lot, lights going and sirens blaring. It was the entire Summerland police force. They slid to a stop in front of the front door to the motor motel, three layers deep, their officers in riot gear diving out and behind their cars, rifles in hand.

Someone flipped the light on again and the Judge twisted to snarl at the night manager, but it wasn't the manager. It was Katy, beautiful Katy in her yellow silk pajamas and yellow silk robe, looking for the Judge, worried.

She took one look at him and screeched, "Oh my God", then clamped her jaw shut, her face changing into that taut 'control all emotion' look he knew so well. The look made to handle any emergency. She marched over, plucked him up off the floor and bullied him down the hall toward their suite where she had her luggage and first aid kit, determined to examine the source of all the blood dripping down his cheek. Ten minutes later he reappeared to answer questions from the police, a huge bandage, partly white, partly spotted dark red, pasted precariously over his left ear, and, of course, Katy in tow.

He was immediately sent out toward two ambulances, one being loaded with a stretcher that held the motel manager, her face twisted in pain, her eyes in shock. The other ambulance team replaced his bandage with a more substantial one taped down to his hair. He knew it would hurt when he had to take the bandage off; likely leaving a wide swath of bald where hair was growing right now.

Johnny was there, directing a forensics team scouring the hillside above the motel in the pouring rain. Johnny waved, then turned back to his work, looking relieved that the Judge was okay.

Blaine came tearing up as the Judge sat on the tailgate of the ambulance, the mandatory blanket thrown over his shoulder, Katy standing over him, fussing.

"Gosh Judge," said Blaine, "I hear you've grown a cauliflower ear!"

The Judge just glared at him, willing Blaine to shut up and go away, which he did.

The Judge spent the next two hours inside the motel's conference room with Johnny and two detectives, answering questions and describing what happened in triplicate. One detective opined that the shooter had laid in wait for them in brush about 500 yards up the bank from the parking lot, and based on the slugs recovered, had used an M4 carbine, the rifle preferred by FBI SWAT teams around the country.

The Mini was towed away as evidence, to the Judge's secret satisfaction, and a driver showed up to drop a new 2025 Cadillac CT4 for their use, rented by Katy from the local car rental joint. She wasn't about to share her Tesla. The Judge announced he'd be driving the rental car.

They were finally allowed to crash into bed in their adjoining bedrooms, Blaine still shaking a bit from their near miss and grieving over the damage to his car, the Judge putting up with Katy's fussing and attention before sliding off into exhausted sleep.

CHAPTER 50

The next evening, Laura and Blaine huddled over a patio table in a quiet corner of the veranda at the Boathouse at Hendry's Beach. They drank glasses of Sauvignon Blanc accompanied by a cheese board. The soft white surf of the blue Pacific lapped just outside the veranda, sluicing up the beach from small waves as the sun started its sink into the sea.

They'd started sharing bits and pieces of their life stories, prompted here and there by pointed questions from the other. But Blaine could see there was something on Laura's mind.

"Did you ever do drugs, Blaine?" asked Laura.

"No. Never did. I never smoked cigarettes, so I didn't know how to inhale to smoke marijuana. One time in college I inserted myself in a small ring of people passing around a joint and pretended to puff on it. The second time the joint came around and I puffed, the girl next to me snarled, 'Get this asshole out of here. He doesn't know how to inhale. He's wasting the joint!' What could I say? She was right. I slunk away in embarrassment."

Laura giggled, her eyes filled with amusement.

"So, what was your first sexual experience like, Laura?"

"It was traditional, in the back seat of my first boyfriend's car. I was sixteen. I was curious and wanted to see what it was all about. And then…and then…the next time, my boyfriend parked his car on our driveway, in front of the front porch. It was late; we figured it was safe. I was trying to give my boyfriend his…and my, first head. And damn if Tom didn't wander out onto our driveway and then casually peek in our car window."

"What did your Dad do?"

"Hah! He spun on his heel and went right back inside the house. Didn't say a thing. Never brought it up. But I was so embarrassed. My face was so red it probably lit up the whole damn neighborhood. And, of course, my boyfriend was shit-faced scared. He zipped himself up so fast…like a scalded cat. He was lucky he didn't snag his plumbing."

Blaine chuckled.

"I had Kenny, that's my first boyfriend, through the rest of high school and my first year of college. He was a nice guy, but not quick, not smart. I got tired of him and broke it off after my freshman year."

"Who was the next boyfriend?"

"There really hasn't been one. I've dated around. You know, the way we modern women do, sexually liberated, intent on experiencing their sexuality, and so on. Met some nice guys, but nobody ever stuck for long. How about you, Blaine? What was your first sexual experience like?'

"I was a slow starter. Finally got a girlfriend in my sophomore year in college, and we stayed together through the next three years. Then, shortly before graduation, we just sort of drifted apart; there wasn't really anything holding us together. I guess it was sex by convenience."

"And since?"

"Occasional affairs here and there. And then there was Kara."

"Your girlfriend that died?"

"Yes."

"I'm so sorry about that."

"It was very hard, Laura. A virus got her; there was nothing I could do."

Laura nodded her head in understanding.

"But," Blaine said, shaking off old memories, "that's the past. You're the present, and the future."

Laura produced a sad smile. "You need to understand, Blaine…I watched all the physical and emotional abuse my mother took. I was the audience for my dad's brutality. He wanted me to watch, and teach me what masculine domination and abuse were all about. As a result, I guess I prefer shorter-term relationships, now. Kenny was the only long-term relationship I've had, and in the end, it was just so dull."

"We wouldn't ever be dull together, Laura. I think we could have a magic relationship that lasted forever. I love you, Laura."

"I…I…I can't love you, Blaine, at least not like that. I'm not ready to love anybody like that. There's no trust left in me. I don't want to get too close to anyone, can't trust anyone, at least not for the long term. The abuse was so awful…and I'm so paranoid about it. It colors my whole life. I'm sorry."

"But we can fix that. We can get you help. Get you over it."

Her chin came up, she reached across the table to take Blaine's hand, their eyes locked.

"There's more to it than just that, Blaine. I need to explain, you need to understand. It's better we don't get any closer. It's perhaps time for me to go."

"What? What do you mean?"

"Listen, Blaine. I'm only twenty-four. Women of my generation have entirely new opportunities in life.

First, we have easy birth control, we can experiment, have fun, and be as randy as you males. We don't have to get caught in the baby trap like my mom did.

Then we have economic freedom. We can hold any job you can hold, and compete with you for any job on equal terms. We can choose any career we want, make our own way, and make our own fortunes. We don't need a man to support us, stick us in some dinky Burb house like a caged canary so we can do the housework and clean his clothes…and put up with his tyrannies, great or petty, trapped by our social and familial ties, and haunted by the opportunities to be fully ourselves, opportunities we let slip by, or decided to sacrifice because we made the mistake of having a child with a man-boy bully"

"We wouldn't be like that, Laura. I wouldn't be like that."

"Blaine, if I decide to have a kid, I don't need a man to make that happen. I can freeze my eggs, choose if and when I want to have a kid or take a lover just for the purpose of getting knocked up. Or I can invest in sperm over the counter and hire someone to watch the kid and part-time raise it while I keep on with my career. I could even hire a surrogate mother to carry it and give it birth.

I need the freedom to work, the freedom to live alone, the freedom to make my own decisions, the freedom not to be tethered to a male lord and master."

"That sounds lonely."

"It's like this, Blaine. I'm focused now on becoming a vet. I like animals. If I want a loyal companion, I'll get a pet. There's no room in my plans for a steady boyfriend right now. I want to travel the world, learn new things, have adventures, dance with every boy at the dance, and leave before I'm once again disappointed by the male of the species. Be thrilled, be wowed, experiment with all sorts of men of every make and color, have fun, experience everything, explore my sexuality, be pursued by lots of potential lovers, and always have the flexibility to walk away. I want everything, Blaine…I guess everything except your vision of our future together. I'm sorry. I let myself get caught up in your excitement, in seeing myself through your eyes, and in your naïve belief in love even though you don't know me at all. Maybe that was part of the appeal, even, your simplified boyish romantic interpretation of how this could go. You're sweet. And this felt good. But all bad relationships start out feeling good."

Laura got up from the table a little unsteadily, her cheeks flushed, leaned over to kiss Blaine on the top of his head, and then walked away.

Out of the restaurant…

Out of Blaine's life!

CHAPTER 51

The Judge and Blaine met early the next morning and walked from the suite motel toward the local Starbucks. The sun was shining, the temperature was moderate, the sky was that vivid blue the way it can get in Santa Barbara some days, and butterflies were floating through the trees. They settled on the sunny Starbucks patio with lattes. The Judge had a large bandage on his ear, covering a chunk taken out by the bullet two nights before, drawing looks from other patrons as he walked in.

"It's over Judge," sighed Blaine.

"Over?"

"Me and Laura."

"Oh. I'm sorry to hear that, Blaine. I know you really liked her."

"I loved her, Judge. I'm really sad right now…and lonely."

"It happened awfully fast, Blaine."

"Sometimes it happens like that, Judge. Can you remember when you first met Katy?"

"Yes. It was magic. I was walking on air. But Laura is very young. She's what? Twenty-four, and you're twenty-eight."

"You're twenty years older than Katy."

"Yes. But it's not just about the number of years, but the time on the planet. Twenty-four is much younger than twenty-eight. Katy was ready to commit, to settle down and declare she'd be my wife forever. At twenty-four a young woman is still mostly a child."

"I suppose that is so," said Blaine. "And Laura was emotionally abused growing up. She's going to need therapy to help her level things out."

"There you go, Blaine. It's probably for the best she let you go. She needs time to get on with working out her issues. Maybe someday when she's older she'll search you out again."

"But why does it hurt so much, Judge? What is love? What does it all mean?"

"That's a question for the ages, Blaine. Far, far wiser men than I have considered it without reaching an answer. Romantic love has been described as a sense of attachment and bonding combined with an idealization of another person. Feeling a deep connection with them and emotional intimacy around them.

But romantic love doesn't last long even when a couple continues their relationship. It moves to a more mature, satisfying sort of loving relationship. Movies try to convince us we'll feel romantic love forever, but I think intense romantic love has an expiration date for everyone. Shrinks say it's the shortest stage in a long-term relationship; that such passion can last two to three years at most, but that most relationships transition into something else much sooner."

"Intellectualizing it like that doesn't help much, Judge."

"No. I guess not. Here's another thought. For me, I prefer to look at my past loves differently."

"How?"

"I believe we never truly get over someone we've loved, Blaine. That there's a part of us that holds on to that person forever. We hold on to the good times, the joyful times, the worst times…that we once shared.

Maybe we're reflecting back over our years, or maybe a memory is triggered by a song, a place, a scent, or a taste, and suddenly we're reminiscing. We consider what we learned, what we took, what we gave, what we shared. We feel the emotions again, being caught up in love, the dizzy heights, the depths of despair, and all the in-betweens, but there's no pain. Our memories of past lovers are now like old, fine wine; bottled memories to be brought out and sampled from time to time.

I believe that once a lover is a part of your life, they're always a part of your life."

Blaine sighed. "Thank you for that, Judge. As I step back now, I see much of what I thought about Laura was only a fantasy…only a dream."

CHAPTER 52

As Blaine and the Judge walked back to the suite motel, the Judge's cell woke up, streaming out the first stanza of Danny Boy, his designated cell phone ring. It reminded the Judge of the Irish part of his heritage, his Irish Catholic grandmother, and the time so long ago now when he was a very young lawyer and had mounted a campaign in a run for congress. Everyone had to have a song to be played when they marched up on the stage to speak at the round robin of debates before various civic and political organizations. The Judge had lost that race. The only thing he'd gotten out of it was a little exposure for his newly budding law practice and his song. The song he'd chosen way back then and had kept.

It was Johnny on the phone, Montecito's finest, and he was so excited he was stumbling over his words. "Barker's guys broke the code on the SD cards, Judge. There are details on nearly fifty murders for hire, spanning approximately five years. Everything: pictures, details of the murders, how it was planned and accomplished, how much the contract paid, and most importantly who hired Olson to make the hit and why. This is sensational. Since the FBI didn't obtain the info on its lonesome, Montecito is getting a piece of the action. This is going to put our department on the map. We're in the process of contacting police departments all over the country, and offshore too."

"What about the Flanders murder, Johnny? Was there anything about Tom Flanders' murder?"

"Afraid not, Judge. No help there I'm afraid. The discs only covered through last Spring. But this is an amazing haul just the same. We're all going to be famous throughout the enforcement community." Johnny sounded like he was ready to dance.

"Congratulations on your haul, Johnny. Blaine and I were glad to help." The Judge signed off, frowning at Blaine across their little table.

"No help on Tom Flanders' murder, Judge?"

"No. I'm afraid not. We're going to have to do some more spadework, Blaine. There are still some things we don't understand." The Judge smiled that inscrutable Charlie Chan smile he liked.

CHAPTER 53

The Judge insisted on having another talk with Iris McGinnes, Flanders' mistress. They knocked on Iris's door twice and then the window in the door opened and there were her eyes, red-rimmed now, peeking up at them. She slowly opened the door and waved them in toward the tired sofa.

"I'm not serving tea today, guys. I'm totally broke."

"We don't need tea. We'll just be a minute, Iris."

"Tom's dead now, you know."

"Yes, it took a while, but he finally succumbed to his injury."

"Injury, shit. My friend's a night nurse. She was on duty. It's a big cover-up. Somebody turned off his alarm and disconnected him from life support!"

"We've heard nothing about that," said Blaine.

"And you probably won't. The hospital, the doctors, the idiot staff, they're all afraid of liability. But I'm telling you. That's the way it happened."

"Do the police know?"

"I don't know. Last I heard the police were treating it as a death from being shot, like you said. But Montecito is a small town. Truth has a way of getting around."

"But the assassin is dead," said Blaine. "He died before Flanders did."

"He did." The Judge looked grim.

"You think that if a person killed Flanders in his hospital room it would have been the one who hired Olson?"

"I do."

"So, the person who hired the assassin must have wanted Flanders dead really badly."

"Yes, and quickly. He was willing to chance getting caught at the hospital, even though Flanders could have very easily never come out of his coma."

"Wow. Together with Mr. Lo and Olson, that's three murders."

"And someone tried to kill us. Seems the person who hired the assassin is getting very nervous."

"And, like you said, impatient. Things weren't looking so good for Flanders as it was."

"It don't mean nothing to me," said Iris. "Dead either way, same difference, no money, and I'm stranded, broke, alone." Iris cast her eyes down to the floor; a single tear rolled down her cheek and splashed on her sweater, leaving a small dark stain.

"You really loved him, didn't you?" Blaine asked softly.

Iris nodded silently, then reached out to grip Blaine's hand.

"Yes. I really did. When he was in a good mood he was wonderful. I miss him so." She pulled a Kleenex out of her sweater sleeve and sniffled into it.

"We're still working to catch the person responsible for setting Tom up to be shot, Iris," said the Judge. "Can you help us just a little bit more with information?"

Iris nodded. Pulling herself together, her chin coming up, sitting straighter in her chair, setting aside her Kleenex, giving the Judge full attention.

"You told us before that Bitsy now has a lover."

"Yes. She does."

"Do you know who it is?"

"No. I only know cause Jerry saw Bitsy and the man making out on Venice Beach."

"Jerry's your former boyfriend, the one Tom scared away?"

"Yes."

"Did Jerry tell you who it was?"

"He seemed scared to talk about it. And anyway, I didn't give a damn what the Ding Bat was doing."

"Could you give us Jerry's contact information? What he saw may provide some answers to why this happened to Tom."

"Jerry didn't want me to tell anyone else where he went when he left Montecito. He was very scared of Tom and what Tom might do. But then Tom can't do anything to anyone now, can he?"

She got up and walked listlessly into her kitchen, a drawer rattled, and then she returned with a small snip of paper which she handed to the Judge.

"That's where Jerry was working. Last time I spoke to him he'd changed jobs, but I don't know what he's doing now."

The Judge took a picture of the number on the paper, thanked her, and handed it back.

She nodded, muttered "I need to be alone now," rose, and showed them to the door.

CHAPTER 54

The Judge stood on the boardwalk and looked out over its low wall to Venice Beach's collection of semi-naked bodies lying under umbrellas or out in the sun. It looked like a rookery of chubby seals. He wondered how much sun damage was being accumulated there; felt sorry for the young people playing in the sand and along the surf line, some with once-white skin now bright pink.

He waited patiently near the surf shop with its closed door and small sign that read '*back in five*'. He'd called the number Iris had supplied, and this surf shop had answered. The kid he spoke to was evasive, but finally let out that Jerry Martel worked there occasionally. Claimed he had no idea how to reach Jerry or what his address was.

Fifteen minutes later, a young kid, perhaps all of eighteen, showed up with a key to open the surf shop door and folded in the four folding doors along the front, opening the entire frontage of the surf shop to access. He had long bleached hair, stringy as though he'd just got out of the shower. He wore beat-up sandals, and faded swim trunks on the hips of a skinny body tanned dark brown.

"Hi there, Bud," said the Judge cheerfully. How's the set?" Exhausting the Judge's entire vocabulary about surfing.

"Small today, man. Not worth dragging your ass out there. But I can rent you a surfboard if you want to try and sell you some trunks to replace those oldie slacks you got on." The young man looked hopeful.

"I was hoping to meet up with Jerry Martel. I understand he works here sometimes."

The young man's face changed immediately from open and friendly to cold and suspicious. "You a cop?"

"No, no, nothing like that. My friend was really close to Jerry up in Montecito, and she gave me this number and asked me to look him up when I came down. She needs a little help."

"If she's really a friend, dude, I'd think she'd ask him herself."

"It's got nothing to do with any trouble or anything serious. I just need to meet up with Jerry and ask him one question."

The Judge reached into his pocket and brought out a crisp twenty-dollar bill he'd put there. The young man's eyes immediately went down to the bill.

"Perhaps I could pay you for the information," suggested the Judge.

The young man wet his lips. He wanted the twenty. Then he looked at the Judge again. "A twenty ain't worth shit these days, man. Don't you understand inflation?"

"Perhaps it could be two nice crisp twenties?"

The young man rubbed one set of fingers against his other palm, looked undecided, then carefully looked around. No one was on the boardwalk outside the shop.

"Kay. Give me the two bills first."

The Judge brought out the second twenty and snapped the bills together, smoothing out their wrinkles.

The young man's hand reached over and plucked the two bills out of the Judge's hand. "Try lifeguard station four out there on the beach. To the left."

The young man turned, lifted a used surfboard out of a stack in the back, and walked to the front of the shop, stepping out onto the boardwalk to lean the board against the corner of the shop, ignoring the Judge as though he wasn't there.

The Judge walked outside, stepped over the low wall separating the boardwalk from the sand, and padded his way out to the edge of the tide sliding up the beach. He turned left and walked along the beach past two lifeguard stations. The third one was marked with a '4' on its flank.

He crossed up the beach and over to it, smiling at the young man sitting on its little platform, legs resting up on a side guard rail.

"Hi," said the Judge.

"Howdy, sir. Need something?"

"Iris McGinnes says hello."

The young man's feet came down off the rail like a shot and he leaped up, a look of fight or flight in his eyes.

The Judge said, "Whoa, I'm a friend of Iris and she just needs a little help. Just one question answered. Just take a second and I'm out of here."

The young man sunk back in his chair, suspicion written across his face. "What's the question?"

"I understand you saw Bitsy Flanders and her new boyfriend down here on the beach. My question is, 'Who's her new boyfriend?'"

"I didn't see nothing, man."

"That's not what you told Iris."

"I told Iris lots of stuff. Doesn't mean it was always true."

"Look, there's a murderer running around Montecito. He's already killed twice. He'll kill again. I need to stop him. I need your help."

"Yeah, I heard about Flanders, couldn't happen to a nicer guy. Shot in the chest, huh?"

"Yes. He's since died. He was in a coma, on life support; looks like someone came into his hospital room and disconnected him."

"Wow. Someone really needed him out of the way."

"Yes. And we don't know who might be next…maybe Iris."

"No. Not Iris. She's the finest girl around. No one would want to hurt her. That couldn't happen."

"This murderer is cleaning up loose ends. If he suspects Flanders told Iris something about him, she could be next."

"Jesus…I'd like to tell you. But I just can't get involved. I had a run-in with the guy once. He and Flanders were the same type, respectable, but vindictive if you got on the wrong side of them. And if a respectable type wants to put the screws to a surf bum, no one's gonna give two craps about it. Why don't you ask Bitsy?"

"I did. She won't talk."

"Ah man, you're putting me in a tough position. I don't want Iris hurt."

"You recognized the man?"

"Sure. He and Bitsy were out on the sand. It was just after sundown. Guess they figured no one could see them in the afterlight. Nobody around, 'cept me, locking up my station. Probably staying in one of the Venice hotels for the weekend."

"And they were close?"

"More than close, man. He was touching her all over, through her bikini.

They were kissing and petting and couldn't keep their hands off each other. I thought they were going to do it right there."

"Did they see you?"

"No. 'Least I don't think so."

"Why don't you just write her guy's name down? Here, on my pad. Don't tell me anything else right now. You're really not telling me anything. Just writing a name."

"Ah man…you really think Iris might be in danger?"

The Judge nodded.

"Okay, here." Jerry took the little notebook from the Judge, scribbled a name on the open page, and handed it back.

"Thanks, Jerry. I know that took guts. But you won't regret it. We're going to catch the killer, and I suspect it will be partly because of what you saw."

CHAPTER 55

The Judge and Blaine were nursing their coffee in the morning sun on the Starbuck's patio. It was a sparkling early morning in Summerland and the Judge was happy, having removed the bandage from his ear over strenuous objections from Katy, "to air" as he'd said, then bolted out the door of the suite motel to meet Blaine before there could be further discussion.

The Judge's cell phone began singing Danny Boy a cappella. The Judge answered, then stood up and wandered across the patio as he talked, nodding his head vigorously at points in the conversation. Finishing the call, he returned to the table and sank into his chair, a relaxed look spreading across his face. "Who was that?" asked Blaine.

"That was a techie friend of mine in Washington who works for the FBI. I'm not keen on the FBI guy we have out here working the case, so I asked my friend for a favor."

"Barker is something of a short and irritating little prick," said Blaine.

"Yes, he is. I sent our copy of Olson's five SD cards we found at the laundry to my FBI friend for a separate look at unscrambling the data. He just reported back and briefly summarized a part of their contents. He'll be sending an email with a complete draft of what he found later today so we can take a look."

"Great. Well, shall get moving?"

"Yes. Let's. After the all-hands meeting, I think we'll come back, pick up Katy, and check out."

"Oh…we're done then?"

"Yes, Blaine. I think we're done."

CHAPTER 56

The mayor and Barker trooped into Johnny's office a little past nine, dragging small metal chairs from the bullpen this time so they'd all have a place to sit.

"Where's the Judge and Blaine?" asked Danzer. "Aren't they coming?"

"I just got a call they're on the way," said Johnny. "May be just a tad late."

"Debutante investigators, they show up whenever they feel like it," complained Craig Barker. "We don't need them. It's already too crowded in here and they never have much to contribute."

"We need all the help we can get, Barker," Danzer replied. "I need this case disposed of *now.*"

"Well," Johnny said, "last time we identified several suspects who had motive. But there was no evidence tying any of them to Flanders or Ted Olson. Do we have any new information that ties anyone to anyone in this case, or are we still at a dead end?" He looked at each person individually. They each shook their head 'no', avoiding his eyes.

"Shit, Danzer," said Johnny, "I don't know what you expect us to do. We can't manufacture evidence out of thin air."

The door opened and the Judge and Blaine squeezed in. Johnny looked at them, sighed, and said, "Gentlemen, we're no closer to determining who put the contract out on Flanders, and killed Olson and Lo, than we were before. Mayor, I'm afraid I'm calling this meeting closed. It's been a waste of time."

The Judge smiled, then said. "I think you're wrong, Johnny. I had a pretty good idea who the murderer was at our last meeting. I just didn't have a motive."

All heads turned, riveted on the Judge.

"And now you do?" asked Johnny.

"Now I do."

Barker smirked, indicating he didn't believe the Judge. "Okay, Judge," he said, "Who does our volunteer Sherlock Holmes and his sidekick, Toto, think the murderer is?"

"Yes," said Danzer. "Explain."

"I met yesterday with Jerry Martel, Iris McGinnes's lover."

"It was him? By God, Judge. I'll get a warrant issued immediately," said Johnny.

"No. It wasn't Jerry Martel. But I had to go down to Venice Beach in L.A. to catch up with him. Martel had the last piece of the puzzle that supplied a motive. He works as a lifeguard down there now. He saw Bitsy and a man lounging together by the ocean. Jerry indicated that it got pretty hot and heavy. As Jerry put it, 'they couldn't keep their hands off each other.'"

"That doesn't prove anything, Judge," said Johnny. "So what if Bitsy has a lover?"

"Bitsy had been abused by Flanders all their married life. Now Flanders was about to cut Bitsy out of his separate property, about ten million dollars worth, the only significant money included in their combined assets. Under our California Estate Law, the ten million was Flanders' separate property, not co-mingled, and Bitsy had no claim to it. Flanders's will left all of his estate to Bitsy, including his separate property. But Flanders had made an appointment to change his will; send the ten million off to a charity in the event of his death. The new will was all drafted but never got signed because Flanders was shot the afternoon before he was to meet his attorney and execute it."

"How do you know that?" asked Barker.

"Because I talked to Flanders' estate planning attorney."

"Huh," said Barker.

"So, there's your motive. The murderer did it in part for Bitsy. For retribution for all of Flanders' abuse, and to assure Bitsy could have a grand lifestyle. Hopefully, a lifestyle she would share with her lover in the future."

"This still sounds all very hypothetical," said Johnny.

"But here's the thing," said the Judge. "Blaine found Olson's secret files hidden in his coat at the laundry, files that contained evidence of the identity of each person over the last five years who contracted with Olson to kill someone."

"Yes, and I gave those to Barker," said Johnny. "He had the FBI decode them, and you got a copy of everything we got, Judge. It was all very incriminating for many people around the country, and even internationally. But there were no documents about a contract to kill Tom Flanders."

"No, there wasn't on what we got back. But, you see, Blaine gave you five SD cards, and we got back an uncoded narrative for only four of them."

"I gave everything Blaine gave me to Barker. Barker, how many cards did you get?"

"I don't remember. Let me look." Barker tore into the box of files on the floor he'd brought. "Four."

"Then Blaine only gave us four. There were only four cards to be decoded," said Johnny.

"It's not worth arguing over. You see, I had Blaine make a copy of those cards while we waited in the laundry for your police team to show up. I forwarded Blaine's copies of the files separately to my specialist friend at the FBI for decoding."

"You did what?" snarled Barker. "You went around me to my agency! You dumb fuck son of a bitch."

"I did. You were just a little too hostile to work with, Barker. And who knew? Maybe the person who took the contract out on Flanders was you. Anyway, I just got the report this morning for all the cards fully decoded." The Judge pulled out a shaft of papers folded lengthwise from his inside pocket. We were late because I wanted to print them out."

"And what does it show, Judge?" asked the mayor. "Does it show who hired Olson to kill Flanders?"

"It does. It was all done over the Dark Web. There's a copy of the murder-for-hire contract, the emails back and forth setting up its terms, a link for the I.P. address of the person who made the contract with Olson, a report from the trojan horse Dark Web Crawler Olson used to backtrack the identity of the person contracting him to have someone killed, an address and telephone number for that person, copies of instructions transferring offshore money into Olson's account, the identity of the owner of that offshore account, and other documentation. It's all there."

"So, who is it?" asked the mayor. "Who contracted to kill Flanders, Judge?"

The Judge looked around the room at all the tense faces, then he swung around to Johnny.

"Do you want to tell them, Johnny, or shall I?"

Johnny suddenly stood, jumped to the top of his desk, and made a leap over the short mayor, aiming for the door. The mayor dived flat on the floor like a marine so as not to be hit. Johnny almost landed on his feet. But his foot caught on the top of the mayor's chair and went sprawling onto the floor, face first.

"I'll be damned," muttered Barker as he jumped over the mayor and straddled Johnny's strewn body, relieving him of his gun. "Guess you amateur private dick fuckers are occasionally useful after all."

CHAPTER 57

They met in the lobby of one of the most expensive law firms in D.C. It was a big lobby, with walls of soft tan wood imported from South America, and a matching floor of light tan, almost white. There were four separate groupings of tan leather sofas and overstuffed chairs, laid out so each grouping had privacy from the receptionist and other groupings. Copies of today's Wall Street Journal and Washington Post adorned antique coffee tables, along with large bouquets of fresh-cut flowers in glass vases. The chubby receptionist in a gray tweed suit, sensing their need for discretion and privacy, showed them over to a grouping in a far corner of the lobby, dark and quiet. The place smelled of money, power, and privilege.

There were three of them. The nervous Junior Senator from Missouri, Franklin Ross, looked like he wished he was somewhere else. Lance Kelly looked like a guy walking on eggshells, as though hoping for something big to happen but worried he might screw it up somehow. The third man was tall, mid-forties, with sharp brown eyes peering out from under a boyish mop of brown hair, looking a bit like an aging surfer who'd finally graduated to tailored suits.

The 'suit' stuck out his hand to the Senator, saying, "Clayton Smith" in a mild Texas accent. "I've replaced Buck Jennings in this matter."

"I didn't think Buck Jennings was replaceable," said Ross.

Clayton Smith smiled. "When you're dealing with oil and gas, we're all replaceable, Senator Ross."

"I'm here to close this deal," said Kelly. "I've got the Complex Atomic Solutions' votes, busted my balls to get them. Seventy-five percent of the outstanding shares have voted to accept the tender offer, as has the Board of Directors. I've got the executed documents from the company's side. And I've got executed share certificates to turn over to the Standard Company. They're all excited to see this deal done back in Virginia, poor bastards."

"I have certain codes for offshore bank accounts," said Smith, "and authority to wire twenty million to each of you once we're done here this morning and the deal is closed."

Ross smiled and nodded, unconsciously rubbing his hands together. Kelly nervously rubbed his hands together, hopeful but cautious.

Just then a portly man stepped out into the lobby, wearing an expensive tailored suit, starched white shirt, and red bow tie. "Mr. Kelly we're ready for you. Would you please follow me to our conference room?"

Kelly jumped up from the sofa and quickly slid across the lobby, a grand smile on his face. His two compadres nodded to one another, then settled back into the luxurious sofa, Smith collecting a Wall Street Journal to read and Ross studying his cell, trying to look invisible.

The private conference room was in the back corner of the floor, two walls of glass providing a panoramic view of Washington D.C., the other two walls with mirrors reflecting the view. Kelly was a little disoriented as he was shown in, too much light and too many angles to digest all at once.

Three lawyers and two executives sat on one side of a long table with a stack of documents in front of them. The bow-tied lawyer showed Kelly toward a seat on the opposite side and pulled a chair out to sit next to him. The lawyers and executives each rose from their seats a little to reach across the table and shake Kelly's hand. Kelly had the feeling he'd just waded into a pool of sharks.

The lead lawyer across the table asked if Kelly had any questions. He didn't. The lawyer asked to see Kelly's documents. Bow Tie slid the documents across the table to him. The lead lawyer paged through Kelly's documents, skimming each page, nodding his head as he went. Then he slid his stack of documents over to Bow Tie, who did the same.

After twenty minutes, the two lawyers nodded their heads together in agreement, Bow Tie produced a pen and started directing Kelly where to sign and five minutes later they were done. The group stood, shook hands formally, then the Standard executives and their lawyers bolted for the door, having other places to be. Bow Tie said Kelly had done good and then dashed after them, leaving Kelly sitting by himself, dazed, unsure of what he'd just done.

Kelly fumbled his way out of the conference room and meandered around corridors, finally finding the lobby, entering it with a smile on his face, displaying a thumbs up to Ross and Smith. Ross fell back deep into the sofa, the tension leaving his body.

"It's closed," said Kelly. "Standard now owns one hundred percent of Complex Atomic Solutions, Inc., lock, stock, and barrel. The stock for the stock tender offer has been consummated. Standard can now do whatever it wants with Complex, and no one can stop it.

Standard can decide to have Complex cease production of small atomic plants, have a fire sale, lock up patents, sell its plant and equipment, close its doors."

"Well done, Kelly," said Smith. "I suspect Complex will no longer be building anything atomic, probably will renege on its army contract for small-size reactors, and simply disappear into the sunset. You and the senator have certainly earned your bonuses." Smith took out and opened his laptop, preparing to transfer funds from offshore funds.

"Gentlemen, sorry I can't celebrate with you," said Kelly, "I'm off to my bank to wire certain funds to Chicago."

It was then the elevator opened in the hallway facing the conference room, and the Judge stepped out, followed by two tall men and a uniformed sheriff. They marched over to the little group in the corner of the lobby.

"Gentlemen," said the Judge, "I'd like to introduce you to J.P. Peters, Esquire, the United States Attorney for the District of Columbia, acting on behalf of the Securities and Exchange Commission, and George Henderson of the I.R.S. I'm afraid you're each under arrest for participating in a criminal conspiracy to commit murder, tax fraud, and a scheme to defraud the shareholders of Complex Atomic Solutions in violation of Federal Securities laws."

EPILOGUE

Blaine, Katy, and the Judge settled at a deck table under a yellow umbrella at Chad's in Santa Barbara for breakfast. It was a sunny morning, the sea clear and blue stretching to the horizon. A lone fishing boat plied its trade out on the ocean and there was a wisp of a breeze off the water that hinted of salt and eucalyptus.

"Okay, Judge, you promised to explain what happened," said Katy. "I'm still a little confused."

"Sure, Katy. It all started with Buck Jennings. For years he's been peddling influence with members of Congress and the Executive Branch. Often in league with oil and gas companies from his home state of Texas and elsewhere."

"Along came Tom Flanders," chimed in Blaine. "A man with a big ego and a taste for money. He'd come to Washington as a young scientist with ideals about promoting the use of atomic energy, but gradually realized the powers that be weren't interested in atomic plants and certainly weren't interested in rocking the boat for the lucrative oil and gas business. He was broke, became jaded, and cynical, and decided if he couldn't beat them, he'd join them. Tom made a career on the speaking circuit down-talking atomic power and getting paid well to do so. But it wasn't satisfying. Tom wanted more."

"So, he paid off people to appoint him as Undersecretary for Atomic Energy in the Energy Department?" asked Katy.

"He didn't actually pay anybody," said the Judge, "but he pledged his influence in the D.O.E. as Undersecretary for Atomic Energy, to stop, slow down, and discourage all atomic energy expansion and innovation."

"So, Tom went to Buck?"

"Yes. Buck and Tom ran in the same social and professional circles, both soaking in the largess of Big Oil and Gas. Tom approached Buck, seeking to be appointed Undersecretary. Buck thought about it, and was encouraged by Oil and Gas interests, who offered him a big bonus if he could place an anti-atomic guy as Undersecretary."

"So, Buck went to Senator Ross, the Chairman of the Senate Committee that approved the Undersecretary's appointment?"

"Right," said Blaine. "Ross was already owed a favor over at the White House for helping get out the vote in Missouri, a swing state. Tom, Buck, and Ross cooked up the scheme to have Tom appointed as the Undersecretary for Atomic Energy. After all, the office was open and up for grabs."

"How did it work?"

"Ross got the White House to nominate Tom," said Blaine. "Tom indicated that as Undersecretary he would discourage atomic power development and use; and of course, back whatever else Buck's PAC-money buddies wanted. Senator Ross canvassed the Senate Committee and sniffed out members who were willing to sell their vote and approve Tom as Undersecretary in exchange for lavish PAC expenditures on behalf of their re-election campaigns."

"So, they sold their vote?"

"They did," said the Judge. "But the pay-off wasn't direct. Instead, the PAC committed to spend its money to independently campaign for the election of the cooperating Senators. Buck's part was to sell the idea to his Oil and Gas clients and get them to donate big to the PAC so there was plenty of campaign money to spread around."

"But is that legal, Judge? Buying votes like that?"

"Unfortunately, it's done all the time. Is it legal?" The Judge smiled. "You can get away with it unless someone can prove otherwise. Then it's not. But there's typically no written contract, it's all done on handshakes over a drink at some bar or men's club. Unless somebody caves, it's practically impossible to prove."

"But it doesn't sound right."

"It's not right. But it's the way our American political system works with the advent of PACs. Big money controls a large part of what happens in our government, quietly, behind the scenes. Votes are secretly bought and paid for, no one knows about it, the rich get richer, and the corrupt politicians continue in office indefinitely."

"So, why did Buck and Senator Ross participate in this scheme?" asked Katy. "What was in it for them?"

"Well, Senator Ross got a guarantee of large direct expenditures by the PAC to further his re-election," said Blaine. "And both Ross and Buck were going to get handsome consulting fees for steering an anti-atomic pawn into the Undersecretary's position, removing the threat to Oil and Gas of competition from atomic power for some years to come."

"But something happened, right Judge. It all blew up?"

"It certainly did. It turned out Tom was still a closet fan of atomic energy, harking back to his early beginnings. Not only that, with his business partner, Lance Kelly, Tom was heavily invested in Complex Atomic Solutions, Inc. a designer and manufacturer of small-scale distributive molten salt reactors. Tom believed he'd make millions on his stock play in Complex Atomic Solutions. Once he was Undersecretary, he began a campaign of talking up the advantages of micro-sized nuclear reactors. Worse from an Oil and Gas perspective, he even arranged to have the Army give Complex Atomic a large contract for the development and manufacture of such reactors."

"So, Oil and Gas got mad."

"Everybody got mad, Katy. Oil and Gas was incensed. They'd been doubled crossed. Those PAC contributors told Senator Ross he could forget about any future PAC money to help him and his cooperating Senators get re-elected. Ross had egg all over his face with his fellow senators, who weren't happy. And worst of all, Buck Jennings had spent twenty years building his relationship as a lobbyist with Oil and Gas, only to see it threatened when his chosen man went rogue. Buck's reputation, the way he made his money and supported his lifestyle, was going down the drain."

"Aww, poor guy!" said Katy, a twinkle in her eye.

"Buck had to do something fast. He had to rectify his mistake, move Tom out of being Undersecretary, move someone more malleable in who would be anti-atomic, and thereby reclaim his damaged relationships with Oil and Gas. He approached Dr. Emma Broadwell, a long-time competitor of Tom's and very flexible with her principles as long as there was money involved. She agreed to be the successor candidate for Undersecretary if Tom were removed. Buck then dictated the threatening letter to Tom, hoping to scare him into resigning. But the letter didn't work."

"Did Emma Broadwell know they were planning to kill Tom, Judge?"

"I don't think so, but we'll see. That will be for the Justice Department to determine as part of their ongoing investigation."

"How did Johnny Marks get caught up in this thing? He's not a lobbyist or a player in D.C. politics."

"That's something I couldn't figure out either. But the former employee of the Santa Barbara County Sheriff's Department has been singing like a canary. Turns out he and Buck and Buck's brother Rex were thick as thieves as kids growing up in Houston. Since Johnny was in Montecito where Flanders lived, and had a position of importance with the police, Buck went to Johnny and carefully sounded him out."

"But facilitating an assassination attempt in your own town, just because an old friend asks you to? Who would do that? That's the most surprising thing. Why would he risk it?"

"Greed, love, revenge, frustration, probably all four, Katy. Johnny has been stagnating in the Santa Barbara Sheriff's Department, turned down several times in his effort to move up the ladder and over to Santa Barbara Sheriff's main county office. I think Johnny was frustrated and embarrassed that his longtime friend Buck Jennings had done so well for himself, and Johnny'd done so poorly."

"Okay, frustration. Check."

"But more importantly," Blaine put in, "Johnny was in love with Bitsy, Tom's almost ex-wife. They'd had a hot affair going for a while behind Tom's back. Johnny knew about the physical and emotional abuse Tom had subjected Bitsy to."

"So, revenge."

"Right," said the Judge. "And now there was a divorce pending and a property settlement under discussion that would leave Bitsy with next to nothing."

"Unless Tom died before he could change his will," finished Katy.

"Right. Johnny truly loved Bitsy, he couldn't stand to see her left penniless after all the years and all the abuse."

"So, love, Judge," said Katy, "What about the greed?"

"Bitsy and Johnny were going to run away together and get married as soon as the divorce was final. It's always better to marry a rich wife."

"Hah!"

"Well, except in your case, honey. You're a real princess, money or not."

Katy smiled.

"Anyway," the Judge continued. "Buck knew nothing of the workings of the Dark Web or murder for hire. So, he turned for help to Johnny, his old pal who was on the scene in Montecito, had a good cover as a cop, and knew a lot more about such things. And, Johnny, for his own reasons, plus the promise of a cut of the Oil and Gas cash Buck would continue to get if they were successful, decided to throw the dice. Besides, it seemed easy and safe; all Johnny had to do was make a secret deal on the Dark Web."

"So, it was Johnny who hired Ted Olson?"

"Yes. Olson knew it was Johnny who'd hired him by using his specialized trojan horse Web Crawler. Olson knew nothing about Buck or Ross. When Olson muffed

234

his shot and didn't kill Tom, the PAC got nervous about the whole plan and refused to advance Buck the money so that Johnny could pay Olson the second installment of his fee. That's when things started to go south.

Olson called up Johnny and threatened him with exposure. Johnny was shocked, he thought his anonymity was protected by the Dark Web. He couldn't risk exposure, now or ever. Johnny set up a meeting at Olson's house on the pretext of making the second payment in person. Olson should have been more cautious, but he had a lavish lifestyle and a habit of spending money before it had been banked."

"I feel almost as bad for him as I do for Buck."

"Olson was probably unconscious when he died. Johnny wanted it to look like a suicide. Johnny searched the house. He didn't ransack it, because this was supposed to be the suicide of an ordinary citizen, not a robbery, or the murder of a greedy assassin with blackmail material."

"Blaine messed that up by finding Olson's secret room," Katy said, smiling at her cousin. Blaine all but said 'aw shucks' under the light of his older cousin's approval.

"That wasn't the only part of Johnny's plan that didn't work out for him. He couldn't find the incriminating evidence Olson said he had. But he did see the P.O. Box bill for Olson's alias and went to Jimmy Lo's laundry after hours. But Lo arrived and caught Johnny breaking into Olson's P.O. Box, so Johnny killed him too.

Meanwhile, Buck was having a meltdown in D.C. because Tom wasn't dead and the Undersecretary position wasn't vacant. Their entire plot was unraveling."

"So, Johnny snuck into the critical care unit and disconnected Tom from life support," said Katy.

"Right. Johnny had been in the service and served as a corpsman. He knew enough about medical equipment and life support to sabotage Tom's hook-up and kill him."

"And because he was a police captain, no one would think much if they saw him in the hospital after visiting hours."

"Right. Buck's plan seemed to be working. Dr. Emma Broadwell was making the rounds in D.C. to be considered for Undersecretary, the post was now open, Oil and Gas grudgingly agreed to reinstitute the PAC funding plan with Broadwell in Flanders' place, and the Senate Committee members were still willing to play ball. The investigation in Montecito seemed to be going nowhere and all was quiet."

"But it all blew up?"

"Yes, thanks to Blaine. Blaine went to D.C. and started turning over rocks, stirring everybody up, especially Buck. Blaine seemed to know way too much about Buck's involvement in Flanders's death, and that scared the hell out of him. Buck panicked."

"So, Johnny decided to take care of Buck too."

"Yes. Johnny could tell that Buck was in a panic, waffling about what to do. Johnny could envision Buck coping a plea with the Justice Department to barter down his own sentence. Their whole plot had turned to shit and now Johnny's only priority was self-preservation."

"So, Johnny poisoned Buck?"

"Yes. He snagged some high-grade fentanyl from the Sheriff's evidence lockup and laced Buck's drink. Buck went to sleep and never woke up."

"And Johnny then decided to eliminate you and Blaine as well."

"Yes. We were way too close to unraveling the entire scheme. We were lucky he mostly missed." The Judge touched the top of his ear. "When I called him from the suite motel when we were taking fire, he said he was up north on the 101, but he was in the bushes outside reloading his rifle. I guess he got a good chuckle out of that."

"What about the take-over of Complex Atomic?"

The Judge smiled. He knew Katy wasn't interested in thinking anymore about his close scrape. "That was another Buck scheme to reinflate his standing with Oil and Gas. He had investigated Tom's steering of the lucrative contract for small box reactors for the Army to Complex Atomic and discovered Tom's ownership in the company, a clear conflict of interest.

After Tom was dead, the shares were in an Inter Vivos trust, with Bitsy as the sole trustee. Who better to persuade Bitsy to vote the shares for a share exchange with Standard, than Johnny, her lover? Kelly went along; he was desperate for funds to pay off gambling debts owed to the Chicago Mob. Senator Ross had to be brought into the deal because he knew too much. As Lyndon Johnson once said, 'I'd rather have him inside the tent pissing out, than outside the tent pissing in!'

Standard, of course, was a shell company with no operations, organized by Oil and Gas. Oil and Gas were licking their chops to get their hands on Complex Atomic as a fully owned subsidiary of Standard, and then mothball Complex Atomics' technology forever. There was a twenty million dollar bonus from the PAC to be split between the three co-conspirators, Buck, Kelly, and Ross, if they could pull it off.

However, a limited number of minority shareholders had to be persuaded to vote for the tender, in tandem with Kelly's shares and Bitsy's shares, for it to happen. The offering materials they used to inform the Complex Atomic shareholders and encourage them to vote for the Tender…out and out lied about Standard's real intent. A clear violation of section ten-b and rule ten-b-5 of the Securities Exchange Act of 1934."

"Judge, when did you know it was Johnny?" asked Blaine.

"I suspected Johnny when we got his report back on the contents of the files we found at the Chinese laundry. It seemed awfully convenient to the murderer and inconvenient to our investigation that Tom's blackmail files only contained information up to last Spring. Tom Olson was clearly very meticulous. His secret room, his thorough records about his contracts and those who had hired him. It didn't seem likely that it would have been that long since he'd updated his back-up stash at Lo's laundry. The problem was it didn't make sense because I could see no motive for Johnny to be involved.

Then I met Jerry Martel on Venice Beach, and he reluctantly identified Bitsy's secret lover. It was Johnny. Suddenly the puzzle all fell together.

Fortunately, Blaine made a copy of the encoded files before we handed them over to Johnny. I immediately sent our copy of the files off to my guy at the FBI, and the report came back including the fifth card. It was all there. Johnny's contract for murder of Flanders, the date and time, the way the money was sent over the Dark Web from Johnny for the first installment of Olson's fee, Johnny's name, telephone number, address…all of it!"

"What a waste of lives," said Katy. "And you two almost got yourselves killed…again!"

"I have a question about Laura," said Blaine.

"I'm so sorry that didn't work out."

"I guess it just wasn't meant to be, Judge. But I spoke to her briefly yesterday and she's all excited. She's come into some significant money. She's floating on air. Shopping for her own condominium to buy. Do you know anything about that? Just curious."

The Judge smiled softly. "I do. I had a private coffee with J. Edgar Travis, the estate planning lawyer, yesterday and eased out of him some off-the-record information."

"Go on, Judge. Don't leave us in suspense," said Katy.

"Remember, Blaine, that there'd been bad blood between Tom Flanders and Ted Olson for years?"

"Yes. We were told it was over a lot line dispute or something. Then Olson told us it was because he used to date Bitsy Flanders just before she married Tom and became Mrs. Flanders."

"That's part of it but it was much more involved than that."

"What was it about, Judge?" asked Katy

" Well, Bitsy was originally dating Ted Olson just before Tom Flanders showed up and wooed her away."

"So, Olson hated Flanders because Flanders stole his girl," said Katy.

"It was more than that.

"What?"

When Tom married Bitsy, they took a long honeymoon. It was eight and a half months before the new couple came back to Montecito."

"She was pregnant!" gasped Katy.

"Yes, and it wasn't Tom's child. A fact Tom never let Bitsy forget."

"What happened to the child, Judge? Did Bitsy give it up?"

"No."

"Oh my God. And it was Ted Olson's wasn't it?"

"Yes. Ted's will left his entire and considerable estate in an Inter Vivos trust to that child. Edgar Travis is now in the process of distributing that estate to the beneficiary. Unfortunately, there will no doubt be claims filed against the estate by various victims in various jurisdictions, families of the people Olson murdered for hire. There may not be much of an estate left when it all settles out. The beneficiary would be wise not to spend money expecting an estate they may never receive.

"And who is the offspring of Bitsy and Olson? Who is the beneficiary?" asked Katy.

"Laura Flanders!"

THE END

XXXXXXXXXX

NOTES FROM THE AUTHOR

The Atomic Energy Commission

The Atomic Energy Commission was the original entity to regulate the use of atomic energy in the U.S.. It was disbanded in 1974, and after being split into two separate entities for a while, and in 1977 everything was consolidated under the Assistant Secretary of Energy for Nuclear Energy at the Department of Energy. The Assistant Secretary of Energy for Nuclear Energy is appointed by the President and confirmed by the Senate. Set forth below is a bit of history on how all this happened, and why, and an update on our National Atomic Energy Program as of July 2024.

"Almost a year after World War II ended, Congress established the United States Atomic Energy Commission to foster and control the peacetime development of atomic science and technology. Reflecting America's postwar optimism, Congress declared that atomic energy should be employed not only in the Nation's defense, but also to promote world peace, improve public welfare, and strengthen free competition in private enterprise. After long months of intensive debate among politicians, military planners, and atomic scientists, President Harry S. Truman confirmed the civilian control of atomic energy by signing the Atomic Energy Act on August 1, 1946.

After concentrating on defense commitments in the early years, the Commission then focused on the development of a viable nuclear industry, only to come under fire in the late 1960s and 1970s for being in the position of regulating the same industry it helped to create.

When President Ford signed the Energy Reorganization Act of 1974 on October 11, the Atomic Energy Commission's twenty-eight-year stewardship of the Nation's nuclear energy program came to an end. On January 19, 1975, the Commission's research and development responsibilities were assumed by the Energy Research and Development Administration, (or ERDA), and the regulatory and licensing functions by the Nuclear Regulatory Commission. Six thousand, three hundred twenty Commission employees went to ERDA while one thousand nine hundred seventy former regulatory personnel became part of the new Nuclear Regulatory Commission."

(From '*The Atomic Energy Commission*', By Alice Buck, July 1983) (Link: https://www.energy.gov/management/articles/history-atomic-energy-commission)

In fall 1977, President Jimmy Carter created the new cabinet-level Department of Energy (DOE), and ERDA became an integral part of the DOE. Since then, the energy policies and programs and the several significant projects and technologies originated and coordinated by the former Energy Research and Development Administration have been carried on by a single agency as a matter of national priority. (See Energy Research and Development Administration -link: https://ethw.org/Energy_Research_and_Development_Administration).

July 10, 2024: Excerpts from a Release from the US Office Of Nuclear Energy

"The President signed the Fire Grants and Safety Act into law chalking up a BIG win for our nuclear power industry. Included in the bill is bipartisan legislation known as the ADVANCE Act that will help us build new reactors at a clip that we haven't seen since the 1970s.

Energy demand is expected to grow over the next decade as data centers, electric vehicles, and industrial processes all search for a clean and reliable source of power. Nuclear will be part of that solution, which is why the United States has already committed to tripling our nuclear capacity and is making moves to help secure our clean energy future. But in order to do that, we need legislation like the ADVANCE Act to help speed up the deployment and licensing of new reactors and fuels, and our office stands ready to support this effort.

The ADVANCE Act builds on the successes of previous legislation to develop a modernized approach to licensing new reactor technologies. Many of the advanced reactors under development use different coolants than what is currently used in our commercial light-water reactors—making the regulatory process more of a challenge. The ADVANCE Act directs the U.S. Nuclear Regulatory Commission (NRC) to reduce certain licensing application fees and authorizes increased staffing for NRC reviews to expedite the process. It also introduces prize competitions that the U.S. Department of Energy (DOE) can award to incentivize deployment. These awards are subject to Congressional appropriations but will cover the total costs assessed by the NRC for first movers in a variety of areas, including the first advanced reactor to receive an operating or combined license. This should quicken the pace for innovation and get shovels in the ground sooner to start building more domestic reactors.

We've already seen some incredible progress in this area. This past year, the NRC certified the nation's first small modular reactor. It also issued its first construction permit for a non-light water design as part of a project that we are supporting through our Advanced Reactor Demonstration program.

Another development in the Advance Act is its focus on small reactor technologies, known as microreactors. These compact reactors will be small enough to fit on a semi-truck and can be deployed around the country, including remote locations and military bases for reliable heat and power. The ADVANCE Act directs the NRC to develop guidance to license and regulate microreactor designs within 18 months. It also eliminates costs associated with pre-application activities and early site permits at DOE sites or other locations that are critical to our national security. Both should expedite the demonstration and deployment of two microreactor projects that are being pursued by our military. Alaska's Eielson Air Force Base plans to build a microreactor at its site as early as 2027. The Defense Department is also gearing up to demonstrate a high-temperature gas reactor design at Idaho National Laboratory around the same timeframe.

The ADVANCE Act also enables the cleanup and reuse of brownfield sites, including retired or retiring coal plants. Our analysis shows that hundreds of these coal sites could be converted into nuclear power plants to help keep high-paying jobs and economic opportunities in these energy communities. The NRC will examine and streamline licensing processes for nuclear facilities at these sites and will also take into account the associated infrastructure as part of the process. The NRC is currently reviewing TerraPower's construction permit application to build its Natrium reactor near a retiring coal plant in Kemmerer, Wyoming. If approved, it would be the first one issued by the NRC for a commercial non-light water reactor and will pave the way for other designs looking to do the same at similar brownfield sites.

Many of these new reactor designs will also require high-assay low-enriched uranium, known as HALEU, which is not yet commercially available in the United States. We have charted several steps to strengthen our domestic nuclear fuel supply chain and grow our domestic capabilities to produce low-enriched uranium, including HALEU.

The ADVANCE Act bill builds on this work and Congress' recent ban on Russian uranium imports by also prohibiting certain fuel products made in China. This move further strengthens our domestic nuclear fuel supply chain as we work to build up an adequate fuel supply for the United States and its allies. DOE recently made up to $2.7 billion available to purchase low-enriched uranium from domestic sources to build capacity here in the states. We also plan to award contracts this summer through our HALEU Availability Program to ensure there is enough material to support the development, demonstration, and deployment of new reactors.

We'll continue working with the NRC to help develop, qualify, and license new fuel concepts such as accident tolerant fuels for the commercial fleet, along with TRISO fuels that can be used in future molten salt and high-temperature gas reactor designs."

Dr. Michael Goff, Acting Assistant Secretary for the U.S. Department of Energy's Office of Nuclear Energy.

Link: https://www.energy.gov/ne/articles/newly-signed-bill-will-boost-nuclear-reactor-deployment-united-states

Political Action Committees

The political action committee or PAC sprang from the labor movement of 1943. Congress prohibited unions from giving direct contributions to political candidates. In response, the CIO formed the first PAC, known as the CIO-PAC, formed in July or 1943.

A PAC is a tax-exempt 527 organization that pools campaign contributions from members and donates funds to campaigns for or against candidates, ballot initiatives, or legislation. At the U.S. federal level, an organization becomes a PAC when it receives or spends more than $1,000 for the purpose of influencing a federal election, and registers with the Federal Election Commission (the "FEC"). At the state level, an organization becomes a PAC according to the state's election laws.

A series of campaign reform laws enacted during the 1970s allowed corporations, trade associations, and labor unions to form PACs. In 1971 the Federal Trade Commission ("FTC") created rules for disclosure, which required all donations received by a PAC must go through a central committee maintained by the PAC, and required PACs to file regular reports with the FEC disclosing anyone who has donated at least $200.

In the aftermath of Watergate, Congress passed the Federal Election Campaign Act Amendments of 1974, which created new limits on contributions to campaigns by PACS. In 1978, the FEC ruled that donors could donate unlimited money to Political Parties, (but not to the candidate), if the party spent the money (so called 'Soft money'), for "party building activities" such as voter registration drives, and was not spent to directly support a candidate's election campaign.

Today, contributions to PACs from corporate or labor union treasuries are illegal, though these entities may sponsor a PAC and provide financial support for the PAC's administration and fundraising. Union-affiliated PACs may solicit contributions only from union members. Independent PACs may solicit contributions from the general public.

Federal multi-candidate PACs may contribute to candidates as follows:

$5,000 directly to a candidate or candidate committee for each election (primary and general elections count as separate elections);

$15,000 to a political party per year; and

$5,000 to another PAC per year.

In its 2010 case Citizens United v. FEC, the Supreme Court of the United States overturned sections of the Campaign Reform Act of 2002 that had 'prohibited' corporate and union political independent expenditures in political campaigns. A 5–4 majority of the Supreme Court ruled that limiting "independent political spending" from corporations and other groups violated the First Amendment right to free speech. The Court left intact prohibitions on corporations and unions contributing "directly" to a candidate or candidate committee. As a result, corporations and other outside groups can spend unlimited money on elections. The justices who voted with the majority assumed that independent spending cannot be corrupt and that the spending would be transparent, but both assumptions have proven to often be incorrect

As a result, today PACs may make unlimited expenditures independently of a candidate, to promote that candidate.

Federal law formally allows for two types of PACs: connected and non-connected. Judicial decisions added a third classification, independent expenditure-only committees, which are colloquially known as "super PACs".

Most of the 4,600 active, registered PACs, named "connected PACs", sometimes also called "corporate PACs", are established by businesses, non-profits, labor unions, trade groups, or health organizations. These PACs receive and raise money from a "restricted class", generally consisting of managers and shareholders in the case of a corporation or members in the case of a non-profit organization, labor union or other interest group

Groups with an ideological mission, single-issue groups, and members of Congress and other political leaders may form "non-connected PACs". These organizations may accept funds from any individual, connected PAC, or organization.

Elected officials and political parties cannot give more than the federal limit 'directly' to candidates. However, they can set up a leadership PAC that makes independent expenditures. Provided expenditures are not coordinated with the candidate, this type of spending is 'Unlimited'.

Leadership PACs are non-connected PACs, and can accept donations from individuals and other PACs. Since current officeholders have an easier time attracting contributions, Leadership PACs are an effective way for current officeholders to raise money. A leadership PAC sponsored by an elected official cannot use funds to support that official's own campaign. However, it may fund travel, administrative expenses, consultants, polling, and other so-called 'non-campaign expenses'.

Super PACs, officially known as "independent expenditure-only political action committees," are unlike traditional PACs in that they may raise unlimited amounts from individuals, corporations, unions, and other groups to spend on, for example, ads overtly advocating for or against political candidates. However, they are not allowed to either coordinate with or contribute directly to candidate campaigns or political parties. Super PACs are subject to the same organizational, reporting, and public disclosure requirements of traditional PACs.

Super PACs are made possible because of two judicial decisions in 2010: the Citizens United v. Federal Election Commission case, and two months later, the

Federal D.C. Appellate Court case of Speechnow.org v. FEC. where the Court held that PACs which do not make contributions to candidates, parties, or other PACs, can accept 'unlimited' contributions from individuals, unions, and corporations for the purpose of making 'independent expenditures'.

Super PACs are not allowed to coordinate directly with candidates or political parties. This restriction was intended to prevent Super PACS from operating campaigns that complement or parallel those of the candidates they support or engage in negotiations that could result in quid pro quo bargaining between donors to the PAC and the candidate or officeholder. However, it is 'legal' for candidates and super PAC managers to discuss campaign strategy and tactics for using the media. And of course, it is 'legal' for Super PACs to support any candidacy on their own as long as there is no coordination with the campaign or party.

The 2020 election attracted record amounts of donations from dark money groups to Super PACs. These groups are supposed to reveal their backers, but they can hide by using a nonprofit or shell company as the donor, or by filing reports only 'after' the election has been held.

In the 2022 election, the following top ten PACs donated a total of $28,051,395 (directly, and via their affiliates and subsidiaries) to federal candidates:

1. National Association of Realtors – $4,001,500

2. National Beer Wholesalers Association – $3,258,000
3. Credit Union National Association – $2,888,500
4. American Israel Public Affairs Committee – $2,664,900
5. American Crystal Sugar – $2,624,000
6. AT&T Inc. – $2,609,400
7. Blue Cross/Blue Shield – $2,561,225
8. International Union of Operating Engineers – $2,533,920
9. National Auto Dealers Association – $2,514,000
10. American Bankers Association – $2,395,950

See:

Wikipedia-Political Action Committees.

(Link:https://en.wikipedia.org/wiki/Political_action_c ommittee#:~:text=or%20candidate%20committee.-,History,direct%20contributions%20to%20political%20 candidates.)

Wikipedia-The Bipartisan Campaign Reform Act.

(Link:https://en.wikipedia.org/wiki/Bipartisan_Campa ign_Reform_Act)

A Little More About Fentanyl

Fentanyl is so powerful that a small amount can be deadly. Just two milligrams can cause an overdose or death. It can also be very addictive. You cannot smell or taste fentanyl.

The signs that someone might be experiencing a fentanyl overdose, according to the CDD, include:

- Small, constricted "pinpoint" pupils
- Falling asleep or losing consciousness
- Slow or weak breathing
- Choking or gurgling sounds
- Limp body
- Cold and/or clammy skin
- Discolored skin (especially in lips and nails)

Overdose can cause stupor, changes in pupil size, clammy skin, cyanosis, coma, and respiratory failure leading to death. The presence of a triad of symptoms such as coma, pinpoint pupils, and respiratory depression strongly suggests opioid intoxication. Being unresponsive to stimuli, slow heart rate, infrequent breathing; deep snoring or gurgling (death rattle) can occur.

Poor Blaine and His Lost Love

The author would be remiss if he didn't add a note about the nature of Love, and poor Blaine in this story with his brief love affair before being brutally dumped.

"15 Ways Love Affects Your Brain and Body. By Crystal Raypole: There's no denying that love can do a number on you, whether you're head over heels, stuck on someone, or completely swept away. You don't need to do much more than pick up a book or turn on the radio or TV to hear about love's effects."

"Even the oldest written love song discovered to date has something to add: 'You have captivated me, let me stand tremblingly before you,' reads the translation of 'The Love Song for Shu-Sin,' which dates to approximately 2000 B.C."

"More modern media examples, including romantic comedies and sentimental tales of soul mates, can sometimes be a little hard to swallow, especially if Cupid's arrows don't strike you quite that hard. But if you've been in love yourself, you'll know the occasional exaggerations don't entirely miss the mark. Many people describe love as something you just have to learn to recognize when it happens."

"When you think of love, your heart might be the first organ that comes to mind. While terms like 'thinking with your heart', 'you're in my heart', and 'heartbroken' make this pretty understandable, you really have your brain to thank — that's where it all goes down. Brain changes triggered by love certainly affect your mood and behavior when these feelings are new, but some effects linger long past the first blush of love, continuing to strengthen your commitment over time."

"Here's a look at some of the major effects.

Euphoria. That giddy, euphoric excitement you feel when spending time with the person you love (or seeing them across the room, or hearing their name)? You can trace this entirely normal effect of falling in love back to the neurotransmitter dopamine. Your brain's reward system relies on this important chemical to reinforce pleasurable behaviors, including eating, listening to music, having sex, and seeing people you love. Simply thinking about the object of your affection is enough to trigger dopamine release, making you feel excited and eager to do whatever it takes to see them. Then, when you actually do see them, your brain 'rewards' you with more dopamine, which you experience as intense pleasure. This cycle plays an important part in mating behavior. Feeling good when you spend time with the person you love makes it more likely you'll keep doing it. From a purely biological perspective, this is an important first step in the process of choosing an ideal mate to reproduce with."

"Attachment and security. When it comes to love, dopamine isn't the only chemical on the field. Oxytocin levels also surge, boosting feelings of attachment, safety, and trust. This is why you probably feel comfortable and relaxed in the company of a partner, especially once your love makes it past the first early rush. These feelings might seem even stronger after touching, kissing, or sex. That's oxytocin at work. It's nicknamed 'the love hormone' for a reason. This release of oxytocin can strengthen your bond, in part, because it may decrease your interest in other potential partners. In short, the better your partner makes you feel, the closer you'll likely want to become."

"Willingness to sacrifice. Most people agree love involves some degree of compromise and sacrifice. Sacrifices can range from small — like going with dandelion yellow paint in the kitchen instead of robin's egg blue — to life-altering. For example, you might move across the country, even to a different country, to support your partner. As love flourishes, you may find yourself more willing to make these sacrifices. It's believed this happens because partners tend to become more synced up, thanks in part to the vagus nerve, which begins in your brain and plays a role in everything from your facial expressions to the rhythm of your heart. This alignment can help you notice when they feel sad or distressed. Since it's only natural to want to keep someone you love from experiencing pain, you might choose to sacrifice something for this reason."

Constant thoughts. Is the person you love front and center in your thoughts? Maybe you think about them so often they've even started to feature in your dreams. This partially relates to the dopamine cycle that rewards these positive thoughts, but…research suggests you can also thank another part of your brain: the anterior cingulate cortex. Experts have linked this brain region to obsessive-compulsive behaviors, which can help explain why the intensity and frequency of your thoughts might seem to creep toward the level of an obsession. Still, when you first fall in love with someone, it's normal for them to be the main thing on your mind. This can reinforce your desire to spend time with them, potentially increasing your chances of successfully building a relationship."

"Less stress. Lasting love is consistently linked to lower levels of stress. The positive feelings associated with oxytocin and dopamine production can help improve your mood, for one. Research … also suggests single people may have higher levels of cortisol, the stress hormone, than people in committed relationships. What is a partner if not someone to vent to, someone who can have your back? It's understandable, then, that the support and companionship of someone you love can help you manage challenging life events more easily.

"Jealousy. While people tend to think of jealousy as something bad, it's a natural emotion that can help you pay more attention to your needs and feelings. In other words, jealousy sparked by love can suggest you have a strong commitment to your partner and don't want to lose them. Jealousy can actually have a positive impact on your relationship by promoting bonding and attachment — as long as you use it wisely. When you notice jealous feelings, first remind yourself they're normal. Then, share them with your partner instead of snooping or making passive-aggressive remarks about their behavior."

"Love affects your body. Whether you feel love in your fingers, your toes, or all around, it'll show up in your body, too. (You may find) Boosted passion. Falling in love can make you feel pretty lustful. What makes you want to get it on all the time? Another set of hormones comes into play here. Androgens, a group of hormones that includes testosterone, increase your desire for sex with the person you love. Having sex also boosts production of these hormones, which can lead to a cycle that's also reinforced by the release of oxytocin and dopamine. Sex with your partner feels great and increases closeness, so it's perfectly normal to want more. No harm in that — sex offers plenty of health benefits."

"Improved physical health. Love, particularly love that develops into a committed relationship, can have a positive impact on overall health. A few of these benefits include: decreased risk of heart disease, lower blood pressure, improved immune health, and faster recovery from illness."

"Longer life span. A loving relationship could help you have a longer life. Research… reviewed 95 articles that compared the death rate for single people to the death rate for people who were married or lived with partners. The review authors found evidence to suggest that single people had a much higher risk for early death: 24 percent, according to some of the studies they looked at. A 2012 study of 225 adults who had coronary artery bypass grafting also found evidence suggesting love can lead to a longer life. People who were married when they had the surgery were 2.5 times more likely to be still living 15 years later. High marital satisfaction increased this rate further: People who reported being highly satisfied in their marriage were 3.2 times more likely to be still living than those who were less satisfied."

"Pain relief. You might have some firsthand experience with the way thoughts of your loved one can improve your mood, and maybe even provide a little comfort or strength when you don't feel well. This effect doesn't just exist in your imagination, according to a small 2010 study. This study looked at 15 adults in romantic relationships established within the previous 9 months. The participants experienced moderate to high levels of thermal pain while doing one of three things: responding to a word-association prompt shown to reduce pain through previous research, looking at a photograph of an attractive acquaintance, and looking at a photograph of their romantic partner. They reported less pain both when completing the distraction task and when looking at a photo of their partner. The study authors also noted that looking at a partner's photo activated the brain's reward system, which suggests this activation may lower your perception of pain."

"What about negative effects? Lovesick, lovelorn, heartbroken: These words only go to show that love doesn't always feel amazing. An awareness of love's less-than-positive effects can make it easier to keep an eye out for them so they don't cause you, or your budding relationship, any harm."

"Increased stress. In a long-term, committed relationship, stress tends to decrease over time. But when you first fall in love, your stress usually goes up. It makes sense; falling in love can feel like a pretty high-stakes situation, especially before you know how the other person feels. A little stress isn't always a bad thing, since it can motivate you to pursue your love. If you can't get anything done because you're waiting anxiously for them to pick up the flirty conversation you had going the night before, though, you might have a bit of a problem."

"Physical symptoms. Your body responds to the stress of love by producing norepinephrine and adrenaline, the same hormones your body releases when you face danger or other crises. These hormones can cause a range of physical symptoms, like that flip-flopping feeling in your stomach. "Butterflies" might sound nice, sure — until they make you feel like you need to throw up. When you see, or even just think of, the person you love, you feel tense and nervous. Your heart begins to race, your palms sweat, and your face flushes. You might feel a little shaky. Your words might seem to tumble out of nowhere. This can make you anxious and uncomfortable, even when there's no one else you'd rather be talking to."

"Sleep and appetite changes. Tossing and turning because you can't get that special someone out of your head? Wondering how they feel about you? Maybe you've already discovered they feel the same way but don't know when you'll see them next. That's just another type of agony. A nervous stomach can also keep you up and make it hard to eat. And when your thoughts fixate on love, food might seem completely unimportant. Rapidly changing hormone levels can certainly affect your appetite and ability to sleep, but eating well and making sure to get enough rest will help you feel more prepared to face whatever happens."

"Poor judgment. Ever done something silly (perhaps a little dangerous) to impress someone you love? Maybe you acted without thinking and did something you'd never ordinarily consider. You're not the only one. When you experience intense love, parts of your brain responsible for helping you detect danger (amygdala) and make decisions (the frontal lobe) go into temporary hibernation, leaving you lacking these essential skills. So, if you decide to confess your love in front of a hundred people at your best friend's birthday party, the consequences might be nothing more than a really embarrassing story you'll never hear the end of. But this lack of judgment can also have more serious consequences, such as making it difficult to recognize red flags."

"Love addiction. There's a lot of debate about whether people can become addicted to love. In short, it is possible to experience a pattern where you crave the euphoric phase of early love or an idealized romantic attachment. People with so-called love addictions might also feel the need to move on from a relationship once they no longer feel 'in love'. If you notice these signs, it might be time to take a brief break from love and dating. Talking to a therapist can help you get some more insight on this pattern."

Written by Crystal Raypole, writer and editor for Good Therapy, Medically reviewed by Janet Brito, Ph.D., LCSW, CST. August 25, 2020

See the entire article here: (Link) https://www.healthline.com/health/relationships/effe cts-of-love.

"Montecito" is a work of fiction. Apart from the well-known locales that are depicted in the book, all of the names, characters, places, organizations, clubs, and incidents are the products of the author's imagination or are used fictitiously. Any resemblance to current events or locales, to organizations or clubs, or to persons living or dead, is entirely coincidental.
Davis MacDonald

****

Thank you so much for reading my book. If you enjoyed it, please take a moment to leave me a review on Amazon or at your favorite retailer.

All The Best

Davis MacDonald

Acknowledgments

The people, organizations, clubs, places, and events depicted in this book are all fictional, and any similarity to any real people, organizations, clubs, or events is unintended. Names have been chosen at random and are not intended to suggest any particular person. The facts, circumstances, plot and characters in this book were created for dramatic effect and bear no relationship to the actual community of Montecito and its denizens.

Let me add that Montecito is a wonderful and beautiful place to live and to visit, with townsfolk who work hard and live in harmony with one another in a delightful Mediterranean-like setting that you really must visit if you have the opportunity.

I'd like to thank my principal editors: Jason Myers, a noted writer in his own right, for his tireless work on this book with me; and Kath Salter, a Lauded Poet, who did the final edit and put it all together. A special thanks to Grey Salter, who assisted on some of the medical aspects of the story. And to Dane Low (www.ebooklaunch.com) for the smashing cover designs on this and all twelve books in THE JUDGE SERIES.

I hope you have enjoyed reading it as much as I have enjoyed writing it, and perhaps here and there it made you smile a little.

About Davis MacDonald

Davis MacDonald grew up in Southern California and writes of places about which he has intimate knowledge. A member of the National Association of Independent Writers and Editors, (NAIWE), his career has spanned Law Professor, Bar Association Chair, Investment Banker and Lawyer. Many of the colorful characters in his novels are drawn from his personal experience.

HOW TO CONNECT WITH DAVIS MACDONALD

Davis.MacDonald1@gmail.com.

Website: www.DavisMacDonald-Author.com

Follow me on Twitter: http://twitter.com/DavisMacdonald1

Friend me on Facebook: http://facebook.com

Subscribe to my blog: http://davismacdonald.naiwe.com/professional-profile/

If you enjoyed Davis Macdonald's Montecito, Book 12 in the series, but have not followed the series from the beginning, consider picking up The Hill, Book 1 in the series, both a mystery and love story of how the Judge and Katy first met.

And please leave a Review on Amazon and help us spread the word.

Davis MacDonald

THE HILL

What follows is the first chapter of "THE HILL". the FIRST book in Davis MacDonald's The Judge series. Available In Fine Book Stores And On Amazon.

If you like, you can download this mystery novel for free on the Davis Macdonald website (www.DavisMacDonald-Author.com). Simply go to THE HILL on the site, input your email, and I'll send you a free electronic copy of THE HILL.

ENJOY!

Davis MacDonald

THE HILL

CHAPTER 1
Friday

Sometimes your destiny is pre-ordained. Sometimes well planned and thought out ahead. Sometimes it gradually sneaks up on you; you look back, surprised at the distance covered. Sometimes it just falls out one day at your feet like the body of a young girl, rolling lifelessly in the surf.

It was early October in Southern California. The day had been very warm early on, Indian Summery, even a little sticky. But as the afternoon dwindled away, the heat gave way to a slight chill as the thin golden rays of the sun vanished below the sea. Soft light spilled like dust over fallen leaves, manicured green-gray lawn and asphalt alike.

Along the coast a stiff breeze had come up off the water, whipped up by a storm to the south in Baja, churning the Santa Monica Bay into frosty whitecaps. It was still a warm wind, but it brought the smell and the taste of the sea to the cliffs of Palos Verdes Estates, a small hidden suburb to the southwest of Los Angeles. The waves had steadily increased in size and frequency all afternoon and now crashed with a heavy rhythm against the beach and sluiced up amongst the rocks. The tide was on the way out but it was still a rugged surf.

The Judge strode along Paseo Del Mar, the ocean bluff street that tracked the city's rocky coastline. He was a tall man. Broad-shouldered and big boned. With just the beginnings of a paunch around the middle, hinting at an appetite for fine wines and good food. He cut an imposing figure in his formal dark blue corduroy sport coat, outfitted with a large collar and casual patch pockets. He wore a light blue dress shirt under, its oversized collar open at the neck, and disreputable-looking jeans of unknown vintage, faded and threadbare here and there. He had the ruddy and rugged chiseled features of Welsh ancestors, a rather too-big nose, large ears, and bushy eyebrows on the way to premature grey.

He had a given name of course, but after he ascended to the Bench people began calling him just "Judge". Even old friends he'd known for years affectionately adopted the nickname. Somehow it seemed to fit. And it had stuck.

As the sun faded, the temperature dropped, and the wind brought color to his cheeks and an added urgency to his gait. With his big hands and feet and his jeans and short-cut dark hair, he might have passed for a dock worker in another locale.

Except that he had large piercing blue eyes, intelligent and restless. Except that his eyes swept the space around him continually and missed nothing. Except that he thought like a judge. Except that this was Palos Verdes, one of the most affluent communities in the United States.

He walked a golden retriever, perhaps a year old, big, clearly untrained, and still a puppy in spirit and energy despite her bulk. The puppy, as he thought of her, despite her size, Annie by name, seemed determined to go in all directions except the one The Judge wanted.

The puppy was recently acquired. An experiment. The Judge was already having second thoughts. Annie was to be his new companion. A fellow spirit to balance out what had become a too-solitary life.

So far she had mostly been a pain in the ass. She strained at the leash every 30 seconds or so, testing his resolve to stay on the road. At 60 pounds she could give a good tug, although hardly a match for his 200 pounds. She wanted to romp the bushes alongside. He supposed the bushes held better smells. Allied with the asphalt, he couldn't compete.

This was his routine at sunset. He walked with the puppy from his house higher up the Hill. Down to Paseo Del Mar, the bluff road which ran along the sea cliff. He went a half mile in one direction along the cliff. Then he reversed. He went half mile past his entry point. And back. It was all so…organized.

The Judge was organized. His life was ordered in tiers of personal interest and professional responsibility. He had been technically proficient as a judge, straight as an arrow on the rules, and enjoyed his part in the drama that worked itself out each day in the courtroom.

It was called the American system of Justice. But it wasn't always just. It wasn't always right. And there wasn't always a legal remedy for those who deserved one. American Justice came down to a system of rules. It operated within its own framework. To the Judge, it was still the closest thing to real justice in this world. There was a certain symmetry to it he enjoyed. It had defined his professional life for more than 10 years. But it was by no means perfect.

In any event that life was gone now. Whisked away in an instant. He'd been dumped on the street. He was no longer a judge. People continued to call him Judge, of course, out of respect, or maybe pity. Who knew?

He'd lost his re-election 6 months ago. It was still somewhat of a shock. After 10 years on the bench, he thought he'd continue indefinitely and then retire a judge.

Now he had lots of time to squander, on things like puppies and walks. It was very different from being a judge.

50 years old, and no law to practice.. He didn't feel up to starting a new law practice again. He'd done it once years ago, before the judgeship. It had been hard. Once should have been enough. But then what the hell else was he to do?

He told himself he wasn't bitter, at least not exactly. Just a mild sour taste. Dumped by his constituents. Ten years and out the door one morning, almost by whim.

The light in the sky was fading quickly now. Just like his career, he mused. It had been a peaceful afternoon. He hadn't seen a soul. No joggers, no bikers. None of the neighbors walking their dogs. They always seemed to know the puppy's name. They never remembered his. There was an orange afterglow puddled against the rim of the sea. It had turned from Indian Summer to cool Fall in the space of an hour, the way it does on The Hill.

Palos Verdes, or "The Hill", as its denizens referred to it, was a discrete series of hills with cliffs, jutting up off the Los Angeles plain and out into the sea to the southwest. A hill and rock peninsula, surrounded on three sides by the sea. Midway between LAX and the Port of Los Angeles, it was the only rocky coast along a line of otherwise flat surfing beaches stretching from Santa Monica to the Newport Coast in Orange County, punctuated by the twin ports of Los Angeles and Long

Beach, and several piers and boat harbors. Twenty-five minutes distance by car to any freeway, by L.A. standards it was an isolated and travel-locked outpost far off the beaten track. It was geographically close but time-lengthy to travel to L.A.'s so called "downtown", to the glitzy Westside, or to Hollywood or the Valley.

The Hill quietly punctuated the Southern California coast line, mostly unknown and unvisited by Angelenos, even though at least one of its communities routinely ranked as one of the ten wealthiest in the United States.

And it was very quiet. People only traveled to The Hill if they lived there.

The judge approached his midway point again on his last stretch before turning uphill on Via Alma. He noticed a battered penny lying in the road. He looked around to be sure no one was watching and then bent over and scooped it up. When he was young he believed in making a wish on such a find. Perhaps he should try. A wish for guidance.

As he bent over the leash slipped from his grasp. Annie scooted off in a flash, plowing into the brush alongside the bluff.

Muttering under his breath, the Judge gamely waded into dry foxtails after her. She thought it was "Catch Annie, if you can", a wonderful game to her pea-sized brain. She dodged away from his reach, waving her tail like a flagman, dashing further into the rough, toward the bluff edge, daring him to catch her.

The Judge waded after. He could feel the burrs in his socks and smell the dry dust they'd kicked up, mixed with the salty aroma from the crashing surf 40 feet below. He was almost to Annie now. He was concerned she might scamper over the edge in her excitement.

But she had stopped at cliff edge and was seriously nosing something in the scrub. His eyes caught the flash of baby blue as the dry grass parted around her legs. He slowed his pace and gingerly picked his way closer to the cliff and the puppy.

He could make it out now. It was a powder blue dress, neatly folded on the ground, as if laid out for someone to wake up and put on. For some reason, it reminded him of the young girl who house-sat his puppy the night before. A pretty high school senior just turned 18. The daughter of an old friend.

He had gone to San Francisco on Wednesday. By pre-arrangement the girl, her name was Christi, had stayed over and puppy-sat Annie Wednesday and Thursday night. Having a puppy was like a small child. He had to hire a live-in babysitter if he left town. It was expected. By the neighbors, by the local vet, by everyone. You couldn't just send the baby to the puppy kennel like in the old days. Lock it up for 24 hours in a secure cage and forget it. Oh, no. The damn animal almost had legal rights.

He'd returned from LAX hours before and paid off his puppy sitter. Annie seemed none the worse for wear. Apparently, the Judge was never missed. And why would he be? The puppy had been ensconced for two nights with Christi, a young thing in a pretty dress, a robin's egg blue dress. This looked very much like the dress.

Two hours ago, he'd given Christi cash that she was quite happy to get. She'd left in a bundle of smiles and good cheer, wrapped in blue.

The Judge was suddenly cold. He didn't want to look over the cliff edge...but he did.

It was a long way down. A sheer drop. A crashing sea below. All foam and green in the fading light.

Rocks jutting up here and there served as the splash base for spouts of sea and froth as rollers hit the shore. There was a continual roar, punctuated periodically by the crash of a particularly big wave throwing itself against the rocks. The wind whipped a fine spray of salt and moisture up the face of the cliff. The judge's hair and face were quickly coated with a light mist. He could taste the salt on his lips. It was an awesome site. All power and wild sea. The judge panned the scene, taking it all in.

Then he saw what he feared.
A bobbing white and pink form, the shape of a young girl, spinning, rolling, half submerged in the sea.

Crashing up against the sharp rocks.

Lifelike but lifeless. In endless motion. A bouncing rolling dancer, captive to sea surge, tide, wind, and merciless rocks.

Chapter 2

The last rays of the vanished sun had pasted colors to the bottoms of countless distant clouds. Pinks, yellows, oranges, a soft blue like the folded dress. But a deeper purple was spreading across the sky now, swallowing the color. The wind had not dropped much but the temperature had. Is that why he felt so bloody cold?

The Judge and the puppy stood together at the side of the road. Annie huddled close, her ears back in dismay, her tail flat to the ground. They were alternately painted in the red of the fire truck lights. The paramedic and patrol car lights had been turned off, perhaps a symbol of their futility here.

The Judge always felt a little unreal standing in the arc of sweeping emergency lights. A little disoriented. Not like the men who ran the machines. The layman had only bad experiences with the arcing red lights. Family emergencies, accidents, death, loss of loved ones, face-to-face recognition of one's own mortality. He pulled his corduroy coat closer around him and brought the puppy against his leg. For warmth, he thought. And maybe reassurance. At least one living thing still cared he was alive.

The Judge had dialed 911 at the cliff's edge. He'd considered bolting down the narrow path to the left, down to the beach. But even from his cliff top perch it was clear the girl lying face down in the water had been there awhile. She was not moving. At least not of her own accord. The surf was the puppeteer here. It danced the body randomly about the rocks in a grotesque fashion, rolling it around and around and slamming it over and under.

And in the deepening dusk the trail was slippery and treacherous. For someone out of shape like the Judge it would have been a tricky effort. He might have ended up a second victim. The fire rescue team had been there in three minutes flat, and down on the beach in five. But reaching the body across the rocks and surf was proving tricky even for professionals.

The paramedics had gone down the trail at a flat-out run, three bronzed young men in their early thirties. They agilely leaped from rock to rock at the surf's edge. After a quick survey, two of them, both wrapped in a fancy harness anchored to the beach, went into the rocky surf and waded the body ashore.

Two policemen, a detective, and a forensic tech, hovered in a tight circle over the body on the sand. There were flashlights spraying in all directions, low voices exchanging notes, and the occasional rogue wave that threatened to wash them away. The firemen were busy too, rigging a stretcher for hauling the body up the path to the comparative safety of the top. Safety for the living; too late for the dead.

Top side a small band of neighbors had formed, augmented by a couple of bikers, a lone jogger, and a Latino gardener dressed in de rigor khaki, the uniform of faceless people who tended the gardens and lawns of the Hill. The gardener faded quickly when the patrol car arrived, replaced by a young couple passing in their car, stopping now and getting out to have a look.

"It was another suicide jump, and right in front of my house too", announced a tall angular woman with clever blue eyes and the feel of Stanford. She wore a violet raincoat, hastily thrown over dark blue pants, an ivory blouse and a blue sport jacket. Early 50s like the judge, she wore the traditional "I am a professional so take me seriously" uniform so in fashion these days with the softer sex. Beside her stood a small Asian woman, likely Japanese, quietly staring with sad dark eyes. She was dressed in a pin-striped charcoal suit coat. Perhaps a lawyer or a banker.

The female half of the young couple kept muttering, "Oh my god…oh my god" under her breath. A sort of mantra that seemed aimed at making the whole scene disappear. She was a brunette, dressed to show. She wore scruffy tight jeans and a tight T-shirt low cut in front to display budding breasts, rigged with an undergarment to push up from below, in defiance of nature and the law of gravity. Her male counterpart was quiet and pale, watching with sad eyes as the stretcher jostled its way up the cliff, born by the firemen. He was dressed in tan pants and a white polo shirt under a blue-striped office shirt, the tail hanging out at the back. He had his arms around her to keep her warm, just a bit too high to be discrete. The judge supposed he'd do the same if he had a pretty girl like that.

The young detective, short in stature and squeaky in voice, strutted over to the Judge, pulling out his flip-top notebook. "You found the body, sir", he said, more a statement than a question.

The Judge hated being addressed as "Sir". It felt like a sly slur, an ugly reminder that the younger person had eternity stretching before him while the Judge was on the edge of the abyss. He supposed it was true. How nice it was to be young and certain you'd live forever. The judge could vaguely remember the fantasy. It disappeared with the years as did many things. Of course, the Judge was quite happy to be addressed as "Judge", but that wasn't going to happen anymore.

"No," he said, "I found the blue dress. Then saw something in the surf below. So I called 911." It sounded like quibbling even to the Judge, but the hell with it. He didn't much like this detective. He didn't know quite why.

"I'm Detective Broadman," he announced, handing the Judge a card. "We think we have an ID: one Christina Benson, just turned 18, a local girl. There was a license in the dress."

The judge's countenance remained impassive, but his heart sank. Then it was Christi.

"Did you know her?' asked the detective.

"I know Christi Benson. Is that her being carried up the cliff?"

"We believe so," said the detective. "Come have a look".

The Judge handed the end of the puppy leash to the tall angular woman, who quite happily took the dog. An opportunity for distraction from the gruesome scene playing out for the cluster of neighbors.

The judge and the detective walked with measured steps over to the top of the trail; the judge's feet felt like lead. The firemen were just carrying the stretcher over the top, a terrible small bundle strapped to it, with a grey blanket thrown over. The detective instinctively positioned them so their broad backs more or less blocked the view of the small knot of community looking on. He raised the blanket, shining a flashlight under.

It was Christi. She wore a skimpy white two-piece swimsuit. It was the only area that had not been battered by the rocks and sand. She was still beautiful, even in death…but different. Her blue eyes gazed up blankly at the judge. Brown, matted, sand-caked hair above pale white skin, marked with cuts, scrapes and bruises, and a huge welt at the side of her head where she must have hit the rocks. Her expression was one of surprise, frozen in time. The image would haunt the Judge.

The lively flashing blue eyes, quick smile, infectious laugh she used to punctuate statements sometimes, the warmth and the glow of a just flowering young woman…..poof…poof….gone.

"Yes," croaked the judge, "Yes….Christi Benson". Mercifully, the detective dropped the blanket back in place. The judge started to move back toward the relative comfort of the small cluster of neighbors, his eyes cast down, unseeing. But the little detective briskly cut him off, flip book in hand again.

"When was the last time you saw Christina Benson," he asked. His squeaky voice had all the warmth of a dental drill.

"About three hours ago", the judge replied. "She house sat, or dog sat, for me last night and the night before. I was out of town."

The detective's eyes narrowed thoughtfully. "So…. you may have been the last person to see her alive?"

The judge shook his head, "I don't know".

"How did she seem? Did she seem depressed, pensive, sad, moody, down, anything like that?"

"No. She seemed happy and full of life. My impression was that she had a date."

"Why did you think that, sir?" That Sir again. "Did she say she had a date? That she was meeting somebody?"

The judge paused a moment to reflect. "I don't know, she left running her fingers through her hair, and doing her lipstick. She seemed happy and…I don't know…animated. No, she didn't say she had a date."

"What was she wearing?" asked the detective.

 "The blue dress"

"Sure it's the same blue dress?"

"Looks the same color", snapped the Judge. "I don't know whether it's the 'same' dress.".

"Of course," said the detective, making another note.

An older white Mercedes screeched to a halt at the curve across the street, causing them both to turn and look.

A distraught woman in her mid-forties leaped from the car, making for the stretcher, panic in her face.

Oh God, thought the Judge, it's Maddie. Christi's mother.

Maddie made a determined bolt between two officers, but they impeded her forward motion with their bulk.

With the help of a fireman, they encircled her and blocked her access.

Maddie was one of the Judge's few friends on The Hill, a rapidly dwindling group. But this wasn't the time to feel sorry for himself. He felt needed now.

He ignored the detective and his flip top book, stepping around him, and went over to take Maddie into his arms.

She started to sob uncontrollably into his shoulder, his sports coat with the grief of a mother who's lost a child.

Finally, she came up for air, pulling herself together and hoarsely muttering, "I want to see her".

"Are you sure Maddie?" he said softly. "It's not the way you want to remember her."

"Yes," she said in a voice suddenly cold and far away, "I have to."

The Judge turned to the two officers who had positioned themselves between Maddie and the body.

"She needs to see her daughter now,", he said.

One of the officers started to object. But the Judge held up his hand imperially, displaying the prestige and force of personality he'd so often used from his bench. Both officers instinctually moved aside.

Maddie walked slowly over to the stretcher, her head held unnaturally high and straight. The Judge moved with her, step for step.

One of the firemen lifted the stretcher blanket and tried unsuccessfully to soften with his hand the light from the flashlight he shined under.

Maddie gasped, steadied herself, and with trembling fingers, reached down and caressed the face of her child.

She bent down to give the cold sandy forehead a small kiss, and then slumped away, seeking the judge's shoulder again for support.

He walked her unsteadily back to her Mercedes and offered to drive her home. She handed him the keys without comment. She trusted him. They'd even been lovers once. So very long ago. Before she met and married Jake, her ex. Before Christine.

Once lovers, always a special connection. Human beings were built to share intimacy. Once shared, it wasn't something that could be put back in bottle as if not opened. Even when things don't work out and you move on you carry some part of that person with you into your future.

They'd been good friends on The Hill since her divorce. Strictly platonic, of course. But he's watched Christi grow up. For some reason, fate had brought him to that cliff edge and now to Maddie's side when she again needed support.

He helped her into the car. She sat there staring blankly out the passenger side window. He retrieved Annie and loaded the puppy in the backseat. Then he drove the three of them slowly away, wondering what words would make any difference.

****

To continue the Story, pick up a free electronic copy of THE HILL from my Website, (google Davis MacDonald – Author, and go to THE HILL tab), or pick up a paperback copy at any bookstore, or on Amazon.